CROWNS
OF
ICE

BOOKS BY KRISTA STREET

SUPERNATURAL WORLD NOVELS

Fae of Snow & Ice

Court of Winter
Thorns of Frost
Wings of Snow
Crowns of Ice

Supernatural Curse

Wolf of Fire
Bound of Blood
Cursed of Moon
Forged of Bone

Supernatural Institute

Fated by Starlight
Born by Moonlight
Hunted by Firelight
Kissed by Shadowlight

Supernatural Community

Magic in Light
Power in Darkness
Dragons in Fire
Angel in Embers

Supernatural Standalone Novels

Beast of Shadows

Links to all of Krista's books may be found on her website.

CROWNS OF ICE

fae fantasy romance

FAE OF SNOW & ICE
BOOK 4

KRISTA STREET

Cover art created by Maria Spada: www.mariaspada.com
Map illustration created by Christopher Srnka: www.dinochris.com

WELCOME TO THE FAE LANDS

Crowns of Ice is the final book in the four-book *Fae of Snow & Ice* series, which is a slow-burn, enemies-to-lovers, fae fantasy romance.

This book takes place in the fae lands of Krista Street's *Supernatural World*. Although Krista's other paranormal romance books also features the fae lands, the *Fae of Snow & Ice* series is entirely separate so may be read before or after her previous series.

Solis Continent

Brashier Sea

Ice Caves
Pentlebim

Kroravee

Isalee

Solisarium

Floating
Meadows

Prinavee

Gielis

Highsteer
Castle

Osaravee

Duval

Harivee

Murlands

Guxbee

Bay
of
Korl

Barvilum

Tala Sea

Glassen
Barrier
Islands

GLOSSARY

Territories of the Solis Continent

Harrivee – the middle southern territory, coastal cities often fighting with the Lochen fae. Territory color is yellow.

Isalee – the northernmost territory, Cliffs of Sarum on its northern peak. Territory color is white.

Kroravee – the northwestern territory, most reclusive territory, very unwelcoming even to other Solis fae. Territory color is purple.

Mervalee – the easternmost territory, richly blessed with *orem,* borders the Nolus continent. Territory color is green.

Osaravee – the southwestern territory, coastal cities often fighting with the Lochen fae. Territory color is red.

Prinavee – the central territory, where Solisarium, the capital of the Solis continent, resides. Territory color is the royal palate: blue, black, and silver.

Seas of the fae lands

Adriastic Sea – the ocean to the west of the Nolus continent.

Brashier Sea – the most northern sea in the fae lands, large icebergs often present.

Tala Sea – the ocean to the south of the Solis continent.

Terms

Affinity – the magical ability that each Solis fae develops at maturing age. Maturing age happens around thirteen years of age in the hundreds-year-long life span of a Solis fairy. A Solis fairy's affinity can be common or quite rare, weak or very strong. Most Solis fae only have one affinity. Very powerful Solis fae have more than one.

Archon – a fairy that holds power over a village, city, territory, or land. There are tiers of archons, and the more land that an archon manages, the more politically powerful that archon is. The most powerful archon on the Solis continent is King Novakin.

Blessed Mother – a magical life force of the fae lands that nurtures growth and life among the fae. The Blessed Mother is not a goddess but a force from nature that is similar in strength and power to the gods. The

Blessed Mother is believed to reside deep within the land at the heart of the planet. This belief is unique to the Solis fae.

Channa – intrinsic Lochen magic that keeps Lochen fae warm no matter the climate.

Defective – a Solis fae who is magicless and never develops an affinity.

Full season – the equivalent of one year.

Ingamy – a derogatory word for a Solis fairy.

Millee – the Solis fae unit of measurement, the equivalent of one mile.

Orem – the magic that infuses the Solis continent, allowing plants and crops to grow in freezing temperatures. *Orem* is replenished by celestial events and comes from the gods.

Salivar – a Lochen fae concubine.

Solls – a term Solis fae use when they clink glasses to celebrate, like Cheers.

Fae races

Solis fae – the Solis fae reside on the icy, most northern continent of the fae lands planet. Solis fae have silvery-white hair, crystalline blue eyes, and wings. They typically live for thousands of years.

Nolus fae – the Nolus fae reside on the central continent. They often have various shades of colorful hair, pointy teeth, glowing skin, and otherworldly strength. They typically live three hundred years, but royal Nolus fae live for thousands of years.

Lochen fae – the Lochen fae reside on a southern continent, islands, and in the seas throughout the fae lands. They can morph into fish-like creatures, similar to mermaids, but they can also walk on two legs and live on land. There are subspecies of Lochen fae that live in fresh-water rivers, lakes, and ponds. The Lochen fae typically have green eyes and varying skin shades and hair colors.

Silten fae – the Silten fae reside on a separate continent across the Adriastic Sea, west of the Nolus continent. They have animalistic features: horns, scales, hooves, and tails, and they are the most varied in how they appear. Most live in underground dens, hollow logs, or wooded forests, but Silten fae with more human-like bodies reside in cities.

Fae plants and food

Acorlis – a root vegetable, sweet flavor with an orange skin, similar to a sweet potato.

Cottonum – a plant similar to cotton.

Leminai – a bright-green alcoholic drink common throughout the fae lands.

Nightill – purple and black wildflowers.

Peteesium – an enchanted flower that creates a very potent hallucinogen.

Salopas – a fairy version of a bar with no serving

staff. There are magically enchanted trays that serve patrons.

Fae animals

Brommel – a stag or deer-like creature that can run so swiftly hardly any fae can hunt them.

Colantha – a large cat that resides in jungles.

Domal – an animal similar to a horse but more intelligent.

Feerily – a deadly sea creature. As a form of execution, the Lochen will feed a fairy to a feerily.

Ice bear – a large bear with a naturally white furry coat and six-inch claws, which stands eight feet tall on two legs. An ice bear's coat can change color to match its surroundings.

Snowgum – the most feared ice creature whose magical ability allows it to become invisible for short spans. Snowgums resemble a large feline.

Tilamy – a sea creature that's lively and non-threatening. They're sometimes kept as pets by the Lochen fae.

Trisilee – a tiny bird with wings that flap hundreds of miles per hour, like a hummingbird.

Ustorill – a wild animal that lives in the forest, similar to a boar.

PRONUNCIATION GUIDE

Names

Ilara Seary – Ill-are-uh Seer-ee

Norivun Achul – Nor-ih-vun Ah-cool

Cailis – Kay-liss

Krisil – Kris-ill

Evis – Eve-iss

Sandus – Sand-us

Balbus – Bell-bus

Patrice – Pah-treese

Haisley – Hay-slee

Nuwin – New-win

Daiseeum – Day-zee-um

Novakin – Naw-vah-kin

Lissandra – Li-sahn-druh

Drachu – Draw-koo

Michas – My-kiss

Sirus – Seer-us

Meegana – Mee-gah-nuh

Georgyanna – George-ee-ah-nuh

Matron Olsander – May-tron Ole-sand-err

Sabreeny – Saw-breen-ee

Tylen – Tie-len

Priestess Genoova –Gen-oo-vuh

Bavar – Bah-varr

God Zorifel –Zorr-ih-fell

Goddess Nuleef – Null-leaf

Goddess Verasellee – Vair-uh-sell-ee

Fae Races, Territories, Seas, & Cities

Solis – Saw-liss

Nolus – Naw-luss

Lochen – Lock-uhn

Silten – Sill-tun

Harrivee – Hair-uh-vee

Isalee – Iss-ah-lee

Kroravee – Quor-uh-vee

Mervalee – Merr-vuh-lee

Osaravee – Oh-sar-uh-vee

Prinavee – Prin-uh-vee

Glassen Barrier Islands – Gloss-en

Adriastic Sea – Aid-ree-ass-tic

Brashier Sea – Bra-zhee-err

Tala Sea – Tall-uh

Derian Forest – Dare-ee-un

Wisareian Forest – Wiss-are-ee-un

Isle of Malician –Muh-liss-ee-un
Pasibith – Pass-ih-bith
Solisarium – Sole-liss-are-ee-um
Vemil Brasea – Vem-ill Bra-sea
Vockalin – Vock-ah-lynn

CHAPTER 1 - NORIVUN

My mate, guards, and I mistphased to the castle's courtyard and landed back in Solisarium by nightfall. Our refuge on the Nolus continent was now behind us—the safety of the inn a distant memory. We would be staying on our northern continent from here on, and we could only pray to the gods and goddesses that our home land would be kind to us.

Moonlight penetrated the pastel-colored clouds in the night sky, the three moons' light like rays of falling snow. The glittering light flickered off the eternal mark that swirled across my finger. A mark I'd received only hours before.

Since we'd reappeared in an area south of the castle's front entrance, one not heavily patrolled during the castle guard's night watch, we were alone. The sparkling ward that encompassed the entire grounds in a dome was thickest here, and the soaring wall at my back was as high as the second floor. Nobody could magically travel to this part of the yard—not unless one was a member of the royal family.

I stared at the huge monstrosity rising above me. Sometimes, I hated this palace. Hated its wealth and decadence. Hated its prestige and pretentiousness. There wasn't one part of this castle that my father hadn't tainted with his brutal hands and malicious intent.

I knew to some, the castle was a residence to aspire to. To me, it had always been a prison I couldn't escape from—nor could my mother.

When the mistphase calmed around the six of us, and our bodies solidified into whole fae once more, I immediately cast an illusion over all of us. My affinity fell like a gentle mist, cloaking us entirely.

"We're fully hidden?" Ryder asked, his sharp cheek-bones looking like a razor's edge in the moonlight.

"We are. I'll keep us cloaked until Drachu's neck-lace and the looking glass are safely stowed."

Ilara glanced up at me with worried violet-colored eyes. Her beautiful white feathered wings stayed tucked between her shoulder blades. "Are you sure your father won't find them?"

The mate bond inside me hummed, and I placed a hand on her lower back, stroking her through her tunic. "He hasn't found anything within my safe before. I'm sure."

She gave a curt nod, and some of her pulsing anxiety through our bond calmed.

Before coming here, we'd all agreed that it was best to stay undetected until the looking glass and Drachu's necklace were hidden. Since the pendant held a stone with the ability to harness Ilara's affinities, she was vulnerable if it fell into the wrong hands. And given that the looking glass proved what the warlock had done in Isalee—a warlock my father had hired—we all knew what the king would do if he got his hands on it.

Until those items were secured within my safe, which was tucked deep in my closet and sealed by my blood and magic, we wouldn't rest easy.

After that, we would find my father, King Novakin, and present Ilara to him as he'd demanded we do after she'd fled following the Rising Queen Trial. But the king didn't know what else we had planned. To him, we were simply returning with my mate. Yet now, Ilara and I were united in an eternal marriage—a bond that not even the king could break.

And our vengeance was coming.

Of course, all of us would know—my father included—that my guards, Ilara, the Fire Wolf, and I had destroyed the veil of death in Isalee's field. Four days had passed since the incident, plenty of time for the warlock to report back to my father, but King Novakin lived under a ruse, his true nature hidden from the council and public. He couldn't accuse us of anything without also implicating himself, so right now, we would do the same. We would pretend we'd done nothing in Isalee until we were able to sway the king's council to our side.

My nostrils flared as my thoughts soared to what we needed to accomplish. The looking glass wasn't proof that my father had hired the warlock who'd created the veil, but perhaps it, along with Lord Crimsonale's testimony stating the king had met with the warlock a full season prior, would be enough to vote my father off the throne, which meant we needed to track down the Osaravee archon as soon as we were able.

Nish scowled at the dark castle. "Let's get on with it then."

We strode across the dim courtyard as snow flew. Footprints were left in our wake, but my illusion covered them as quickly as they formed.

A gust of wind lifted the cape billowing at my back while my silver hair tangled in front of my face.

Stones encrusted with snow and ice felt slick beneath my boots when we climbed the steps toward the door. My gaze shifted upward to the towering castle, and my wings splayed out. Power radiated along my limbs, stirring my magic as my mate and guards kept pace at my sides.

Three weeks had passed since I'd left these walls. Three weeks in which I'd been hunting for my mate and trying to undo all of the damage my father had inflicted on our fae and my wife. And three weeks in which my father had been waiting for my return.

Ilara also tilted her head up, gazing at the castle's opulent spires, turrets, and towers. Inside lay the throne room of the Court of Winter—the room my father was likely occupying at this very moment.

Worry strummed from her along our mate bond again, and the dragon within me stirred.

"What do you think he's going to do to me?" she asked as the door neared.

My nostrils flared. "Most likely, he'll send you off to your chambers. Since we're eternally bound, he can no longer insist that you marry Lord Arcane Woodsbury." Just saying the words tasted like acid on my tongue. "He'll be forced to accept you as the true Rising Queen."

Her throat rolled in a swallow. "He's going to be so angry." Midnight locks trailed down her back, curling and swaying in the breeze, gathering around her magnificent wings. "And your mother? Will he punish her in my stead?" She turned her violet eyes upon me again, and I wanted to crush the growing alarm swirling within them.

"I'll do my best to keep her safe."

Ilara nodded, but her shoulders remained stiff, and I hated that my words rang hollow. Because there had been so many times that I hadn't been able to keep my mother from the king's rage. So many times that my mother had been abused because I hadn't stopped it.

But that had been before, when I hadn't been willing to challenge the king. Now, I would taste his blood upon my tongue before I would see my mate or mother harmed again.

I swung the door open, and a large hall lit with fairy lights waited.

Warmth from the castle hit me. I strengthened my

illusion Shield around us, keeping our voices hidden from any passersby. Thankfully, no one was about to see the door open and close behind us.

Ilara stepped inside, and began to walk silently down the corridor, my guards at our backs. "Do you think he's already scheming to have that deadly veil re-instilled within Isalee?" she asked.

"Knowing my father, yes."

My guards growled quietly, and Ilara's nostrils flared as we strode down the hall toward my private wing.

While I wanted to outright accuse my father of what he'd done and what he undoubtedly was currently doing, such a tactic would prove fruitless. The king would simply deny any involvement. Worse, he was probably already covering his tracks and ensuring any link between him and the warlock was erased.

If we'd been able to come sooner, perhaps we could have caught him unaware, or if we'd been able to kill the warlock after he'd confronted us in Isalee's field, then it was possible my father would have never known what we'd done, but we'd been too weak to accomplish that.

The spell we'd found to counteract the veil of death had drained all of us entirely of our magic. We'd been too depleted to kill the warlock, and in that state we would have been too vulnerable to return to Solisarium to expose my father. The risk would have been too great.

But now, after four days on the Nolus continent,

resting and recuperating, we were ready to meet whatever was to come.

Familiar scents of roasting meat drifted through the air when we passed the kitchens. Guards were positioned intermittently, but none of them glanced in our direction since my illusion kept us invisible.

Ilara kept pace beside me, my guards moving just as swiftly. I didn't pause. Securing Drachu's necklace was paramount. I wouldn't expose Ilara to my father until it was safely hidden.

ONCE DRACHU's necklace was locked within my safe, I dispelled the illusion cloaking us. We still stood in my bedroom chambers, my wards firmly in place.

"Ready?" I placed my hands on my hips, eyeing everyone.

Sandus's silver beard shone in the fairy lights when he nodded.

Haxil crossed his arms, his round cheeks for once not lifting in a smile.

Nish's usual scowl made an appearance, and Ryder's braid settled between his wings when he tucked both hands behind him, close to his swords.

Ryder nodded toward the door. "After you, Your Highnesses."

We left my private wing and entered the common halls. We didn't mistphase. I wanted our return known now that the pendant and looking glass were safely stowed.

Servants froze in every corridor the second they beheld us and my mate's white wings. Whispers immediately erupted behind cupped hands, and the night staff became a tizzy of activity.

Since Ilara was entirely transformed within her angel affinity, her usual blue irises now shone like amethysts. And those rare eyes and equally unusual black hair among Solis fae made for a magnificent sight.

When we entered the convening area of wings, only a short distance from the throne room's entrance, the castle commander strode toward me.

"Prince Norivun?" The commander's gaze cut from me to my guards. Two palace guards flanked the commander's sides, their eyes bright yet apprehensive. Cocking his head, the commander added, "I see you've finally returned."

"Indeed we have," I replied dryly.

Not surprisingly, word had spread before we reached the throne room, the servants no doubt taking flight through their magical corridors and hidden halls that allowed them to navigate this monstrous castle at a high rate.

The commander took a step closer to my mate while assessing her white wings. His brow furrowed, a line appearing between his eyes. "Lady Seary?"

Ilara's chin lifted, her eyes defiant. The earlier nervousness I'd detected from her was still there, still strumming along our bond, but she hid it admirably. "I've returned."

"As I can see. The king's demanded you be brought to him." The commander reached for her arm.

"Be careful how you touch *my wife*," I growled.

The commander's arm whipped back, and I lifted my hand for him to see the mark that was inked into my skin. It was the supreme symbol that united all of the gods and goddesses—a circle with an array of connecting swirls and stars—a sign of our eternal marriage that declared we'd been bound before the gods.

"You're—" His mouth opened and closed. "She's your *wife* now? Your eternal wife? But Lady Endalaver—"

"Shall never be married to me." I clasped Ilara's hand, our inked bindings flashing in the fairy lights. "Lady Seary and I are eternally wed. Not even the king can alter that."

The castle commander gaped.

We strode past him, heading toward the throne room doors.

Ilara's wings shimmered like glittering snowflakes in the wide hall. The bright lights illuminated the space as the familiar tapestries holding scenes from all of the territories decorated the walls.

At the final ice doors, the guards' eyes were wide, their mouths hanging open.

"Have you forgotten your jobs?" Nish snapped

when we stopped before them, and the doors remained unmoved.

"Sorry, my prince. Very sorry." They both bowed and opened the doors simultaneously.

The six of us strode inside without pause, my steps increasing in speed when my father and mother appeared at the end of the large throne room, on their dais with a few nobles surrounding them.

The second my father's attention alighted on Ilara, he sat straighter on his throne.

Our footsteps echoed in the huge room, and when we reached the bottom of the dais stairs, we bowed automatically.

"Leave us. Now." My father's cold words cut to those around him. The nobles scattered and disappeared out the doors until it was only the guards, my mate, and my parents.

Gray hairs streaked through the white hair at my father's temples, but despite his middle age, the king's eyes were sharp and his body fit. My mother appeared as she always did. Calm. Poised. Regal. Long hair draped down her back, white from the illusion I'd hidden it under. Without my illusion, her hair was as black as my mate's.

"You go too," my father said icily, eyeing all four of my guards. "Out. I would like a word alone with my son and the female."

My jaw locked, and my nostrils flared. *The female.* I could defy him, insist that my guards stay, but if I did, they would, and their disobedience to their king could send them to the dungeons.

Black wings rippled around my guards' backs, their magic soaring as their warrior affinities heated their limbs, but I shook my head. "Do as he says," I commanded.

The king scoffed when my guards responded to my bidding after hesitating at his. It was only when they'd left the room that he muttered, "Such insolence." His attention snapped to the queen. "Lissandra, return to your tower. I meant it when I said I wanted a word alone with Norivun and the female."

My mother stiffened and then stood. Her complexion was clear, no bruises present as had been the case the last time I'd seen her, but that didn't mean the rest of her remained unscathed. Yet one would never know from the strong way she held herself.

"As you wish, my king." She glided down the stairs, and her attention drifted to Ilara's and my hands. They were hidden behind our thighs, our eternal marks unseen, yet I knew my mother was aware of them when a tiny smile lifted her lips.

She brushed against me when she passed, her smile growing broader. As much as my father tried to suppress her affinities, he never had been able to completely.

"Well done," she whispered so quietly that I knew the king hadn't heard.

The ice doors opened and closed when she exited, the sound resonating through the room.

Ilara's chin rose higher as King Novakin leaned back on his throne. My father flicked a hand toward the guards at the doors, his fingers making a strange movement. When I turned to see what new activity was to follow his subtle order, both guards had left.

We were truly alone with the king.

King Novakin stroked his jaw. "So, you've finally returned." His words sounded neutral, but ice shone in his expression when he assessed my mate. "And you've brought the female from Mervalee, just as I requested."

His words lacked the smugness I would expect if he truly believed we'd come innocently.

Magic roiled along my limbs, and I stepped closer to my mate. I wanted to shield her with my body, but I knew she wouldn't like that. Ilara could handle herself, as she'd proven time and time again. "I have, Father. Just as you requested."

"How long have you been gone, Lady Seary?" The king continued to run a finger along his lower jaw. "Has it been three weeks? Three weeks of you defying my command?"

Worry strummed from her, yet she replied in a steady tone, "Yes, I did flee and defy your command, but only because I could not watch my mate marry another."

The king's eyebrows rose. "Ah, *mate*, now is it? Does that mean . . ." His words hung in the air, like icicles suspended from a fall, before he inhaled through his nose, then began to chuckle. "You *are* mated. You each carry the other's scent now. How tragic it is if you're fully bonded to one another. You do know that my son will be marrying Lady Endalaver in only a week's time, don't you?"

"I won't be," I growled. "Ilara and I have eternally wed. I'm bound to her for all time. Even *you* cannot break that bond." I held up our hands, the marks of our eternal marriage glittering in the fairy lights.

"You—" Wings whipping out, my father shot to standing. "You enacted the ancient bond?" His face mottled, and his hands fisted. "You dared defy *me?*" His voice boomed through the throne room like exploding glass.

Ilara jumped, her pulse fluttering in her neck.

Seething, I stepped closer to him and snarled, "You gave me no choice. The wedding to Georgyanna is off. Ilara will be the next queen."

A moment passed, and then another as the king stood as still as a statue. His aura clouded around him, the air in the room dropping to freezing temperatures from his air elemental affinity even though his expression gave away nothing.

"You truly defied me. Both of you." His attention snapped to Ilara.

I bared my teeth and stepped in front of her. "She's my *mate*. Did you really think I would ever marry another?"

The king's nostrils flared, and then he took a step down the stairs, first one, then two. He took his time descending, watching Ilara's quickened breathing and widening eyes. When he reached the bottom of the stairs, he stood before me.

We were the same height with similar builds. But whereas my hair still held the pure silver color of youth, his had turned snowy white with gray at the temples from middle age. His age didn't detract from his intimidation, though, something he relished.

My jaw clenched. I didn't flinch. I held eye contact with him, not once looking away. It wasn't the first time we'd danced this dance.

Veins bulged from his neck, and his eyelid twitched. "I am the *king* of the Solis continent. My word is law."

"And Ilara and I are eternally bound. Even *you* cannot break our marriage."

His lips quivered, and he snarled low in his throat. "Guards! Apprehend this female!"

Two sets of boot steps reached my ears, letting me know the guards had returned. My death affinity rose, and I said on a low growl, "You're *not* to touch her. I'll kill you if you do."

For the briefest moment, my father's eyes widened, and in that expression I knew he understood how serious I was. I would kill him, here and now, and damn the consequences if he so much as laid a hand on my mate.

But as soon as that fear was upon his face, King Novakin laughed, the sound low and cruel as the approaching footsteps grew louder. "Is that right? You think you could actually kill me? On the contrary, I believe I can do whatever I want with her. You both defied me, but since you're the crown prince, and imprisoning my own flesh and blood would be seen as distasteful among our kind, I won't apprehend you, but *her*—"

He rounded on Ilara, who'd turned as white as snow. "She shall join her village archon in the dungeons where she belongs."

"No!" My bellow rang throughout the throne room, and my death affinity rose. Movement flashed in my peripheral vision.

"Nori!" Ilara screamed as her fear slammed into me.

But my death affinity was too fast to heed her concern. It shot out of me, aimed right at the king, just as Ilara tried to wrench me away.

"Behind you, Nori! Move out of his—"

A firm hand clamped onto my shoulder.

My death affinity's tendrils ensnaring my father's soul disappeared into oblivion, like mist in the wind, and the magic that perpetually rumbled along my limbs *vanished* as all of my magic, power, and affinities locked down inside me so tightly that it was as though they'd never been.

Sputtering, I spun around to confront whatever guard had touched me.

"No!" Ilara cried again. "Mother Below!"

Shock blasted up my spine when I beheld green eyes, blond hair, and light-brown skin.

"Hello, Prince Norivun," Tylen inclined his head— the Lochen fairy with magic strong enough to null any fairy's powers. "We meet again."

CHAPTER 2 - NORIVUN

I yanked out of Tylen's grip, my eyes wild. The doors to the throne room burst open, and a dozen guards ran in, jogging to flank the Lochen prince's sides. Two stayed behind, locking the doors with a solid bar of Isalee steel.

Dread worked up my spine, and my arm shot out, propelling Ilara backward, keeping her away from all of them, but the king was at our back, and the guards and Tylen surrounded us.

I called for my magic, begged it to heed my command, but Tylen's contact hadn't been fleeting. He'd clamped a hold of my arm, prolonging his nulling magic until it barreled through my system unchecked. My heart thundered as the strength of his power slammed down on my abilities, and given how long he'd touched me, I didn't know when I would be able to access them again.

Disbelief rendered me momentarily frozen, as was

Ilara, but then I snarled and advanced on the Lochen king's son.

Tylen's eyes flashed wide, and he bolted out of the way just as Drachu sauntered around a curtain near the window.

Ilara's heart thundered along our bond as my thoughts shifted rapid-fire. *How? How is Drachu here?*

The Lochen king smiled.

"What's happening?" Ilara gasped.

"Seize her," my father commanded. "*Now.*"

The dozen guards moved forward, and I realized whatever strange signal the king had done prior with his fingers had been to enact this attack.

Before I could blink, eight of the guards surrounded me, and four encircled Ilara. Swords pointed at my neck, abdomen, and back. Just as many pointed at my mate, but she quickly erected a Sheild around herself.

I advanced, but one of the swords sank into my skin, and a trail of blood appeared. The guard holding it trembled, but his grip held steady even when I growled.

"I would think twice about resisting, Norivun," the king said in a smug tone. "My guards have orders to detain you using whatever means necessary."

Ilara's gaze shot to mine, but despite the king's warning, she threw her air Shield until it covered me too.

"Nish! Ryder! Haxil! Sandus!" I yelled for my guards, but Tylen was suddenly there again.

He moved in a flurry of speed until his hands brushed against Ilara's Shields and then her arm. She spun away from him, but in a blink, her wings and violet eyes snapped out of existence. Terror flashed in her expression as the king's guards moved in on her.

Tylen moved quickly away, holding his hands up. "I'm sorry," he said so quietly that I almost didn't hear him. "But you left us with no choice."

Rattling came from the throne room doors.

"My prince!" Haxil yelled from the hall.

"Open these fucking doors!" Nish shouted.

Pounding came next as my guards tried to break their way in, but the Isalee steel held.

My father let out a booming laugh. "Mother Below, this is going even better than I thought it would."

I swirled around, seething at the tyrant on the throne, but my father's guards moved with me, keeping me caged in.

King Novakin wore a malicious smile. He fluttered his hand toward the Lochen prince. "Thank you, Tylen. You may retreat for now."

Tylen nodded stiffly, then walked briskly back to the curtained area. A curtain that hid a servant's passage.

"Fucking coward!" I snarled after him. The bastard had been *hiding* when he'd entered the throne room, then ran to do my father's bidding when he'd been summoned.

"We were set up," Ilara whispered as she stood frozen in the center of the guards surrounding her.

Drachu crossed his arms, watching everything with an impatient expression. The Lochen king wore a full set of clothing, unlike his usual attire, and the reality of our situation hit me like a ton of falling stones.

My father had known all along that Ilara and I would be coming. He'd known since we'd destroyed the veil that it was inevitable we would appear.

And he'd been waiting. Planning. Plotting.

"What do you want?" I bit out through clenched teeth as devastation rippled from Ilara along our bond.

The king crossed his arms, and his eyes narrowed into slits. "I believe you know exactly what I want."

More grunts and shouts came from my guards locked out of the throne room, but despite their efforts, they couldn't break in.

"Nori?" Tears filled Ilara's eyes as the guards began to pull her away. Fear pulsed toward me on our bond anew, and rage clouded my vision as my mate waited for my direction. Waited for me to tell her if now was the right time to rebel. The right time to act. She didn't know my father as I did, but *fuck him* for doing this to her.

"Fight them," I said to her in a deadly quiet tone.

I lunged toward her, but a sword to my stomach stopped me in my tracks. I knocked it to the side, not caring when another laceration grazed my skin. Snarling at the guard who wielded it, I continued to advance, but just as quickly, the other guards moved in to block me.

A flare of determination lit Ilara's eyes. Her hand whipped out and caught the first guard right beneath his breastbone. He coughed and staggered back.

She was already aiming for the second when the king said in a cold tone, "I would advise against that. You're to do as I command, Lady Seary, unless you would like your sister and friends brought before the court to bear punishment for your crimes?"

Ilara's next hit slowed, and her face paled. Her arms fell slack at her sides, as the first guard, still wheezing from her punch, grabbed hold of her again.

Her stricken face met mine. Cailis might have been safe at my hidden refuge on the Cliffs of Sarum, but Birnee and Finnley weren't, neither were Meegana or Beatrice. Ilara's village friends could be apprehended at any time, and the other two Rising Queen Trial participants were only steps away.

My features twisted as regret fired through me. *I should have ensured they were all safe.*

The king arched an eyebrow. "Lady Seary, your insolence has earned you time in the dungeons until I say otherwise. Should you choose to flounce my command again, I shall do what's necessary to ensure your obedience."

Her jaw dropped completely.

"Father, how *dare* you," I seethed.

The king swung his frosty blue eyes to me. "No. How dare *you*, Norivun," he spat. "You come into *my* throne room and act as though you've bested me, but you haven't." He stepped closer until I could see every wrinkle in the corners of his eyes. "I know what you did in Isalee."

His statement was said so low, so quietly that I knew no one else had heard him.

My eyes widened for a fraction of a second. My father had just admitted what he'd done to our continent. He wasn't trying to hide it any longer, not from me. He felt that confident in his victory despite what we'd done.

"Norivun!" Ilara's scream was wild, her eyes wide as a horrible, unsettling feeling swept through me.

My father was truly going to lock her away. Perhaps indefinitely.

My chest heaved, and I reached for my swords. My arms were sluggish, my affinities still gone, but I would *not* allow them to take my mate. "She stays with me."

"Take her to the dungeons," the king called to the guards. "Lock her in the cell next to her village archon, Vorl, or whatever his name is."

Ilara's face turned ashen.

My wings whipped out, fury pulsing through me. The eight guards who surrounded me all widened their stances.

"My prince!" Ryder bellowed from outside another door to the throne room. That door also rattled but refused to budge.

I swung my sword as half a dozen guards tried to tackle me, but I darted out of the way. One hissed when my blade sliced along his abdomen.

"Father, don't do this!" I roared as I fought my way to Ilara.

With each second that passed, she was being

dragged farther and farther from my side.

Another guard leaped into my path. I cut him down as two more guards jumped onto my back.

Fury propelled me forward as my mate was forced through the corner exit. Her cries rang down the hall, and my heart exploded in pain.

"Father!" I bellowed as my sword found its mark on another guard's shoulder. "Don't. Do. This."

"Bring him down!" my father commanded.

Six more guards came in through the back doors, but even though I fought and creeped my way toward where they'd taken my mate, I was one against a dozen.

I lashed out, cutting down two more guards before the remaining tackled me to the floor.

I thrashed and punched, refusing to give up, but without my magic, I was simply a magicless male with nothing other than my size and training to guide me.

And it wasn't enough.

Lashing magic from the guards' restraints bound my wings, encircled my ankles, and cuffed my wrists. All of the guards were panting, their eyes wild as they beheld the Death Master in chains before them.

But as much as I yanked and pulled on my trapped magic to assist me, it wouldn't respond.

Regret ravaged my soul so sharply that pain sliced through my heart.

"Ilara!" I roared.

"Norivun!" Her answering call was faint. Distant. Blessed Mother, they were already dragging her below.

Ryder, Haxil, Nish, and Sandus appeared in the

courtyard outside of the throne room a second later. They each grabbed stones from the garden, then pulled their arms back to throw them at the glass.

I was about to yell at them to go after Ilara when my father said, "Don't. I'll shave their wings, then have them hanged for defying me."

The windows and glass doors shattered. All four of my guards blurred to my side, swords in hand and lips peeled back. Vengeance consumed their auras.

"My prince!"

They skidded to a stop at my side, snarling at the guards surrounding me. Ryder and Haxil immediately pulled me to my feet, then lifted their swords.

"Don't." I hung my head. With my limbs and wings restrained, I stood immobile before them.

"Don't?" Nish yelled, and the guards at my side flinched and stepped back.

"Correct. Don't," I repeated. I would die for my mate, but I wouldn't give my guards' lives for a fruitless endeavor. There were too many under my father's command. Too many for us to fight.

The king snickered.

With fisted hands, I gritted my teeth. Just as my father knew he could control me with my mother, he knew, too, of the depth of my affection for my guards. They were brothers to me. I would sooner cut off my own hand than give one of their lives for naught. Despite the torture unleashing upon my soul as Ilara grew farther away, I wouldn't have them die for a lost cause.

My mate would have to protect herself until we could free her.

Mother Below. A snarl of absolute rage threatened to work up my throat.

Drachu crossed his arms, watching all of the fighting and bloodshed as he drummed his fingers on his forearms. "Are we done yet?"

King Novakin inclined his head. "I believe so."

Given Drachu's bland features, I knew the Lochen leader didn't care what theatrics occurred in the Court of Winter. All he wanted was his damned pendant.

I spat on the floor since he was too far away to spit in the face. If not for him commanding his son, my affinities would be useable, and my mate would be free.

"My prince?" Sandus said, despair in his tone. The four of them still surrounded me, still waited for me to change my mind.

I shook my head. "Return to your chambers."

Nish's jaw dropped, and Haxil snarled. Ryder stepped toward me, but I cut them all an unrelenting look.

I said, *"Return to your chambers."*

All four of their chests heaved. They still didn't move.

Finally, Ryder, bowed. "As you wish, my prince."

He jerked his chin toward the ruined glass doors, and the four walked stiffly away. Away from me. Away from my mate.

But we couldn't win today.

My father clasped his hands beneath his great black

wings. A cruel smile lifted his lips. "Well, as I'd been about to say earlier, I had some visitors in your absence, as you can see." He cocked an eyebrow at Drachu, then waved toward where Tylen had retreated. "It seems you've been busy during the past three weeks."

Drachu's lips peeled back. "He certainly has."

"I believe you own something of the Lochen king's." My father *tsked*. "Really, Nori. Such bad manners to steal something that doesn't belong to you."

A sound came from the exit. I tensed and listened. My mate's calls were barely discernible now she was so far away, but every distant scream from Ilara was like a stab in my heart.

"You won't win," the king said calmly. He strolled in front of me again.

Fuck. Fuck. Fuck.

The king rounded on his guards. "See that he's taken to his chambers and locked inside. Our new, dear friend, Tylen, has agreed to stay at the Court of Winter until my son returns what belongs to Drachu. I would like Tylen to visit the prince hourly if needed to ensure Norivun does as I command."

I staggered back, nearly tripping since my ankles were bound. *Hourly?* I would never be able to fight my father if Tylen continually suppressed my magic.

The palace guards dragged me away, and Drachu and my father grinned.

It was the last thing I saw before the doors closed behind me.

CHAPTER 3 - ILARA

The guards forced me down a spiral staircase. Down, down, down. I called for Norivun just to let him know that I wasn't giving up, that I wasn't going to go quietly. But eventually his answering yells grew faint, then so silent I could no longer hear anything other than my own breathing and the guards' heavy steps.

Fairy lights dotted the stairwell's walls, illuminating the stark interior. Dank, cold stones slipped beneath my feet. With each step that passed, the air grew frostier, muskier, and damper. Closing my eyes, I tried to pull on my air affinity, in hopes it would give me a hint of what was at the bottom of the stairs, but . . . nothing. My affinities were still entirely suppressed, but I took some comfort in knowing that Tylen's touch had been so fleeting. With any luck, my magic would be back by the time we reached wherever we were going.

"Where are you taking me?" I asked.

"The dungeons are at the very bottom of the keep, m'lady," the guard on my left replied. He was young, probably no more than thirty winters. His jaw was tight, his eyes wide. He kept glancing over his shoulder, as though waiting for the Bringer of Darkness to appear like a phantom from the shadows and exact his horrific revenge.

I scoffed. "You should be afraid."

His throat bobbed, and his grip on me tightened. "Is it true that Prince Norivun is your mate?"

"Yes. We're eternally bound."

The guard on my right sneered. "Bollocks. The prince is to marry Lady Endalaver."

I hissed. "Look for yourself." I tried to whip my hand up for him to see, but the restraints held them behind my back, and with my affinities and magic still locked down, I could barely move.

Their footsteps slowed. Each of them glanced at one another over my head.

"You look," the one on the right finally said with a grunt.

They stopped, and the younger one bent down and turned my hand. When his thumb brushed against the raised silver ink on my finger, he shot to standing, his eyes widening as he plastered himself to the wall. "Ock, Sillian, it's true! She's his eternal mate. Oh Mother, oh Blessed Mother, he's going to kill us. Surely, he'll—"

"Shut the fuck up, Earlish! We're doing as the

king's commanded even if she's not lying. We can't be held liable for that." Sillian's tone faltered when he added, "Surely, the prince will see that. Now, come on. Let's get her down there and get out of here."

They continued our descent until we reached the bottom of the stairs. Two new guards flanked an arched steel door with dozens of locks and bolts.

"Newest prisoner?" one drawled.

"She's the crown prince's mate," Earlish replied. "Lady Seary. She competed in the Rising Queen Trial."

The second guard straightened, then actually looked at me. When he assessed my black hair and wingless back, his eyes widened. "What's she doing here?"

"King's orders," Sillian grunted as his grip on me tightened. "She defied his command."

The guard's eyes widened. He fumbled with his keys to open the door. "Ock, the prince'll kill all of us for this."

"That's what I was saying," Earlish replied, his voice cracking.

"He can't," Sillian growled. "The king commanded it. We're just following orders."

I smirked. While I knew they were simply doing as they'd been told, as they'd been trained to do, I couldn't help the thrill that ran through me.

An answering stroke came on the mate bond, and I knew Norivun had felt my moment of glee. I closed my eyes and pushed my love toward him, guilt filling me that he'd only felt my terror in the throne room, but I wouldn't let that continue.

I will not be afraid. I will not subject my mate to my fear. I can handle whatever's to come.

The Mother knew this wouldn't be the first time I'd faced cruelty in my life.

I pushed another stream of love toward Norivun and was careful to hide my apprehension at what lay ahead. At least I could still feel my mate. Even Tylen's nulling magic didn't have the power to suppress our mate bond born of the gods.

A dark spiral of Norivun's fury coasted back to me. Jagged edges of wrath and rage twisted from him. I had no idea what the king had done to him, but my mate was furious.

I took another breath, forcing myself to remain calm. I didn't know how long I would be kept down here, but I would survive it.

When the door finally creaked open, both guards made the sign of the Blessed Mother when Sillian and Earlish dragged me past.

Ahead, a long, dim corridor sprawled before me. Cells lined each wall with iron bars. Inside the cells, chains hung from the walls with shackles at their ends. The door closed with a solid bang behind us, then I was alone with the guards in the dank dungeon.

For a moment, my resilience faltered. I gazed at what lay around me. Most of the cells were empty, but a few we passed held males, and one female from the looks of it. All were dirty and haggard-looking. Blood drained from my face when the guards propelled me forward.

Surely, I won't be here long enough to start looking like that.

I closed my eyes and felt again for my affinities. A faint stirring answered in my belly but nothing yet between my shoulder blades. *Crap.* They were still too weak to use.

Reality crashed into me when I realized that even if I could access my magic, I couldn't defy the king. Not yet. Even knowing what I knew, King Novakin still ruled this land. Despite the king being the one who should be locked within these cells, until the king was removed from power, overtly defying him would land me on the executioner's block. So I would have to endure his ruling . . . for now.

Earlish nodded toward the end of the corridor. "Her archon's at the end. He said to put her next to him."

Sillian grunted, and the two propelled me forward.

One of the prisoners stood at his bars and leered when I passed, then made a licking motion with his tongue. His teeth were rotten, his putrid breath detectable even from the distance.

"Aren't you a pretty thing." His gaze raked over my wingless back and dark hair. "Wings shaved, eh? Or are you Nolus?" He eyed my hair again. "What's your name, female?" He began to stroke himself, blatantly growing aroused for everyone to see.

I bared my teeth.

Earlish replied, "She's the Death Master's mate. I'd think twice before doing anything like that."

The prisoner's eyes rounded, and he whipped his hand out of his pants. I stared him down, lip curling, not once flinching, and he shifted back from his cell bars.

Despite my bravado, rivers of ice flowed down my spine. Without my magic, all I had was Sandus's training to protect myself if one of these males broke into my prison chamber.

When we reached the end of the hall, Earlish and Sillian stopped at the last cell. Hay lined the floor of the small enclosure, and the windowless stone held bits of frost.

With a twist of his key, Sillian opened the door and pushed me inside. I flew forward, landing on all fours. I seethed over my shoulder at him.

The youngest one's throat bobbed. Once my door was locked, they both stepped back.

"We only did this 'cause the king commanded it." Earlish made the sign of the Blessed Mother. "Please tell the prince that."

Sillian jabbed him in the side. "He won't kill us. If he does, he'll answer to the king. Get moving, boy."

Wings tight to their backs, they ducked down the hall, and when they reached the end, a loud creak followed as the dungeon's main door opened and closed. After that, the dungeon grew eerily quiet. Everyone's eyes fell upon me, and then their whisperings began.

I knew if I strained to hear, I could probably decipher what they were saying, but I didn't want to. If it wasn't lewd comments, it would likely be questions or wanting to know why the crown prince's mate had been locked up. None of those curiosities were anything I would reply to.

I shifted my attention to the cell next to me. A wall of bars separated us, and a male lying on the floor was plainly visible. He hadn't moved since I'd arrived. Huge, limp wings flopped to his sides. Overgrown hair hung past his ears. The only reason I knew he was alive was from the slight rise of his chest.

"Vorl?"

His head lifted slowly, and I crept closer to my cell's bars so I could see him better. Shock bolted through me. "It is you."

Vorl pushed to sitting, his eyes going so round I thought they'd pop out of his head. "Ilara?"

I tried to hide my reaction, but I'd never seen him look so *defeated*. "Fancy seeing you here."

My wry comment had a cruel smile curving his lips, and inadvertently, my heart began to race.

But it was an age-old response. A learned response from seasons of abuse under this male's hands. But I wasn't weak or defective anymore. And I wouldn't be his prey again.

My fingers curled around the cell bars that connected us. Our gazes locked.

Dirt covered Vorl's face, and the stench reeking from him made me wonder if he'd been allowed to bathe at all in the three months he'd been down here.

Knowing the crown prince, probably not. And considering Vorl hadn't used his magic to self-cleanse, I couldn't help but wonder if my former archon was also being starved to suppress his affinities. He was certainly thinner now, his bulky muscles leaner and more defined.

Vorl rolled to his feet. Life seemed to flow into him when he prowled toward me, but I didn't back up.

Another tingling of my affinities rumbled in my belly. The brief touch from Tylen was beginning to wear off, thankfully, but that wasn't the only reason I refused to cower. Never again would I show submission before this male.

"I knew he'd tire of you." Vorl's smile grew. Despite his once-huge build looking considerably thinner, his demeanor hadn't changed. A familiar sadistic gleam entered his eyes. It was a look I'd spent my entire childhood running from. "Did the prince finally tire of his favorite whore?"

My eyes narrowed. "What did you call me?"

Vorl spat on the floor, then grinned. "His whore. It's what you are, isn't it?"

"I'm his *wife*."

His eyes flared briefly, but then he laughed and said sarcastically, "Oh, right, his wife, because a member of the royal family would undoubtedly be sent to the dungeons."

I scoffed. "Ock, Vorl. Suit yourself. Believe what you want."

"Oh, I will, just as I know that you *are* his whore."

My jaw locked, the muscle pulsing in the corner. I gripped the cell bars tighter. "Don't you feel any remorse for what you did to me? Do you feel any regret at all for how much you abused me?"

"Regret? When you were a subject under my command? As your archon, it was within my right to treat you as I saw fit."

"That's not true, and you know it. Being an archon doesn't give one the right to hurt another."

Vorl shrugged, and his wings lifted higher along his back, making him look more like the male I remembered. "I disagree."

My jaw dropped. "You've really learned nothing during all of the months you've been down here? You truly don't believe you ever did anything wrong, much less feel remorse for it?"

"The only remorse I feel is not killing you when I had the chance." Vorl strolled forward until only the bars separated us.

Another stirring of my affinities swirled inside me, and I stoked that flame of magic.

He smirked. "Besides, something tells me if you're here, the prince and king agree with me that you're nothing but a worthless fairy who deserves every bit of punishment I ever inflicted on you."

Before I could react, his hands whipped through the bars and encircled my throat.

For the briefest moment, shock rendered me frozen, but then I jerked my arms up fast enough that they

34 ❄

blurred, and I had Vorl's thumbs in my grip in a move Sandus had taught me months ago.

Before Vorl could blink, I wrenched his hands off me as his thumbs remained in my grasp. I knew I could let him go. Knew I could end it here.

Yet this male hadn't learned anything from his time in the dungeons.

He truly would never change.

And if these hands couldn't be used to hurt me, then they could certainly be used to hurt another.

A small shadow of darkness slithered through me until it beat in a throbbing hum.

"You'll *never* hurt a female again." I snapped Vorl's thumbs back with a wrenching twist.

Resounding *cracks* echoed through the dungeon as my former archon let out a howl of pain. He staggered back, staring at his thumbs, which now bent at unnatural angles. And I knew without a healer to assist him, his fingers would never work properly again.

"You witch!" Disbelief shone on his face as spittle flew from his mouth. His teeth clenched, and then roaring, he charged and hit the bars so hard that they rattled. He thrashed, trying to reach me despite his fingers growing swollen and purple.

I crossed my arms and arched an eyebrow. Howls of laughter and hooting came from the other prisoners.

The sound of locks being turned came from the main door, followed by creaking and groaning. When the final lock unclicked, the dungeon door swung open, and the two guards came to investigate.

"What's the meaning of this!" one of them yelled.

Vorl snarled and continued trying to grab me.

I stepped closer to him and knocked his thrashing limbs to the side. He howled when I made contact with a broken finger as the guards marched toward us.

"You know, at first I told the crown prince not to torture you," I said quietly. "I asked him to show mercy as I thought any fairy deserved." The guards grew closer. The other prisoners' jeers rose higher while they avidly devoured the scene I was causing. "But I see now that you haven't changed at all, and you never will."

Vorl's lips curled back in a snarl. *Mother Below.* He looked more animal than fae right now, and I had a feeling I was looking directly into the eyes of the beast I'd always known he was.

I leaned closer and hissed, "I think next time I'll stay and watch what Norivun has planned for you."

I kicked precisely through the bars, hitting him at a calculated angle in the knees, which knocked my former archon to the ground just as the guards reached our cells.

Vorl yowled again, but he immediately pushed himself up.

The guards scowled and looked from me to him, then back to me.

"What did you do?" the taller one asked.

I crossed my arms. "Something I wish I'd been able to do a long time ago."

And for the first time, I felt the truth in those words.

While I still was and always would be Ilara Seary, daughter of Mervalee Territory, the female who believed in kindness and justice for all fae, I was also the true victor of the Rising Queen Trial.

And a queen knew when to let her vengeance rise.

CHAPTER 4 - NORIVUN

I paced in my private chambers as Balbus scurried about, doing everything he could to appease my foul mood.

Three days.

It had been *three fucking days* since Ilara had been taken from the throne room and locked in the dungeons while I'd been locked in my chambers like an errant toddler.

"My prince, I'm sorry. What can I do to assist you?" Balbus twisted his hands. "That horrid Lochen prince will no doubt be back within the hour, but perhaps I could help you escape, and then your affinities could finally return. Please, my prince, tell me what I can do."

My faithful servant's jowls jiggled he was talking so fast, but there was nothing he could do to help me. Not unless I was willing to risk my father's wrath if he found out Balbus had assisted my escape, but I wouldn't do that to a male who'd been nothing but loyal to me.

I would have to find a way out of this myself, but as long as Tylen returned and suppressed my affinities every hour, I would remain significantly impaired.

Growling, I tore a hand through my hair. I couldn't mistphase. I couldn't enact my affinities. I couldn't even self-cleanse since my magic was so suppressed. Worst of all, I couldn't speak with my guards or see my mate.

My father had stationed two of his guards outside my bedchamber doors, and they refused my exit or anyone's entry other than my servants and Tylen, although they didn't know about Nuwin's secret visits.

Thankfully, Tylen was growing weary. The male hadn't slept properly in three days, and it was beginning to show. Fatigue lined his features. On his last visit, it'd taken him a long while to suppress my power since during nighttime hours, he'd been woken every hour since I'd returned. We both knew he couldn't keep this up indefinitely. He needed sleep.

But since I refused to give Drachu the pendant he so desperately coveted, this ridiculous game would continue until either I caved or Tylen wasn't able to be roused to come to my chambers.

But I wouldn't give in. Even if my father ordered my torture, I wouldn't betray the pendant's location. If I did, my mate would be forever vulnerable and at the Lochen king's mercy.

My jaw locked when I pictured Ilara in the dungeons, and I swallowed the howl that wanted to work up my throat. I was failing her. Totally and completely failing her.

My pacing increased, and Balbus twisted his hands. *How? How can I free her?*

I swung back around in front of my fireplace as snow beat against the window. I clasped my hands behind my back and trailed a finger along my wrist.

I stopped short.

Of course. How have I not thought of it sooner?

I swirled toward my servant. "Balbus, there is something you can do for me, but I'll need you to be discreet."

ANXIOUS ENERGY COILED in my stomach as I waited for my servant to return. I stood at the window, my wings as tense as my shoulders while I stared outside. Tylen was due back within the next thirty minutes, and I needed to conduct the ritual before then.

"Do you want me to try and get it?" Nuwin stood at my side, his hair tousled and eyes bright. My brother's clandestine visits during the past three days had only been possible because of the trap door in my sitting area's chambers. Our father had banned his visits too, yet the king didn't know about the secret passageways Nuwin and I had constructed over the seasons.

"No. The risk is too great. Balbus will find it. It's best that you stay near Mother and try to keep Father away from her, and that you keep trying to see my mate." I dragged a hand through my hair again. "Have you been able to get in the dungeons today?"

Nuwin's eyes dimmed. "No, it's the same as the last three days, but I'll keep trying even though the guards are staying resolute. It doesn't help that Father's threatened all of them. They're too worried they'll meet the executioner's block if they defy him and allow me entry."

"What about Ilara's friends? Did you go to them as I asked?"

Nuwin nodded, and the light caught on his silver hair. "I was finally able to get them alone. Meegana and Beatrice said they'll visit her today before one of their lessons. It's the time they're the least observed, so they're hopeful their royal marriage tutors won't notice their absence. With any luck, the guards will let them in. I doubt those two are in Father's thoughts. He has too much else going on."

My nostrils flared. "Good. Just get somebody in there. I need someone she trusts to check on her."

"I will. I'll try again tonight if her friends—"

"My prince!" The door flung open behind me, and then Balbus was racing to my side. With wide eyes, he bowed hastily before thrusting a book toward me. "I believe I found it. Is this the one you spoke of?"

My eyes gleamed when I beheld the book of ancient spells. "It is. Thank you as always."

Nuwin smiled broadly. "Well done, Balbus."

"A pleasure, my princes. Truly. What else can I do to assist?"

"Nothing, other than stand back." I hurriedly thumbed through the book, looking for the spell I'd recalled seeing back in my university days when I'd been testing and evaluating my ability to scry.

The words leaped out at me when I reached the section titled, "Fairy Bargains: Necessities and Toils." I read it quickly, memorizing the spell.

When finished, I snapped the book closed, then grabbed my crystals from my safe. I would need them with my magic so suppressed. It would take the crystals' power to channel what I could.

Balbus watched on, twisting his hands continuously, and Nuwin bowed his head.

"Good luck, brother."

"Let's hope this works." Nostrils flaring, I closed my eyes while concentrating on the crystals in my palm. Because if this plan didn't pull through, I was out of options to save my mate.

CHAPTER 5 - ILARA

"This is dreadful, truly dreadful!" Meegana held my hands through the bars of my cell as Beatrice nodded from behind her. Their surprise visit following my sorry excuse for a supper had been the most joyous thing I'd experienced in three days.

But given their expressions, they were anything but joyful. Still, a genuine smile streaked across my face.

Meegana shook her head, despite my demeanor, and tears formed in her eyes. "How can the king lock you down here? You've done nothing wrong, not truly."

I shrugged. It just felt *so* good to see someone I knew and cared for, and I gripped her hands even tighter through the bars before saying ruefully, "I did defy his command. I refused to marry Lord Arcane Woodsbury."

Meegana grasped me harder. Despite her small build, her grip was sturdy and strong. "And I'm to marry that vile Lord Waterline, and Beatrice is to marry Lord Brusher." She shuddered.

"While I'm not thrilled at an arranged marriage either, Lord Brusher does seem the least despicable of the three." Beatrice lifted her wide athletic shoulders. "But I still would rather not marry him," she added with a sour expression.

"I'm sorry." I squeezed Meegana's hands one last time, then gripped Beatrice's. "I'll try to help you both find a way out of it, if I ever get out of here."

"Oh, Ilara," Meegana cried. "This is just dreadful!"

I forced a smile, but she wasn't the only one concerned about my state. Through the bond, Norivun's rage strummed toward me. He'd been like that for three days straight, yet since I was still locked up in the dungeon, I knew his father had found a way to restrain the crown prince too.

Meegana dabbed at her eyes. "Did you know that my wedding to Lord Waterline is in less than two weeks' time, only a week after the crown prince was supposed to have married Georgyanna? Unlike you, I'm not eternally wed to another, so I'm not sure if there is a way out of it."

"This is a dreadful situation for all of us," Beatrice agreed just as a distant shudder shook the walls.

Meegana cocked her head and glanced upward. "Did you feel that?"

I frowned. "I did." A tingle of heat flared on my inner wrist. My frown increased when the single petal —the mark that had disappeared after Norivun and I had obliterated the veil in Isalee—glowed on my skin, then began to throb. My eyes widened when another rumble came from above. "How odd," I murmured more to myself than them.

"What's going on up there?" a familiar female voice called from down the dungeon's hall.

Beatrice groaned. "Ock, don't look now, but it seems you have another visitor."

I rolled my eyes when I spotted Lady Georgyanna Endalaver sauntering toward us. All of the prisoners whistled and made rude gestures toward her when she passed.

The Kroravee witch wore the crown she'd won in the second test, the gemstones glittering in the dim light. A lilac-colored gown covered her lithe frame, the bright and cheerful color looking completely at odds with the dark and dank dungeon.

"Well, look who's here," Georgyanna called. "I thought I saw you two sneaking down the stairwell." When a third rumble shivered the stones around us, she reached a hand to the wall to steady herself. Some of her bravado faded before her spiteful expression returned. "If it's not the biggest losers in the Rising Queen Trial, all together in one place." She adjusted the crown atop her head and twirled a curl of her short silver hair around the glittering stones.

Beatrice made a sound of disgust.

"You wanna come visit me, pretty thing?" one of the prisoners called to her.

Georgyanna sneered in his direction, then gave him

her back and flexed her wings. Despite her slight figure making her appear delicate, she was anything but. One only had to know her soul to realize her fragile exterior was all for show. The female held a core of pure malice and wasn't afraid to use her affinities as weapons.

"What do you want, Georgyanna?" I asked in a hard tone.

"Isn't it obvious?" She stopped before my cell. "I came to gloat. You're finally exactly where you belong." She gave Meegana and Beatrice each a pointed look. "Oh, and I just told your tutors that you weren't to be found in the sitting room practicing your pianos as you'd been instructed." She twirled a piece of hair around her crown again. "Best hurry along before they venture there and find you gone."

"You're such a witch!" Meegana huffed. "And this place is more like where *you* belong. Perhaps you and Ilara should trade places."

Georgyanna bared her teeth at Meegana while Beatrice gave me an apologetic look.

"I'm sorry, but we should go." Beatrice squeezed my hands again. "If Georgyanna ratted us out, Meegana and I are going to get an earful. We were lucky to get away when we did without them noticing."

"We'll come again soon, though, just as soon as we're able," Meegana added.

Beatrice curled her lip at Georgyanna. "Sorry to leave you in such sorry company."

Georgyanna flicked her pinky finger at them as they gathered their skirts.

"Thank you for coming. It meant the realm to me." I blew them each a kiss, and both smiled, ignoring Georgyanna completely before they swirled away.

I gripped my cell bars, poking my face through the slats to watch my retreating friends.

"Stay strong, Ilara." Meegana turned to walk backward. She brought a fist to her chest. "The crown prince won't allow you to stay down here forever." She let out a squeal when one of the prisoners tried to grab her through the bars, then cast worried-looking eyes my way, but I forced a smile even though inside my heart was breaking.

I made my smile stay wide, though. But I desperately wanted to know what was happening above. If they'd been able to stay longer, perhaps they could have told me how Norivun fared or what the king was up to, but Georgyanna had to come and ruin it . . .

I scowled. *Alone once more with nothing but hideous fae surrounding me.*

I eyed Vorl. He'd kept quiet during the brief visit with my friends, but I knew he'd listened to every word of our conversation.

Once Meegana and Beatrice were gone, Georgyanna crossed her arms. "You know you'll probably die down here. I heard the king has no intentions of letting you go. *Ever.* Then the crown prince will have to be with me despite your eternal bond, and—" A huge boom rocked the walls. The Kroravee witch immediately ducked and scurried to the corner of the hall. "What in the realm was *that?*"

I gripped my cell bars when another boom, even stronger than the previous, rattled the entire floor above us. Dust sprinkled from the ceiling, falling on Georgyanna's perfectly styled hair and glittering crown.

The tingling on my inner wrist increased. My lips parted when the petal throbbed anew, then my breath sucked in when understanding hit me.

Something was happening, and I would have bet rulibs that it was related to my fulfilled bargain with the prince—the bargain that stated I would replenish the *orem* in our land's soil.

But how can that be? Our bargain was completed when we destroyed the veil of death in Isalee, and the *orem* had been allowed to surge to the surface.

Righting herself, Georgyanna glanced warily at the ceiling again, then she narrowed her eyes and adjusted her crown once more. Straightening to her full height, she sauntered back to my cell. "As I was saying . . . I also wonder what our citizens will think when I tell them how you deceived and tricked Prince Norivun and that he never wanted to actually marry you, but you forced his hand at the altar, and—"

CRACK.

A huge creaking sound came from above, and then a large fissure zigzagged across the dungeon's ceiling, splitting the stone.

Georgyanna screamed, and my stomach bottomed out.

"Dear gods," I muttered, no longer caring that Georgyanna had visited me simply to spew vile comments while forcing my friends' visit to be cut short.

"What's happening?" Georgyanna shrieked.

"It must be a very powerful earthquake." Vorl huddled in the corner of his cell, as far away from me as possible. The other prisoners began to yell and shout.

The mark on my wrist flared *again*. Brow furrowing, I shook my head. "I don't think it's that."

"Then what is it?" Georgyanna shouted as the other prisoners rattled their bars and called for the guards to free them.

"It's the gods." The castle shook again, and my heart beat harder. While I didn't think the dungeon walls were going to cave in, I also didn't know for certain that they wouldn't.

Either way, I had a feeling it wasn't safe to stay here, but I didn't know how to escape, and I didn't know why the gods were exacting revenge now. But the more time that passed, and the more explosions that came from above, all while my mark continually tingled along my skin, the more certain I was that such an event was occurring.

Especially when satisfaction barreled toward me on the mate bond.

Norivun. My heart surged.

My mate must have done something.

CHAPTER 6 - NORIVUN

My heart thudded, and its steady beat filled my ears. I held up my wrist. The shattered heart symbol that had disappeared after Ilara and I had destroyed the poisoned veil within Isalee was returning. It throbbed faintly along my skin. I now knew why the gods had chosen that symbol for me. My mate was imprisoned and being kept from me, and everything inside me was tearing apart at what my father was doing to her. My heart was indeed breaking, although shattering would have been a more accurate description.

Another rattle shook the castle, the entire floor rumbling beneath my feet.

Balbus's eyes widened. "My prince! Your power's returning. How wonderful. Perhaps Tylen's grown too weary to suppress—"

"It's not me, Balbus." When more tremors shook the

walls, my lips twisted in a cruel smile. I grabbed the window frame to keep from falling. That rumble had been even stronger than the first.

Outside, the guards practicing their drills in the courtyard all looked to my window warily. When another huge vibration rocked me to the side, a scream sounded faintly from down the hall.

But unbeknownst to them, these vibrations weren't from my expelling Outlets.

A glass window shattered in a chapel across the yard. *Pity.* I'd rather liked that stained-glass rendition of Solisarium. But I had no doubt that window hadn't been a random target.

Lightning abruptly zigzagged through the sky, and a crash of thunder boomed across the land.

A stone wall crashed to the ground, and more screams came.

"My prince!" Balbus's jaw dropped when a bolt of lightning hit the ground right outside the king's private chambers. "What in the realm is happening?"

I turned from my window and strode toward the door. "The gods are angry, Balbus. My father isn't allowing Ilara's end of the bargain to be fulfilled. The bargain guaranteed that she would be allowed to return to Mervalee to live in peace, and I just reminded them of that when I called for them to listen."

My servant's lips spread in a smile. Another terrible rocking of the castle shifted the stones beneath our feet. "That's what you needed that old book for?"

I gave a brief nod, then jumped back when my entire bookshelf crashed to the floor, and books flew everywhere. "Correct, that spell can force the gods to listen in regards to a bargain."

Because the bargain Ilara and I had made guaranteed she would be allowed to return to Mervalee Territory to live in peace. And by the king banishing her to the dungeons, locking her up possibly indefinitely, he'd ripped that choice away from her.

Inadvertently, King Novakin had altered what the bargain had promised my mate, but since it'd been a week since Ilara and I had completed our bargain, I'd needed to remind the gods of that. Most likely, their fickle interest had already shifted past us, but now—at last—the gods' revenge was coming.

The tremors turned even more vicious, and Balbus gasped, his smile faltering, but I didn't care. I welcomed the destruction of this entire palace.

Because not even a king was above the gods' wrath, and it was time I enlightened my father to that.

In the hallway, stones were shifting beneath one's feet, and servants were flying through the corridors, screaming and crying. Chaos was ripping through the royal castle while the rest of Solisarium remained untouched. It made it easy to get past my father's guards.

"Balbus, check on my mother and Nuwin. Please," I called as I strode down the hall while my servant scurried behind me.

"Of course, my prince."

Since I couldn't mistphase, I picked up a jog and ran the entire way to the throne room, dodging and dipping around crumbled walls and fallen pillars. When I reached the hall that led to my father's favorite room, I didn't even slow.

"My prince, you can't go in—"

I shoved aside the guard who stood at the entrance to the throne room. One of the ice doors had cracked completely, a huge jagged line cutting through the enchanted frame that kept it frozen inside the warm hall. It lay on the floor, leaving a huge gaping hole to the entrance of the throne room.

I stepped over the wreckage, satisfaction igniting inside me at the destruction.

Inside the throne room, my father was yelling at his guards and castle staff. Everyone was running about, some flying through the air even as walls shifted and glass shattered. Rocking *booms* shook the walls and floors every few seconds, and more and more of the castle began to crumble.

"You shouldn't have locked her in the dungeon, Father!" I roared from across the room. Wind whipped through the huge hall as an epic display of lightning continued outside. "You've angered the gods. This won't stop until you free her."

Fury filled the king's eyes when he rounded on me. "You!" He pointed an accusing finger my way. The rage on his face increased when he cut a path through the room toward me.

Cracks filled the floor, and his precious throne chair sat at an odd angle on his dais. Never before had such carnage caused a manic glee to rise inside me as it did at this very moment.

"What have you done?" The king seethed when he reached me. Wildness filled his eyes. He was losing control, and he knew it.

My lips twisted in a cruel smile. "I've done nothing. It's *you* that has angered the gods. They'll keep targeting you and your darling palace until you free Ilara."

Drachu appeared at my father's side, coming from a section of the throne room that had not yet crumbled. His dark hair was tangled and unkempt. Dust lined his forehead, and anger flashed in his eyes. "Give me my pendant, you bastard."

I bared my teeth at him. "Never."

The king shot forward and curled his hands into my shirt, his fingers like claws. "Stop all of this *now*."

My brutal smile turned sharper. "I couldn't even if I wanted to. A bargain Ilara and I made promised that she could return to Mervalee to live in peace. She fulfilled that bargain a week ago, so that promise needs to be kept, yet she hasn't had a chance to return to Mervalee, and now *you've* thrown her in the dungeon with no hopes of escape. No freedom. No peace. You've condemned her indefinitely, and the gods see that. Until you free her, this destruction will continue."

Veins bulged in my father's neck. "But *I* didn't make a bargain with her!"

I shrugged. "Perhaps not, but you know how the gods are. If a fairy isn't given what a bargain promises, punishment follows."

As though to prove my point, the ceiling above us shattered when an explosive bolt of lightning hit it. All of us ducked, covering our heads as my father cast an air Shield around us at the last moment. Debris rained down, and Drachu's cursing ratcheted up when more screams filled the air.

"What kind of kingdom is this?" Drachu's green eyes narrowed upon my father. He coughed and fanned the air. Dust billowed around us. "You can't even control your firstborn."

Smirking, I straightened and crossed my arms as the ground shifted beneath us again. Far below, beneath the keep in the dungeons, my mate waited. I knew she felt the carnage above. Fear bled through the bond, but something else did too—curiosity. She was still safe. The gods wouldn't allow her to be harmed in their wrath, but it could prove tricky getting to her if my father didn't free her soon.

"Stop this now!" my father bellowed in my face.

Drachu muttered a sound of disgust while I dusted my fingernails off on my shirt. "It will stop, my king, just as soon as you free Ilara Seary, daughter of Mervalee Territory, and allow her to return home."

The king's nostrils flared, and his cheeks turned a blazing crimson. His entire body vibrated, and I'd never felt such satisfaction in all of my life.

"Guards!" he abruptly yelled. "Release Ilara Seary!"

CHAPTER 7 - ILARA

Hope began to beat in my chest. The sound of groaning came from far above, and Georgyanna let out another shriek. The Kroravee native's gaze darted fearfully upward, then to the exit.

"Are you done with your gloating then?" I eyed Georgyanna vehemently through the bars.

The witch fumed even though fear shone in her eyes. Atop her head, her glittering crown was now covered in dust. I knew she'd worn it on purpose. It was as though she was doing everything in her power to rattle me and remind me that she'd ultimately won the Rising Queen Trial, and that she was going to remain the victor even if I was mated and eternally bound to the crown prince.

Until an hour ago, I would have been inclined to agree with her, but now . . .

Perhaps the gods had another plan in store for me that my mate seemed hell-bent on fulfilling.

Georgyanna's lip curled. A tendril of her oily manipulation affinity coated my Shield. Another blast echoed at the castle's surface just as Georgyanna tried to work her way through my protective magic.

And feeling her affinity try to take a hold of me, in a time when I was already stressed and anxious, just as she'd done to me at the stadium during our final test . . .

Snarling, I surged forward in my cell until my fingers curled around the cold bars. Magic rumbled in my gut. I called upon my air affinity. Shooting it toward Georgyanna, I punched right through her Shield until my affinity spiraled down her throat and coiled around the air in her lungs.

Her eyes widened, and she clutched her neck.

Another *boom* shook the castle, rattling the dungeon's bars, as I drew all of the air from Georgyanna's chest.

"You're not the only one who can make threats, Georgyanna." I forced her toward me on a gust of air, then with lightning-fast reflexes that had my warrior affinity humming, I spun her and had my arm locked around her neck, trapping her in a headlock with her back against the bars.

She thrashed, kicking and struggling, but my warrior strength held her firm.

Leaning through the bars, I whispered in her ear, "If you ever hurt me or anyone I love ever again, I'm coming for you." I held up my hand, showing her the

❄ 58 ❄

eternal mark that glimmered subtly on my finger. "You will *never* be queen of the Solis continent. The prince and I are eternally wed. The only one who will ever wear the queen's crown is Queen Lissandra, and if not her, then me."

I pushed Georgyanna away from me just as I released my air affinity's hold on her.

She fell to the ground, coughing and hacking. Tears filled her eyes when she glared up at me.

I bared my teeth, and she recoiled. I could only imagine the sight I made. No bathing had been offered in the dungeons, but I'd been able to self-cleanse using my magic. But even strong magic couldn't conjure a comb. And dust had been raining on my head since the destruction started. No doubt my hair was a fright.

A howl of rage worked up Georgyanna's throat, but then she shot to her feet and took off down the hall before taking flight, flapping her wings as fast as they could carry her. More dust fell from the ceiling as whatever battle was being waged above strengthened.

The cell block grew eerily silent after the steel door banged closed behind her. All eyes fell upon me. More than a few of the prisoners' gazes were wary and fearful, although some shone with respect. But when I shifted my attention to them, they all quickly looked away and went back to yelling and calling for the guards to free them.

Only Vorl remained watching me, but when I glanced his way, he ducked his head.

He still sat in the corner of his cell, his jaw tight as

another rumble shook the castle. I had no doubt that if I had Norivun's sensory affinity, I'd be detecting fear in his scent.

Since the first day I'd arrived here and shown him a hint of my powers, my village archon had kept a wide berth from me, never looking me in the eye nor muttering snide comments.

At least one of the bullies in my life had finally learned their lesson. With any luck, Georgyanna would be next. I could only hope that what I'd just experienced with her was the last encounter I would ever have with the Kroravee witch.

Another tremor shook the castle. All of the prisoners now stood at their cell bars, gripping and shaking them.

"Let us the fuck outta here, you fucking scum!" one of the prisoners yelled toward the door.

"Can't you hear us?" another one called.

But since Georgyanna had fled, the dungeon door hadn't budged, and neither of the guards standing outside had bothered to look in.

True fear began to run through me, but so did a strum of curiosity when my mark burned even more. If this truly was happening because of the gods, as my tingling mark implied it was, then would any harm come to me? Surely not.

The lights flickered, and a shift in the stone above caused a huge moan to reverberate through the dungeon.

Or maybe it would.

I gazed upward as my fear strengthened, and then I began to pick at my fingernails when the crack in the ceiling widened.

"We're all going to die in here!" one of the prisoners yelled.

But the rumbling abruptly stopped. Complete silence descended. Everything grew so still that I could detect Vorl's breathing.

A few prisoners shuffled their feet, most looking nervously about.

The steel door abruptly crashed open to the dungeons, and then the crown prince of the Winter Court stormed inside.

Wings as black as the night, with obsidian talons at their tips, scraped along the ceiling's stone. Eyes glittering with savage victory zeroed in on me, and a surge of the prince's devotion zoomed toward me on our bond.

My heart felt as though it would burst.

All of the prisoners gasped or made the sign of the Blessed Mother when he passed them, but Norivun's attention had locked onto me and me only.

The mate bond within me sang and brightened as my love for this male barreled through me.

A satisfied smile spread across his face when he stopped before my cell with two quaking guards in tow. Darkness gathered around his shoulders, and his tantalizing scent of cedar and snow wafted around him, but I didn't detect his aura.

My teeth ground together. *So Tylen has still been visiting him.* It would explain why he hadn't come sooner, but despite his suppressed magic, it didn't detract from my mate's strong presence and commanding demeanor.

"Release my wife," he snarled at the guards.

The second *wife* left the prince's mouth, renewed whispering and mumblings disturbed the air, but I didn't pay Vorl or any of the other prisoners any attention.

The guards fumbled with their keys and unlocked my cell door with a flourish.

"After you, my love," the prince said with an amused bow.

After three days with no magic or affinities, my mate had still found a way to come for me, and somehow, the prince had called upon the gods to seek vengeance when his own had been stilted.

I grinned and flung my arms around him.

Norivun ushered me out of the dank hall and up the castle's spiral staircase.

"Are you all right?" he asked quietly while his hand stayed glued to my lower back.

"You managed to find a way to free me from the dungeons and thwart your father, and you're asking me if I'm all right?" I arched an eyebrow as we walked quickly up the stairs. "Do you always ask such *asinine* questions, my prince?"

His lips curved, and he let out a low chuckle. "Ah, there's that sharp tongue that I love so much."

I laughed.

His grin slid slowly away. "We need to find my guards. Can you mistphase?"

I nodded as the scent of ashy magic being cast filled the air, growing stronger with each step I took. "What's that smell?"

"Our fae with constructo affinities are trying to repair the damage the gods caused. Their affinities can leave a lingering odor when they're working nonstop."

I rubbed at my wrist, where my mark had been flaring. It had disappeared again, only smooth skin once more. "So it *was* their wrath I was feeling. Does that mean you called for the gods?"

He grinned wickedly. "Indeed. It was the only thing I could think of. With Tylen visiting me every hour and my father refusing to set you free, I could think of no other option."

I paused and hugged him again, catching him entirely unaware in the stairwell. He crushed me to him, righting his balance as I whispered, "Thank you."

He enclosed me in his grip, his arms like steel bands around my waist. He dipped his head into the crook of my neck and inhaled deeply. "I'm sorry it took me so long."

"Don't be. It's not your fault."

He held me like that for a moment longer, then reluctantly let go. "Were you hurt down there?"

"No, quite the opposite in fact. I'm pretty sure Vorl will never touch me again."

A sly smile lifted his lips. "I wish I could have watched whatever you did to him."

"I'm sure you would have thoroughly approved, especially when Georgyanna came to visit, and I didn't spare her either. She was just here."

"I know." His lip curled in disgust. "I passed her on my way down. She was in quite a state." His curled lip turned into a grin again.

I laughed once more, unable to help it as we resumed our upward march. "Was anyone hurt during the commotion?" I pointed upward, toward the destroyed castle.

"Not severely. I heard some rumblings that a few were hit with falling debris, but nobody was killed."

"Good. I don't want any innocent fae hurt on my account."

His lips lifted in another crooked smile as fairy lights pierced my eyes the closer we got to the top of the stairs.

"So, where are we going now?" I asked when we reached the main floor. The prince stopped me before we could be seen, his arm curling around my waist.

"We need to get my guards, and then we need to find Michas. I have the looking glass with me. Michas needs to see that his father was right."

"Why Michas? I thought we were going straight to Lord Crimsonale with it?"

"If we could, I would, but that will prove tricky. All

of the councilors have been summoned due to the castle's destruction. They're busy right now, but Michas isn't. If we hurry, we'll be able to show him this and ask if he thinks it's enough evidence for his father to sway the other councilors to our side."

I nodded. "All right, let's find him."

We climbed the remaining steps. At the top of the stairwell, the door hung at an odd angle off its hinges, and when I pushed it open, I gasped.

Servants ran everywhere, and the constructo fae were hard at work as their affinities hummed around them. Chaos reigned. Dozens of fae were crying or blubbering, and those with authority were issuing orders.

Nobody noticed us.

Yelling and shouting came from all of the halls as the smell of the constructo fae's magic increased. I could only imagine the state the castle was in. Every wall and floor was cracked or crumbled. It was a miracle the palace hadn't imploded.

Before my eyes, a constructo fairy wielded their affinity. A huge split down a wall was repaired and sealed as though it'd never been cracked in half.

The prince leaned down and said quietly, "We'll have to go to Mervalee Territory after we speak with Michas. The gods will demand it. Until you've been returned home and then choose to leave on your own, forsaking your life of peace, their wrath will follow."

My brow furrowed. "Would it be better if I chose to stay in Mervalee and not return here?"

The prince eyed me, his expression going carefully blank. "Would you rather stay home?"

"I would rather stay with you, but at what cost to our fae?" I indicated those running around. "This destruction happened because of me."

"This happened because of the *king*." He lifted my chin, then traced his lips softly over mine. "War's coming, my love. It's either my father who starts a physical war with the Nolus, or we start a political war with him. Either way, it's happening. But if you would rather stay in Mervalee, I won't judge you for it."

I shook my head, then ran my tongue along his lower lip. He growled appreciatively.

"No, I'm staying with you. I would only stay in Mervalee if it benefited others and kept you safe." I inclined my head and ran a finger over two protruding stones near the stairs that were teetering and nearly falling out.

Norivun brushed a lock of hair from my face. "Is your magic strong?"

I nodded. "Tylen hasn't been visiting me. My magic has fully returned. And yours?"

His lips thinned. "Fully suppressed still, so you can mistphase all of us?"

"I can."

"Then I'll need you to take me and my guards with you. Until enough time has passed that I've recovered, you'll have to be the one protecting us."

My lips curved upward. "It would be my pleasure, my prince."

I mistphased us to the guards' chambers, and my shoulders sagged in relief when the prince's four guards all stood before us unharmed. "Thank the Mother you're all here."

"Mother Below, you got her out!" Sandus exclaimed to the prince before he pulled me into a hug.

I embraced him in return, not even minding when his bushy beard scratched my cheek. Once he let go, I gripped Nish, then Ryder, and Haxil into hugs just as fierce.

"Ock, Ilara," Nish mumbled. "I've never been so happy to see you."

Haxil chuckled and ruffled Nish's shorn hair. "I knew she'd win you over sooner or later."

"How did you get her out?" Ryder asked my mate.

"My father called for her release. I told him that until Ilara was freed and allowed to return home to

Mervalee to live in peace, as our bargain deemed so, the gods' destruction would continue."

"So that's what was happening." Ryder scratched his pointy chin. "We were placing bets on who fucked who to make the castle begin crumbling to pieces."

Nish smirked. "We were all wrong, obviously."

The prince placed his hands on his hips, a small smile on his lips, but it quickly disappeared when he eyed the door. "We need to find Michas and show him the looking glass. It's too risky right now to go to Lord Crimsonale since my father may learn of what we're attempting to do. We need to hurry. If Ilara doesn't return home soon, the gods' revenge will follow us."

"Ready?" I asked.

They all dipped their heads, and I whipped my magic around them in a blaze of mistphasing power.

We mistphased to the wing where archons and nobles stayed while they were at court, exactly to where Norivun told me to go.

The hall we landed in was dim. Nighttime had fully set in, and light from the moons penetrated the cracked and shattered stained glass windows high above us.

"This way." Norivun nodded toward a door. We stopped outside the young lord's chamber and knocked.

Silence.

The crown prince raised his hand to knock again, but then the sound of faint footsteps came from the other side.

All four guards gripped their swords just as Michas swung the door open.

The young lord's eyes popped in surprise. Not waiting for a response, Norivun pushed past him, getting a startled cry from Michas, before the crown prince shut the door behind us.

Michas glowered when all of us crowded in his chambers. "I wondered when I'd see you next." He waved his hand toward the destruction in his room—an overturned table, a cracked wall, a broken bed frame. "I'm assuming I have you to thank for this?"

The prince locked the door. The ring of the bolt filled the silence since none of us had deigned the young lord with a reply.

Michas's nostrils flared. "What in the realm is going on? My father was here not too long ago, telling me to stay safely locked within my chambers until he could learn more of what the king knows. Are you aware that the king is asking about her and all of you?" The young lord shot an accusing finger at me.

Norivun growled. "I'm sure he is, but he knows Ilara must be returned home if he wants to avoid the gods' wrath and keep his castle standing."

"So that's the reason for the destruction." Michas crossed his arms and arched an eyebrow.

"This conversation would be better held under a silencing Shield." I swirled my hand through the air, encasing all of us within a protective dome. "Go ahead," I said to my mate. "Nobody can hear us."

Norivun extracted the looking glass from his pocket

and angled it to Michas. "This is why we're here. Your father was right. This is who he overheard speaking with the king last season. It's a warlock from the *other* realm, and his magic is the reason behind the dying crops."

Norivun activated the looking glass, and the scene began to play out. Michas's eyes bulged, then his jaw dropped. I shivered when the image came to the battle. It was deadly and brutal, and even though it was only a recording of what happened a week ago, a river of ice skated down my spine.

Crossing my arms, I looked away and tapped my foot as we waited for Michas to see it in its entirety.

When it finished, I raised my eyebrows. "Do you think this is enough proof to convince the council of the king's involvement? If your father testifies to what he heard last season, and we show them this, do you think it'll be enough to vote the king off the throne?"

Michas's jaw worked, and he rubbed the side of his face. "Let me watch it again." Norivun replayed it, but when it came to the end the second time around, Michas shook his head. "It's certainly enough to convince my father that his suspicions were right, as well as Lady Wormiful since she's my father's ally, but I'm concerned that the other councilors won't accept it as enough proof."

"Even with your father's testimony accompanying it?" I pushed. "Surely the two together mean something."

Michas smiled ruefully. "Of course, they do, and I

would like to say that my father would testify against the king, but unless there was a guarantee that King Novakin would be removed from power, I highly doubt my father would risk it."

I scowled, and magic rumbled in my gut. "You're saying Lord Crimsonale won't testify to the council about what he overheard?"

Nish grumbled as Ryder hissed under his breath.

"What a coward," Sandus muttered.

Michas narrowed his eyes at all of them. "My father makes his decisions based upon risk and reward. You can't fault him for that."

I stepped closer to the young lord as more magic roiled in my gut. Keeping my tone as calm as I could manage, I said, "Now is the time to act and take a stand. Surely, your father knows that."

Michas's chin lifted. He studied me, his gaze skimming over my features, before his expression hardened. "My father knows the time is coming, but I can also guarantee that he's not willing to risk his neck. Not yet. If he did testify against the king with that looking-glass recording, there's a good chance at least one of the councilors won't side with us. And then what? My father will be exposed."

Norivun's power rumbled. Placing his hands on his hips, he said, "So you're saying that unless we find absolute proof that the king is behind the dying *orem*, your father will continue his two-faced dance and won't act."

Michas's nostrils flared. "You can't blame him for protecting himself."

"Mother Below!" Norivun cursed under his breath and tore a hand through his hair.

All four of his guards grumbled or scowled, yet none of this was surprising—as I was sure they all felt too—considering what kind of fairy Lord Crimsonale was. Despite all that was happening and all that was at stake, he was still more interested in his personal agenda versus saving our fae.

Norivun's lip curled, and he concealed the looking glass within his pocket. "Fine, if that's how it's to be, then we'll get solid proof. Proof that will require *everyone* to act and won't rely on a testimony from your father." My mate leveled me with his crystalline blue eyes. "Ilara?"

I gave a firm nod, and with a swirl of my magic, the six of us disappeared in a flash of mist and shadows, air and wind.

I MISTPHASED us to another area in the castle, and when we reappeared, Norivun's spine jolted upright. "Why are we at my mother's tower and not in Mervalee?"

"I know we need to get back to my home, but if Michas and Lord Crimsonale want absolute proof, then it's likely they're not the only ones who will be skeptical of the king's true nature. We need one more thing."

"What?" Norivun asked, a curious light entering his eyes.

"You'll see." I didn't explain further as we all began to climb the stairs of the queen's tower.

I knew we needed to return to Mervalee. Knew that I needed to be standing on home soil when I made the choice to forsake a life of peace.

But seeing the Crimsonales' unwillingness to act without absolute proof made me realize what we were up against. If Lord Crimsonale was reluctant to take action, a male who knew of the king's previous actions, then the other councilors certainly wouldn't side with us, and neither would the Solis fae.

We needed to build a strong and formidable case against the king if we were ever to dethrone him and keep him from reclaiming his power in the future.

Which meant we needed *everyone* on our side.

And there was only one way I could think of to do that.

An hour later, I finally mistphased all of us to Mervalee Territory just as the destruction in the castle threatened to start up again.

We reappeared in my childhood home, and after everything that had happened in the past three days, the scent and feel of the one place in my life where I'd always felt safe nearly undid me. I turned slowly around, soaking everything in. The worn table, scarred counters, cracked windowpane, old floorboards. All of it.

The scent of my family still hung in the air even though dust motes flew around us. The room was cold, the air chilled, but with a wave of my hand, my fire affinity ignited the wood within the hearth.

Flames flared within the fireplace, slowly taking the chill from the air, while Norivun's four guards eyed everything with curiosity. The last time I'd been here had been on my one and only official Trial date with the prince. He'd taken me home, brought my sister and friends along, and we'd enjoyed a carefree night of laughter and drink.

How long ago that date now felt.

"Are you doing okay?" Norivun asked softly.

I gave a stiff nod even though heavy emotions clogged my throat. "I am."

Norivun leaned forward, clasping my hands in his. "Are you sure you want to do this? The bargain protects you. If you choose to stay here, you'll be allowed to live in peace. My father can't take you again, lest he wants to anger the gods and goddesses a second time."

"He may not be able to take me, but he can still start a war, and not even the bargain could protect me from that." My long hair fell over my shoulders when I gazed up at him. "Besides, you know I would never agree to be parted from you. I belong where you are."

He cupped my cheek and ran his lips along mine softly. All four guards turned, giving us their backs and what little privacy they could in such a small space.

I fingered the silver eternal mark on Norivun's finger before declaring, "Bound forever, remember?"

His jaw worked, the muscle tightening in the corner as the firelight danced in his glittery sapphire eyes. "Forever."

Tilting my chin upward, I stated in a loud voice, "I've been returned home and have been given the option to live here in peace, but my answer is no. I wish to leave and fight the king."

A flare abruptly burned on my inner wrist, and the leaf once again made an appearance just as Norivun's did the same before both marks flashed out of existence, and this time, I knew they would never return.

From here on, my mate and I were on our own.

Norivun pulled me closer and wrapped me in his embrace. "The gods heard you, my love, and they've answered. They won't protect you from the king again."

"I know, and I don't want them to. I want to fight by your side as I was destined to always do."

He inhaled along my neck, and a spark of hope billowed through me that perhaps his sensory affinity was beginning to respond. "How's your magic?"

He lifted his head just enough to press kisses along my jaw. "It's starting to come back. It's been long enough since Tylen's last visit that I'm beginning to feel hints of it."

"How long do you think it'll be before you can access it?"

"With some food and rest, a few hours, but it'll be a day or two until I'm fully well."

"Then we'll stay here for the night. My garden is likely to be overflowing by now. I'll dig up some acorlis and harvest some of the vegetables and berries. We won't have any meat, but it'll be enough to get you recharging."

Norivun nodded. "We can all help."

Without waiting for an order, Haxil, Nish, Sandus, and Ryder all went to the back door, and Haxil pulled it open. Cold air immediately blew into the kitchen, but I flamed my fire higher in the fireplace, and it chased the chill away.

The six of us ventured outside into the cold, dark night. Several feet of snow covered the land, yet the path to my garden was still visible. Light from the three moons guided the way, sparkling off the snow like diamonds.

My heart swelled when my garden appeared in a haze of pulsing *orem*. The snow stopped at its perimeter, and a cloud of magic created a dome over it. Even though snowflakes scattered in the wind, when they hit my garden's magic, they fizzled out of existence.

I stepped over the edge of its barrier, and the familiar tingle of magic brushed against my skin.

A smile split my lips. All of my crops shone in a rainbow of colors. They all appeared healthy, happy, and well cared for, even though it'd been months since anyone had tended to them.

"Hello, my friends," I whispered and kneeled down to caress one of the pea pods.

"'Tis quite the home garden you have here, Ilara." Haxil surveyed all of my plants and fruits. "Most impressive."

My grin stretched, and I nodded toward the shed. "Gather whatever tools you need. There's plenty here to feed all of us."

TWO HOURS LATER, we were all sitting in front of the warm fire, our bellies stuffed with rich acorlis, sweet berries, fresh salad, and herbed potatoes. A portion of meat would have helped, but I didn't dare venture to old Dorn's home to request a hen. It was possible the king would send fae to hunt for me if he learned that I'd forsaken a life of peace, and the less I involved my fellow villagers, the safer they would be.

The only fae we'd alerted to our presence were Birnee and Finnley. While the guards had been working in my garden, digging up food for us, Norivun and I had ventured to their homes.

We'd warned them that the king might use them against me if I defied him again. Their eyes had grown wide, and after a brief discussion, we all felt it was best not to take any chances.

Norivun and I had wanted to take them to the Cliffs of Sarum, but with how drained Norivun's magic was, he wouldn't be able to open a rip in his illusion.

So we'd all agreed it was best to mistphase them to a small island off the coast of Osaravee. Birnee had an old aunt who lived there. Few knew of her, so we hoped it would provide some protection.

It wasn't a perfect plan, but it would keep them safe. For now.

Releasing a breath, I leaned back into my chair and thought of how my entire family and all of my friends' lives had been turned upside down because of me.

Norivun nudged me, his gaze stormy as my worry strummed right out of me and into him.

"Come here." He pulled me on his lap. The fire crackled in the hearth as he cradled me to him and trailed a hand up my back. I'd released my angel affinity, allowing my back to be bare as we all rested in my warm home.

"How's your magic?" I asked.

He leaned back in his chair, getting a groan from the aging wood. He continued those lulling motions along my back, and a shiver danced up my spine. "Returning. My sensory affinity is nearly fully replenished."

"And the others?"

"Useable, but still weak."

I gave a swift nod and kept my life-giving affinity ignited along my property's perimeter. If anyone came near, friend or foe, it would give me enough warning to mistphase all six of us elsewhere. We couldn't risk the king capturing any of us again.

"So what's the plan on the morrow?" Haxil raised an eyebrow from where he stood near the door.

"We begin our hunt for complete proof of what the king's done," I replied.

"And how do you propose we do that, Princess?"

Ryder stood near the front window, his attention frequently drifting to the small yard and dark night beyond.

Norivun's lips curved, and he glanced down at me. He didn't speak for me, and I knew this would be how we ruled our land. Both of us leading. And when one of us was weakened, the other would stand in their stead, just as he'd done while I'd been locked in the dungeon.

I entwined my fingers with his, and the pad of my thumb grazed his eternal mark. An answering stroke of love came along our bond.

Addressing Ryder, I replied, "We need to find that warlock. If we can somehow get a confession from him, we may have the proof we need to convince the council and the Solis fae of the king's involvement."

Ryder's eyes narrowed, and he cocked his head. "That doesn't sound easy to accomplish."

I nodded. "I don't imagine it will be."

Nish scowled as he shifted from where he stood near the bed chambers. "But how are we going to find him?"

I glanced at my mate, and Norivun frowned, his heavy brow drawing together as that daunting task loomed over us.

"I suppose we'll need to hire the Fire Wolf again," Norivun replied.

"I was thinking the same." I inclined my head since we had no idea how to navigate the *other* realm, much less find a warlock as powerful as the one we'd battled. "Which means, we'll need to return to the Nolus continent to ask for Bavar Fieldstone's assistance again. He helped us find the Fire Wolf once. Perhaps he'll do so again since we have no means of contacting the hunter ourselves."

Nish gave an exaggerated sigh. "Back to the endless warmth and blooming flowers, then."

Sandus snorted and crossed his arms. The movement made his wing's black leathery membranes catch the firelight. "Are you truly complaining about getting out of the snow, just for a wee while?"

"He is," Ryder replied for him. "Just wait. If we have to venture to the *other* realm again, I'm sure his griping will reach a whole new level."

Sandus laughed. "Our plan is sorted then. Tomorrow, we'll venture back to the Nolus capital."

A glimmer of excitement danced across Haxil's features. A similar response unfurled within me. Despite all that had happened, the guard and I shared a conspiratorial wink.

"Do you think we'll be able to meet some of the magical species in the *other* realm if we go there?" he asked me in a low tone.

"I was thinking the same thing." I grinned. "Wouldn't it be wonderful if we could converse with them?"

Haxil's eyes lit up, and Norivun chuckled.

My mate leaned down and whispered into my ear, "Your curiosity and endless wonder are endearing. Have I ever told you that?"

I kissed him softly, and the feel of him stirred the

bond inside me. It'd been so long since we'd been intimate with one another. The past few days away from him had been agonizing, and it didn't help that prior to that, his guards were always around, leaving us little privacy. Our encounters had always been brief with the threat of danger looming over our heads. What I wouldn't give for weeks on end with nothing but our bed chambers and perpetual peace surrounding us, so I could finally enjoy my husband as I'd been wanting to.

The prince's nostrils flared. "Is there something you're thinking about, my love?"

A blush stained my cheeks, and his guards snickered.

Norivun drew me closer, then nipped my ear. "Soon."

"Is that a promise?" I whispered.

"Indeed, Princess."

CHAPTER 9 - ILARA

The next morning, we ventured back to the Nolus continent. Norivun's affinities were all responding once more, even though he wasn't fully recharged, but he insisted he was strong enough to carry on.

So we landed near the same gates we'd entered the first time we visited the capital. The sprawling city covered a large hilly mound that stretched upward at the heart of it. Thousands of stone and thatch buildings lined the rising landscape, stretching along zigzagging streets, and at the top of the large hill stood the opulent golden palace.

We approached the gates as we had our first time here, and the sentries' expressions didn't falter. I couldn't help but wonder if they remembered the supernatural creatures they assessed each day. Likely, hundreds if not thousands of visitors entered the capital on their watch.

But if they remembered us at all, their expressions belied nothing. As before, when they assessed us, their black eyes turned to pure silver. When finished, they released their spears and allowed us entry.

Thankfully, unlike the first time we'd arrived in this city, Drachu didn't have the pendant that controlled my powers. It was still hidden in Norivun's safe, still concealed under his illusion spell. It was just one more thing that we would have to figure out at some point.

Still, walking up the familiar streets very close to where Drachu had sucked my affinities caused a shiver to skate up my spine.

"What is it, my love?" Norivun stepped closer to my side, his shoulders so broad and his aura so potent that several Nolus fae skittered away.

"I was thinking of Drachu, his pendant, and what he did at this exact place."

A low growl rumbled in Norivun's chest, and his hand drifted to my lower back. "He'll never control you again."

"But what are we going to do with that pendant?"

"We'll have to find a way to free your magic from it, which will likely take returning to the Adrall Temple to find that priestess."

I gazed up at him, shielding my sight. Bright sunshine streamed down on us. "What if she refuses?"

"She'll remove it unless she wants to meet Lucifer." Menace rolled off him in waves, and I knew it was only because we'd been so busy that both of us had pushed our concerns about the necklace to the side. But that very pendant was why Drachu had ventured all of the way to the Solis continent. It was why he and Tylen had stayed in King Novakin's castle, waiting for our return.

"We'll figure this out." Norivun drew me closer, extending a wing around my shoulders.

"I hope so."

We carried on, climbing the golden walkway as we headed toward the palace.

Every fairy and supernatural creature we passed gave us a wide berth. Most didn't even try to conceal their stares. My angel wings were out, and given that I strode with four Solis warriors and the crown prince down the cobblestone pavement, we did make quite a sight.

When we reached the castle door, the sentries called for Bavar Fieldstone, but when a servant reappeared and shook her head, a sentry stated, "He's not in residence at this time. You'll need to return another day."

"Of all our luck . . ." Nish glowered and placed his hands on his hips. "Now what?"

"Do you know when he'll return?" Norivun asked the golden-skinned sentry.

The sentry stared down at us from his imposing height. I had to tilt my head all the way back since my line of sight put me right at his breastbone.

The sentry's expression didn't change when he replied in a monotone voice, "We do not share the royals' schedules."

"Of course, you don't," Ryder said under his breath.

"Are you able to reach him?" I asked. "Could you send word to Sir Fieldstone that it's important for us to see him, and perhaps we could meet him wherever he's currently residing?"

The sentry inclined his head as though thinking for a moment.

I was still unsure if the Nolus sentries were actual beings with beating hearts and thought-filled minds or merely complex puppets blessed with animation magic. I'd certainly never seen a species like them before.

"Wait here." The sentry retreated inside.

Minutes passed, and Sandus tapped his foot.

"'Tis always so warm here." Nish sneered at the sky. It was another clear, cloudless day.

Haxil laughed and patted Nish's shoulder. "Are you angry at the weather now?"

"I don't see why not," Nish replied. "There's not even fierce wind or angry clouds. Just sun and warmth and endless blooming—" He fingered a vine near the castle's main door, and from his look, I had a feeling even the flower offended him.

A red petal curled around his fingers as it moved and writhed on the vine. Nish scoffed. "Even their plants are happy."

My lips curved. I trailed my fingers along the small buds that turned toward the sun. "Hello, my friends. What a beautiful day for you to enjoy. A shining sun and endless warmth." I caressed as many as I could reach, whispering to all of them.

A push of contentment came from Norivun along the bond, and I raised my eyebrows.

"Our first night in High Liss, you also spoke with the plants." His eyes sparkled in the sunlight, and his white teeth flashed in a smile. "You spent all of your time floating in that pool conversing with them."

My cheeks flushed. That night, I hadn't known he'd been watching. I'd been entirely uninhibited in those bathing pools, swimming, floating, and stroking every plant and vine on the water's edge. "I've always spoken with plants."

He nodded, his eyes hooded. "'Twas probably your affinity that created your desire to speak with them. You've connected with life since you were young. It's not unusual in powerful fae to see signs of what they're to become."

"Does that mean you connected with"—I swallowed, not sure how to politely word my question—"death?"

Norivun snorted as Nish snickered.

"He was never that morbid, love," Sandus replied. "But I'll never forget what Queen Lissandra told me when I first came to work at the castle. When the prince here was a lad, if fae angered him, they'd often fall ill in the following days, some even needing to be in the infirmary for days at a time until they mended. The healers were always baffled about why their illnesses appeared so suddenly."

My eyebrows shot to my hairline. "That was your affinity doing that without your knowledge?"

CROWNS OF ICE

Norivun shrugged. "None of us knew at the time exactly why those fae fell ill, but my mother had seen what I was to become. She had a fairly good idea that traces of the magic that were inevitably going to manifest in me were seeping out. It was her that taught me to better control my emotions."

My lips parted. "Queen Lissandra is a seer?"

"She is." His look turned pensive, and then he frowned. "She was the greatest seer on our continent until my father caged her power."

I squeezed his hand, hating the thought of his mother suffering.

The sentry opened the door again. "Sir Fieldstone has asked that you join him in Idaho."

My mouth dropped. "Idaho? Where's that?"

The sentry showed us a map of a land with oceans, continents, and seas that I'd never seen before. He pointed to an area on it, on a country labeled *United States*. "This is Idaho. Sir Fieldstone said you were to go to Boise, to the Supernatural Headquarters. He's given specific instructions with where you should portal transfer."

"The Supernatural Headquarters in Idaho and Boise." Sandus cocked his head. "Three locations in one?"

"Boise is a city in the land of Idaho," the sentry replied, his monotone voice never once showing an ounce of emotion, making me more and more convinced they were animated puppets. "The Supernatural Head-

❄ 87 ❄

quarters is an area of employment that Sir Fieldstone frequents."

"Oh, right! That is where he works in the *other* realm, remember?" I said to Norivun. "He must be working there right now."

"Do you suppose this Idaho is like the land of Europe?" Haxil scratched his chin.

Norivun shrugged. "You would know better than me. What have your studies told you?"

But Haxil only shook his head. "There are so few texts on the *other* realm upon our continent. I'm afraid my knowledge of its geography is limited."

"For the Mother's sake." Nish rolled his eyes skyward. "Another new place in the *other* realm. What is my job coming to?"

Sandus and Ryder elbowed him simultaneously.

"'Tis for the Solis that we do this, Nish," Ryder reminded him. "We need to find that warlock, and without Bavar telling us how to reach the Fire Wolf, how else are we to locate him?"

Nish nodded, for the first time looking contrite. "You're right. 'Tis for the Solis."

The sentry extended his huge hand, then opened it to reveal half a dozen portal keys in the center of his palm. "Sir Fieldstone has asked that we give you several of these to use."

"Thank you." I picked up the portal keys, and a shiver of excitement buzzed through me at where we were about to venture. I turned shining eyes upon my mate. "Ready?"

Norivun shook his head, his lips curving despite the apprehension billowing toward me on the bond. "Life is not going to be boring with you, is it, my love?"

I grinned. "Not if I have anything to say about it."

CHAPTER 10 - NORIVUN

We all joined hands, and I whispered the words to activate the portal key, the same words that the Fire Wolf had taught us to use when we'd been in Sven's cabin.

The realm disappeared around us as I firmly anchored my thoughts on the land of Idaho, specifically the location of the Supernatural Forces Headquarters.

As before, when we'd traveled to Europe, the feeling of being ripped apart and torn to pieces from the inside out made magic swirl in my gut.

I ground my jaw, and when we landed in a field, with a blue sky above us and long green grasses swirling around us, I once again had the urge to vomit.

Nish keeled over and emptied his stomach in the field as my other guards and Ilara all rested hands over their bellies while taking deep gulping breaths.

It was only luck that I also didn't grow sick, especially when the magicless air swirled around us and that *off* sensation bore down on my senses.

"Yuck." Nish wiped his lips, and a pulse of his magic cleansed his mouth and cheeks. "This realm is quite simply foul."

I gazed around, searching for the Supernatural Forces Headquarters while Nish continued to grumble.

Hills covered the landscape, and strange-looking trees towered over each hill's surface. The sun's light bathed the fields and rolling hills in a reddish-gold as green grass swayed in a breeze that flowed around us.

My eyes narrowed when I spotted a fine glowing red ribbon that stretched across the field before it disappeared into trees farther away. The red line waved and shimmered, as if manipulated by the wind, but I doubted nature's elements affected it. I sensed strong magic coming from it.

"Look, that's magical," Haxil waved toward the red line, and Ilara clapped in excitement.

"Let's investigate." She strode toward it, and Haxil followed her like an eager pup before I could stop either of them.

Nish rolled his eyes and looked to me for direction.

I sighed. "They're right. That line is indeed magical. Perhaps it's part of the Headquarters we seek."

We all strode toward the line, stopping just short of it. I let puffs of magic out to assess it more.

"Do you taste that?" I asked everyone. "This barrier has a flavor. Mint and anise."

"I taste it too," Ilara said with a nod. Her black hair

draped over her shoulders between her beautiful white wings.

"Same," Haxil replied as my other guards also confirmed they sensed it.

I cocked my head. "It's a barrier of some kind, and —" The air rippled around the red line. I peered closer at it. A shimmer appeared, just a vague sense of a Shield of some kind. "Illusion magic is at play here."

"Can you see past it?" Ilara asked.

I shook my head. "It's too different from mine. Perhaps with time and effort, I could learn to see through it, but at the moment, no."

"What's that over there?" Sandus pointed farther down the red line.

An arched doorway appeared, made up of the same glowing red line as the barrier but in the distinctive shape of a door.

"Perhaps that's where we enter?" Ilara looked at Haxil, who was grinning, before the two once again took off.

Ryder sighed. "Those two are as eager as young children."

Nish sneered. "I don't know why. This place is . . ." He shuddered.

Snorting at his typical pessimism, I followed my mate and guard as the other three prowled behind me.

As soon as I stood before the door, a strange-sounding voice said, "Prince Norivun Deema Melustral Achul and guests, welcome."

Nish jumped. "Ock! What in all the realms. The air is speaking to us!"

A glowing flat surface appeared from out of thin air, with the outline of a hand on it. The strange other-worldly voice again said from nowhere, "Please scan your palm before entering."

"Strange magic." Ryder shook his head. "Strange magic indeed is at work here."

"How fascinating!" Ilara grinned ear to ear.

Haxil leaned closer to inspect the flat surface. "It doesn't appear malicious." He straightened. "How intriguing. Do you suppose one lays their hand on it?"

"I would assume so." I studied the strange flat, glowing contraption again. I also didn't sense any sinister intentions and figured this was part of the Supernatural Forces' magical process, but before I could lay my palm on it, Nish stopped me.

"Let me, my prince. In case it bites you."

Haxil laughed, but Nish's guard instincts were obviously running at full throttle as he laid his palm on it. His jaw ground while the glowing screen assessed him.

"I'm impressed, Nish." Sandus grinned. "I thought you would have cleaved it in two with your sword instead of trusting it."

Nish glowered. "I was considering it."

"Access denied," that same strange voice said, "Should you need assistance from the Supernatural Forces, please contact your local agent."

"Denied? Ock." Nish whipped his palm back to his

side and scowled at the contraption. "What kind of useless magic is this?"

"Perhaps I need to do it since it initially said my name." I laid my hand on the screen, and magic heated my palm.

"Welcome, Prince Norivun Deema Melustral Achul and guests. Please proceed to the identification processing room." The red outlined door before us shimmered, and then the entire interior of it turned opaque, as if a pearly soup.

"I suppose we step through it?" Ilara said.

I trailed a finger across it, and my hand disappeared into the strange door. Nothing but air greeted me on the other side. I pushed a pulse of my elemental affinity out of my fingers, sensing the other side with my air magic.

Nothing but solid floor, walls, and a ceiling responded to my phantom fingers. "I think you're correct. It appears to open into a hall, and no other fae or supernatural creatures are present."

"Shall we enter?" Ilara glanced up at me with eager eyes, not even an ounce of hesitation coming from her on the bond. "Perhaps there are directions once we pass that tell us how to get to the identification processing room."

I sighed. "Yes, but I'm going first. I doubt anything nefarious is in there, but I won't risk any of you." When my guards grumbled, I added, "That's an order."

I had to duck since my wings were too high for the door, and for the briefest moment, the opaque air surrounded me, and then I stepped right through it into the hallway that I'd sensed.

The long hallway was lined with gray walls and a strange smooth flooring that appeared like stone but was entirely without divots or crevices. At the end of the hall, another walkway appeared that ran perpendicular to this one. No signs lay anywhere.

"How odd," I muttered. I stepped back through the opaque door and nodded toward it. "It's safe. Let's all proceed."

When all six of us were inside the strange building, we began walking along the long hallway, searching for directions of which way we should go. But before we reached the end, Bavar Fieldstone careened around the corner as a delighted smile streaked across his face.

"Ah, you've arrived. Welcome!" His dagger, looped through his belt, glimmered in the bright lights overhead. He was as tall as I remembered him, and he wore some kind of otherworldly uniform that was entirely black and covered him head to toe.

Bright orange hair was artfully arranged on his head, and his lips lifted in a smile when he reached us. Bowing, he said with gusto, "I would have been in the field to greet you, but I wasn't entirely sure where the portal key would drop you. I'm so pleased that you managed to make the journey here without peril, and—"

His jaw dropped when he saw Ilara. His gaze traveled over her wings. "What in all the realm? You're an angel? I thought you were a Solis fairy?" He leaned closer, studying her violet eyes that always manifested when her angel affinity was activated.

"I am Solis," she replied a tad defensively as the SF commander continued his inspection, even circling around her. "But I have an angel affinity."

I inhaled, detecting disbelief in the commander's scent. His reaction was similar to how Sven had been when he'd first seen Ilara with her affinity manifested. Apparently, other supernatural creatures found angels fascinating.

Bavar faced all of us again, his eyes still on Ilara. He clapped once. "How magnificent. You're telling me that your Solis affinity has given you angel powers?"

Ilara frowned. "Yes, it gave me wings, if that's what you mean."

Bavar's mouth dropped. "Oh my, you don't know?"

We all shared a look, and Ilara's trepidation tumbled toward me on the bond. A low growl threatened to work up my chest. I stepped closer to her, then laid a hand on her lower back, right beneath her folded wings.

"Know what?" she asked with a flare of hesitation in her tone.

"Of an angel's true ability, the ability to heal any ailment?"

Her eyes widened as her shock billowed toward me. "Are you saying my angel affinity has given me more than just wings?"

Bavar inclined his head. "Truth be told, I don't know. You Solis have strange magic, but your wings and violet eye color are those of an angel, a divine creature, and angels have *extraordinary* healing capabilities. The likes of which most in this world have never seen."

Ilara peered up at me, disbelief and intrigue strumming out of her. "Do you think Matron Olsander would be able to teach me how to access that part of my affinity if I'm able to train with her again? Assuming what Sir Fieldstone says is true?"

"Major Fieldstone," Bavar corrected. "I'm only referred to as Sir Fieldstone when I'm home in the fae lands." He rolled his eyes. "Royal formalities and all, but I prefer Major Fieldstone."

I canted my head as Ilara offered a smile of apology before I said to her, "Matron Olsander was able to teach me how to control my dragon affinity even though it was a divine gift and rare among our kind, so I would assume she would also be able to instruct you on the depths of your angel affinity if such a healing gift is a part of it."

Bavar's mouth dropped. "Dragon affinity? Did you say *dragon affinity*? Does that mean you can shift into a *dragon*?"

I growled low in my throat. While I had no issue with Bavar, I didn't reveal my dragon form to many, preferring the ability be kept guarded in the event that I needed to shift and use it strategically, as I had when Sven's blaze-bands had restrained us, or how I had with the warlock when he'd nearly murdered Daiseeum.

"That's knowledge I typically don't share with others," I said in a clipped tone.

Bavar immediately dipped his chin. "Ah, apologies. My lips are sealed, but truly"—he shook his head—"you Solis are entirely fascinating. Tell me, have you ever considered spending more time on Earth? Your capabilities could prove extremely useful to the SF. I'm sure General McCloy would offer you positions if you're interested?"

"No," all six of us replied simultaneously.

A hint of pride rolled through me that even Ilara and Haxil had been quick to deny such an invitation, which only secured my belief in where their loyalties lay. While their curious minds and love of learning made them inquisitive about this land, their allegiance was to our fellow fae on our continent. And while even I had enjoyed our journeys to the strange lands of the *other* realm, this wasn't where any of our priorities lay.

Bavar sighed. "Very well, but if you should ever change your mind . . ."

Out of courtesy, I replied, "Thank you. If any of us endeavor to be employed by your facility, we shall be sure to communicate those wishes."

"Very well." Bavar clapped again. "Anywho, I'm most intrigued to learn what brings you here today, and I do apologize that I was unable to see you in the Nolus capital. When my staff contacted me, alerting me to your return visit, this was the best compromise I could think of. I'm afraid my SF squad is dealing with a bit of a situation at the moment, so I was unable to depart from Earth."

Ilara and Haxil shared another curious look, and I knew it was from Bavar's reference to a *squad*.

"But that's none of your concern." Bavar grinned again. "Please, follow me. Per SF protocol, we must visit the identification processing room before you proceed farther. I don't have much time, but if more issues have arisen on the Solis continent, then I do indeed want to be informed. I'm assuming that's what prompted this visit today?"

I nodded as we followed him along the gray-walled walkway. "You would be right. War is coming."

"War?" Bavar's orange eyebrows shot up, and all casualness left his expression. "You're marching upon the Nolus?"

"No," Ilara cut in. "Civil war. We're working to dethrone the Solis king, and we have no doubt the king will viciously fight such an attempt."

"Oh my." Bavar brought a hand to his chest. "While wars on the continents do occur, as tragic as they are, I must be honest and confess that I'm relieved to hear my homeland won't be involved."

"And it shan't be if we're able to stop it," I replied. "We have no interest in your land or extending our border. We merely want the wickedness of my father to stop and peace to return to all Solis fae."

Bavar dipped his head. "Of course. As do I, but that is most troubling. Most troubling indeed."

※

THE SF COMMANDER led us to a large room within the strange building. The hallways we'd traveled all had the same drab gray color. There were no decorations, no tapestries, no murals, nor flowers. And only a few of the halls had windows, which revealed an entire array of buildings and training facilities outside. None of which had been visible behind that red, wavy barrier we'd encountered in the field.

"Does an illusion hide all of this facility?" I asked just as we entered a huge room. A handful of *other* supernatural creatures, along with several Nolus fae, appeared hard at work. A long workstation ran along the perimeter of the circular room. Several of the workers sat in front of strange foreign devices with images that appeared real but were see-through. *How odd.*

"Indeed it does." Bavar sauntered toward the desk. "We conceal our activities from the humans. Illusions are a necessity. Our sorcerers come in handy for that." Bavar turned toward one of the workers. "Eliza? Would you be so kind as to process my guests' identities? I would like to take them to a conference room to discuss their concerns, and I'm afraid time is of the essence."

One of the females pulled off a strange headband that had a floating string attached to it that angled to her mouth, and she rushed over. "Of course, sir." Her cherub cheeks lifted when she smiled. She was a Nolus fairy with slightly glowing skin and purple hair. She bowed at all of us. "Welcome, fine fae of the Solis continent." She dipped her head, bringing a fist to her chest. "I have not seen your kind in many years."

Haxil canted his head. "You've met Solis fae before?"

The female nodded. "Indeed. My name is Eliza River, and I hail from Elsfairdasvee. We occasionally have your kind upon our land."

"Ah!" Ilara smiled and brought her fist to her chest before bowing in traditional greeting. "It's a pleasure to meet you. I'm Ilara Seary, daughter of Mervalee Territory. My home territory is just across the border from your village."

Eliza grinned, revealing her pointy teeth. "It is a pleasure to make your acquaintance." She pulled a strange-looking device from her belt. "Will you kindly hold out your inner wrists so I may scan you?"

When all six of us frowned, Eliza said in a rush, "This device will scan your skin and will reveal your true species. I'm afraid it's required for all visitors for safety purposes."

Grumbling, Nish lifted his sleeve as the rest of us did the same without complaint.

I exposed my inner wrist, allowing her to point her device at my bare skin. An eruption of strange-looking lights emitted from the device. Following that, a warm tingling sensation shot up my arm before a symbol glowed on my wrist briefly before disappearing.

"Fairy, not surprising." Eliza held her device over Ilara, and it scanned my mate's wrist. The device made a beeping sound, and Eliza cocked her head. "Fairy and Angel. Interesting."

My mate and I shared a side-eye before my four guards were assessed.

"All fairies, and one is also part angel," Eliza called to Major Fieldstone. "They're cleared for entry under your care."

Bavar bowed. "Many thanks." He waved toward us. "If you would kindly follow me."

Ilara drifted closer to my side as we followed the commander. "Do you think their device called me a fairy and an angel because my angel affinity is currently activated?"

"That's what I assumed too," I responded. "I could have called forth my dragon to see if the beast's skin would change their reading on me, but I doubt they'd appreciate that."

She laughed softly, and the sound was like a soothing balm to my soul. "I have a feeling you're quite right."

We walked through the strange circular room, and I studied the glowing sphere in the center of it when we passed it. It was also made of those strange see-through lights.

"That's a 3D holographic rendition of Earth," Bavar nodded, pointing at the globe.

I canted my head in appreciation, but truth be told, this land was strange, and I didn't particularly care to learn more about it. Of course, Haxil and Ilara both stepped closer to Bavar to ask questions.

"Are those the continents and seas on Earth?" Ilara nodded toward areas on the sphere as we reached the exit.

"Indeed they are." Bavar ushered us into another spectacularly boring gray hallway.

"How many continents are on this planet's surface?" Haxil asked.

"Seven." Bavar strode ahead but answered all of their questions with a smile. "Although one is so far south and so cold that no one inhabits it."

Nish grunted. "Sounds like our continent." He huffed a breath. "Not surprising the species here are also too weak for such a climate. Only the Solis fae are strong enough to survive such conditions."

Bavar merely shrugged, and I slugged my guard in the shoulder as Sandus leaned closer and hissed, "Manners, Nish. We're guests here."

When we entered a room with a square table and chairs, Ryder's long braid whipped between his wings as he glanced about. Nothing was interesting about this room either. One thing was for certain, they were sorely in need of a fairy with a beauty affinity. I could only imagine what Ilara's lady servant would think of this entirely drab building.

"Please, have a seat." Bavar waved toward the chairs, then dipped his head. "I apologize. We don't have any species with wings here, so I'm afraid the chairs don't have divots."

"We'll manage." I swung my chair around and

straddled it, allowing my wings to drape comfortably behind me. My guards did the same.

Ilara, however, calmed her angel affinity, and her wings disappeared in a wink of magic, allowing her to sit normally.

Bavar's mouth dropped. "Your wings . . ."

"They can come and go as I call them forth," Ilara explained.

Bavar merely shook his head. "So fascinating." Clapping his hands, he continued, "Right, now tell me more about what you need. What brings you all the way to Earth today?"

I crossed my arms over the chair's back and leveled him with a stare. "We need to find the warlock that conspired with my father, which means we need to once again hire the Fire Wolf."

CHAPTER 11 - ILARA

Bavar's eyes narrowed. "You need to find a warlock?"

Norivun inclined his head. "The same warlock that created the deadly veil on our continent."

I settled back in my chair and crossed my arms. "It's essential we find him."

Bavar's jaw dropped. "The *king* of the Solis continent was working with a warlock?"

"Yes." My mate inclined his head.

Bavar frowned, his expression turning even more serious. "Warlocks are hunted by the Supernatural Forces. Whenever we become aware that a sorcerer has turned dark, we send a squad to execute them. Their kind are killed on sight since warlocks are only created when a sorcerer turns to dark magic, which requires killing innocent humans and supernaturals. If such a warlock exists in this realm, he must answer to the SF."

"What if he answers to us instead?" I arched an eyebrow. My warrior affinity hummed inside me, its jagged edges and cool stone igniting. "He's responsible for murdering dozens of innocent Solis fae. He must answer for that." Memories of Daiseeum lying upon his altar pummeled my thoughts. I bristled. If we'd arrived even seconds later than what we had, the warlock would have sacrificed my lady's servant. My hands pumped into fists. "He *must* answer to us first."

Norivun's hand drifted to my thigh. He squeezed gently. My balled hands loosened, and I laid my palm over his, but the need for revenge still heated my blood.

"Are you implying that you're willing to execute him?" Bavar's orange hair glinted in the lights when he cocked his head.

"We would be happy to once we get the information we require from him." Norivun's tone turned low, deadly, and a rumble of his great death affinity undulated through the room.

Bavar shivered and waited for my mate's aura to calm before saying, "Such an act is entirely against SF protocol. We do not allow citizens to take the law into their own hands."

"But we're not citizens of this realm." Nish's lip curled. "We're Solis fae and answer to Solis law. This warlock committed atrocious acts on our soil, *not* yours."

Bavar tapped his chin. "Well, that's not technically true. When you're on Earth, the SF is the law.

However, I do understand your logic, and your reasons for being here are entirely unique. If you did find this warlock before the SF did, what is it you're hoping to seek from him?"

"We need a confession from him or proof that he worked with King Novakin." I drummed my fingers on the table. "We must prove that he was conspiring with King Novakin. Until we do, the king's council will not side with us, and it will be us against the entire Solis race."

"I see." Bavar let out a heavy sigh. "And if King Novakin has committed such a heinous act and is also planning to ultimately march upon the Nolus continent, then I do wonder if your roguish request should be allowed. Still, I'm afraid my hands are tied. I cannot make such a decision. I shall need to consult with my superior. If you would please excuse me."

The tall Nolus commander left the room with a frown upon his face.

Once we were alone, all six of us shook our heads.

"Was it a mistake revealing so much?" I asked the crown prince.

Norivun's lips thinned. "I hope not. If we're to work with Major Fieldstone, we must develop trust. If he were to learn that we withheld important information from him, I fear what the consequences would be, especially if our plans go awry and we find ourselves with little to no allies. At the moment, he still stands with us. That counts for something."

"I agree," Sandus piped in. "We've risked a lot simply by venturing here, but without that warlock and proof of what the king's done, we've reached a standstill. It will be our word against the king's, even with the recording of the Isalee field. We wouldn't win."

"Indeed." Ryder canted his head. "We need the king's council in agreement with us. For that, we need the warlock, and since none of us have a tracking affinity and this realm is so bizarre, I'm in agreement that seeking the Fire Wolf is our only option. We made the right decision by coming to Bavar and revealing what we have."

Haxil and Nish also voiced similar beliefs just before the door opened, and Bavar entered with a male who was entirely *other*. He was an older supernatural with graying hair and rounded ears. He definitely wasn't fae, not even a glamoured one given his aura, and since his build was large and his aura incredibly strong while distinctively different from a fairy's, I couldn't help but wonder if he was that species Haxil had told me of—a werewolf.

All six of us stood, bringing a fist to our chests before bowing.

The male stopped short and gave Bavar a side-eye, then mimicked our actions.

After the formality finished, Bavar gestured toward the chairs again. "This is General McCloy, the man who leads our organization. Please sit, and let's discuss."

❄

GENERAL MCCLOY LISTENED PATIENTLY AS we reviewed our reasons for venturing to his realm and what we hoped to achieve. And as the minutes ticked past, we all discussed and eventually compromised on the best way to handle this situation.

The general agreed that we could interrogate the warlock if we found him, but once that was finished, he insisted the Supernatural Forces take over. Essentially, we wouldn't be murdering the dark sorcerer. The SF would take that responsibility.

"Shall we seal this decision with a fairy bargain?" Norivun asked as we all stood.

The general shook his head. "That's not necessary. The SF always honors its word."

"I see." Norivun nodded curtly.

The general placed his hands on his hips. "We'll be monitoring your movements, and remember, it's imperative that you hide your whereabouts from the humans. I must insist that you all wear glamours." He eyed our wings, his eyes lingering even longer on mine. I'd released them again while Bavar had been gone. "Are you all able to retract your wings?"

"Only I can," I replied, and in a whisper of magic, I calmed my angel affinity. My wings disappeared from existence in a rush of magic.

The general's eyes widened.

"Ours are permanent, not created by an affinity," the crown prince explained. "However, hiding them and our fae appearance isn't a problem." A light dusting of my mate's magic puffed out of him, and the feel of his illusion affinity clouded around me and drifted toward the guards. When it dissipated, the prince bowed. "Done."

The general blinked, and his mouth slackened.

Haxil grinned as he glanced at Sandus, Ryder, and Nish. "You all have rounded ears and no wings." He laughed. "And your clothes are rather odd. 'Tis most amusing looking. Who would have thought you'd all appear so plain?"

In addition to hiding our fae appearance, the prince had crafted our clothing to resemble what the Fire Wolf had worn. The strange pants with pockets on our backsides covered all of our legs, and simple tops concealed our upper halves.

"How do I look?" I asked. I could see my clothing, but even though the style had changed, the feeling of it had not.

Norivun smirked, then arched an eyebrow. "You're as beautiful as ever. You hardly look different at all." He curled a lock of black hair around my ear. I touched the tip. My fingers still encountered the delicate point of a fae ear. "Is it hidden?"

The prince nodded. "Indeed. No one will see past my illusion. Your ears appear rounded."

"Are you wearing glamours?" The general's brows drew together, his aura increasing with what I could only assume was awe or curiosity.

"Illusion masks." The prince crossed his arms. "It's a specialty of my affinity."

"I see." The general stroked his chin. "Major Field-stone has told me of your powerful and unusual magic. Tell me, have you ever considered joining our—"

"No," we all replied in unison.

The general's mouth snapped shut.

Bavar leaned closer to General McCloy and whispered, "I already asked. I'm afraid that's not an option they're willing to consider at this time."

The general inclined his head, then waved toward the door. "In that case, I've had my staff in contact with the Fire Wolf. He's currently in Chicago. We shall give you portal keys for your transfer, and considering the strength of your magic, I would advise that you all take a potion we've readied for you that will counteract any fae lands withdrawals. Now, if you would . . ." He gestured to the door, and a moment of buzzing energy filled me.

We were one step closer to finding the warlock and revealing the Solis king for who he really was. With any luck, come nightfall, we'd have the warlock in sight.

THE PORTAL KEY took us to an area in the land of Chicago that Bavar and General McCloy called the Gold Coast. According to them, the Fire Wolf was currently having lunch with two individuals but had agreed to meet us in one hour's time. And since our reasons for being here would involve possibly finding a warlock the SF hadn't even known existed, the general had stated the SF would cover all of the Fire Wolf's hiring fees.

"So no more rulibs will be needed from the castle vaults?" I said to Norivun just after we materialized in an alleyway.

"Probably for the best." My mate shrugged. He glanced around, and his aura rose as he inspected our whereabouts. "My father has probably sealed access to my accounts. Of course, I have other accounts he's unaware of that I could withdraw rulibs from if needed, but it's best to conserve our funds in case we need them later."

Steam rose around us, and a rotting scent filled the air. A large green bin filled with overflowing trash stood next to us.

We'd been instructed to materialize in this precise location due to its proximity to the hunter and the ability to conceal us from the humans. It wasn't an area I would have chosen to inhabit, though.

"This place is entirely foul." Nish waved a hand over his nose. "They don't even properly dispose of their waste." He sneered at the bin, and my nose wrinkled.

Its stench truly was horrid.

"I take it we head that way?" Ryder nodded toward the alleyway's opening.

A street ran perpendicular to where we'd materialized. Strange-looking creations flew past on the road and seemed to resemble metal boxes on wheels. They were loud and smelly but moved quickly.

"How strange," I murmured as I studied them further and also waved the air away in front of my nose. When that didn't deter from the stench, I called upon just enough of my air affinity to create a weak Shield around my face, blocking the fumes.

"Ah, those must be the cars we were warned of!" Haxil elbowed me, and I slowly smiled as I studied them.

The odd-looking vehicles, which we'd been told were the normal form of transportation for the humans since they didn't have wings, enchanted carpets, or mistphasing abilities, were of different shapes and sizes. I was in agreement with Nish, though. They were rather repugnant in their stench, much like the rubbish bin near us, but to have created such a thing when one had no magic was truly remarkable.

"They must be clever, these humans," I surmised, "to have invented such a thing in a magicless state."

Haxil canted his head. "I was thinking the same."

"Now, remember," Nish said sternly, "we're not to stare at anything. General McCloy said humans don't look twice at cars."

I sighed. All I wanted to do was stare.

Norivun prowled closer to the alleyway's mouth, his guards flanking him. "The Fire Wolf is supposed to be meeting us at a salopas on the corner. Try to blend in."

Initially, when the prince had glamoured all of us, our hair color had remained the same. Silver locks had still covered all of their heads, while mine had remained black. However, when the general explained that such coloring was oftentimes only seen on the elderly population of this realm, and he'd recommended we adapt more earthly coloring, the prince had complied.

As a result, the prince had midnight locks similar in shade to mine while Sandus's hair was a color the species here called *blond*. Haxil and Ryder both had brown hair that looked entirely drab and reminded me of domal dung, and Nish, of course, had insisted on something else entirely.

When one of the SF staff had said that some humans colored their hair to appear the same shade as a Nolus fairy, the surly guard had insisted on bright blue. Of the six of us, his coloring was the most cheerful. The irony wasn't lost on any of us.

We reached the end of the alleyway and emerged near the street.

All of us studied the humans walking by. They were of different shapes and sizes. Some were males, others were females. It didn't appear they had more than two genders in this realm, similar to ours.

Several glanced our way, but I couldn't help but wonder if that was because my mate and his guards had such large builds. They towered over most of the species here.

"Do you think we stand out?" Ryder asked quietly, a sharp groove appearing between his eyes.

"I think we're managing to blend in," the prince muttered, but apprehension strummed toward me on the bond as we began walking down a strip of stone.

"Hi there, sugar," a female said to Nish when we passed her on the stone walkway that ran the length of the street.

Nish scowled. "I am *human*. I am not a sweet sustenance, thank you very much."

The female's eyebrows shot to her hairline, and the guard prowled forward. Shaking her head, the female frowned and scurried the other way.

Haxil snorted a laugh. "I don't think that was her meaning, Nishy."

Nish scoffed. "If that wasn't her meaning, then what do you think she was implying by such a derogatory statement? To compare one to food is appalling."

"I think she was coming on to you." I elbowed the grumpy guard. "She may have enjoyed getting to know you a little better."

Nish's chest puffed up. "Truly?" He ran a hand through his blue hair. "Do you think it was the hair color that attracted her?" He glanced over his shoulder toward where the female had disappeared to, but she was long gone.

"Well, we know it certainly wasn't your sparkling personality," Ryder replied in a bored tone.

Everyone snorted or laughed except for Nish.

Nish slugged Ryder in the side. "My mother always told me that my personality was like a fine wine."

"What do you think she meant by that?" Haxil arched an eyebrow. "That it was best left on the shelf to age and never be opened?"

Nish scowled in his direction. "I think there might

be an insult lying in that comment somewhere. However, I'm choosing to ignore it. But for your information, my mother always said that my character would appeal to a select few who were astute enough to appreciate my fine taste."

Sandus laughed. "It sounds like your mother was trying to tell you that you're a pain in the arse but in a nice way."

"Are you implying that my mother—"

The crown prince held up his hand. "There's the Fire Wolf."

We all ground to a halt. On the corner just ahead, the hunter waited. He stood with his hands in his pockets, his expression devoid of emotion. Dark hair fluttered around his head, grazing the tops of his rounded ears. Similar to when we'd first met him, his powerful aura drifted toward me. Even here, in this non-threatening environment, his magic and strength were as evident as my mate's.

I scanned his abdomen, searching for a sign of weakness. The last time we'd seen the hunter, he'd been sliced open by the warlock, but the Fire Wolf had insisted he would be fine. I assessed how he moved, and my frown disappeared. I couldn't detect even a trace of any ailment.

"He looks healthy and strong," I murmured. "No sign of that laceration he suffered from in the Isalee field."

"I was just thinking the same thing," my mate replied.

We strode ahead to meet the Fire Wolf, and we all stopped on the stone walkway at the entrance to what I could only assume was a clothing store.

The Fire Wolf inclined his head in greeting, then looked at me and the prince. "I've been told you need my services again. Has something gone wrong?"

"Unfortunately," my mate replied. "We appreciate you seeing us."

"Indeed," I added, forcing my curiosity away from the store. "We need to find that warlock. We must prove to the king's council that the king hired him."

"Ah, that warlock again." The hunter scratched his chin. "That could be difficult."

The prince growled. "I was wondering if that would be the case."

Two females passed us on the street, nearly bumping into the hunter and prince. They appeared young and had hair the shade of domal dung. Both of them stared at the hunter and my mate as they passed. Then they began whispering to one another, sneaking additional glances over their shoulders at the males.

I bared my teeth, not liking the heated way they were staring at my mate. When one of the females spotted me, she smirked, and her comment drifted toward me on the breeze.

"There's some nice eye candy for you," she whispered to her friend.

I frowned just as Nish turned toward the other guards with a glower. "Ock! What is the meaning of this? Referring to others as though they're sweets or desserts?" He grumbled, then shook his head. "It must be an odd human thing. Perhaps I shall try it if I ever interact with one."

"You're going to interact with a human?" Ryder's eyebrows shot up.

Nish shrugged, then scowled. "I was considering it. I thought perhaps I would say she looks like a beautiful lollipop. Do you think that sounds flattering?"

Sandus snorted. "I think you should try it."

Haxil and I laughed as the hunter leaned closer to my mate. "Are they always like this?"

Norivun sighed. "Yes."

Haxil scratched his chin. "The world has truly turned upside down if Nish is now considering speaking to the humans."

"Keep your comments down," the prince reminded them when another human gave us a confused side-eye.

The Fire Wolf placed his hands on his hips. "Anyway, back to the matter at hand. I'll be able to find your warlock. I haven't met a prey I can't eventually track, but I'm warning you, it could take weeks to discover his location."

I nibbled my lip. "We don't have weeks."

The prince reached into his pocket and extracted a piece of fabric. "Would this help? In my realm, I would use this to scry for him, but I'm unsure if that magic will work here."

My eyes widened. "Wait, what? You own something of the warlock's?"

Nish crossed his arms. "Don't look so shocked, Ilara. The prince has a habit of swiping items his enemies possess."

I rolled my eyes and remembered how Norivun had once admitted that to me. "But how did you get it?"

Norivun shrugged. "I'm guessing it's part of his cloak. Bits of fabric were left behind in the rubble on the night he tried to murder Daiseeum, and since it didn't match Daiseeum's clothing, I'm assuming it's the warlocks."

My jaw dropped. "How did you get it?"

"I had Patrice retrieve it when you were locked in the dungeons. It was missed by the constructo fae in the cleanup process."

"Dungeons?" The hunter raised his eyebrows. "Your lives sound nearly as exciting as mine."

"A malady we're trying to correct." I glared at my mate. "Is there a reason you didn't tell me you possessed this?"

Norivun smiled slyly. "I figured you'd learn about it soon enough."

"Is this like when you told me I'd eventually figure out all of your affinities since you like to see me guessing?"

His grin grew. "Maybe?"

"You do know that you still haven't revealed your sixth affinity to me, right?"

He shrugged. "I might be aware of that."

Huffing, I nodded toward the cloth that the Fire

Wolf plucked from my mate's fingers. "Will that delightful piece of fabric speed the process up?"

The hunter smirked. "Perhaps. I'll give it a try."

CHAPTER 12 - NORIVUN

The hunter requested that we follow him to a different area in his realm, a place called the land of Portland.

When we reemerged at our newest destination, the portal key we'd been given from the SF snuffed out of existence. I'd followed the hunter's instructions precisely, yet when we were in another alleyway, I couldn't help but frown.

Given the tall buildings on either side of us and the underlying scent of rotting garbage in the air, we were in a second city. White clouds drifted high above, barely visible through the narrow strip of sky above the alley's floor. In the distance, a bridge stood out. Similar to the land of Chicago, a single street ran perpendicular to the alleyway's mouth.

I sighed. "The species of this realm do seem to prefer these unpleasant, narrow streets between buildings."

The hunter, having already been waiting in the alleyway before we arrived, just shrugged. "Wait here. This won't take long."

Before any of us could comment, the Fire Wolf disappeared through a brick wall.

"Ock, is he a master at illusions as well?" Nish went to the wall, but when he placed his palm on it, his hand didn't push through the solid surface.

"Not an illusion." I also placed my hand on the cool red stone. "Strong magic, though. This wall is hiding something."

"Any idea what?" Ilara asked. Annoyance strummed from her along our bond. I knew she was still irritated that I hadn't revealed my final affinity to her.

"Your guess is as good as mine." I placed a hand on her waist and leaned down, nuzzling her neck. She pushed me away at first, but when I nipped at her skin, she began to soften.

She sighed. "Why can't you just tell me what your last affinity is?"

"Would it bring you peace if I did?"

"It would certainly appease my curiosity."

I kissed the dip of her throat, right where it met her collarbone. "How about I show you instead, next time I'm able to?" When I lifted my head, a small smile was tugging at her lips.

"Can you show me now?"

I chuckled. "I can't, honestly, but I will when we get home."

Her smile grew. "Now I'm *really* curious. Do you

❄ 122 ❄

promise to show me? No more games, no more guessing?"

"Yes, my love. If it's bothering you that much, I'll show you when we're done with this realm."

The irritation that had been flowing from her eased. She leaned up on her tiptoes and wrapped her arms around my neck. A low growl rumbled in my chest when she pressed her body flush against mine.

"Thank you."

I gathered her to me, kissing her in earnest while running my hands along her soft curves. "If I knew I would get this kind of response, I would've promised to tell you a long time ago."

A laugh spilled from her lips, and my guards snickered.

"Do you need us to give you some privacy, my prince?" Haxil asked with a bemused smile.

"Haxil!" Ilara admonished.

The guard shrugged. "No judgment here."

Nish nodded. "It wouldn't be the first time one of us fucked a female on the streets. Sometimes you just need to make do with what you have."

Ilara's cheeks turned so red that a rumble of laughter shook me. "They're just trying to rile you. They don't actually engage in provocative activities in alleyways. At least, not regularly."

My mate hid her face against my chest. "Is it horrible that their attempts to rile me are working?"

I chuckled and whispered, "Just give it another

hundred winters. You'll be so used to their crude humor by then that you won't bat an eye."

"Lovely. I look forward to the future."

I laughed just as the hunter materialized through the wall. When I beheld his dark expression, my amusement fled. "Did you find the warlock?"

The Fire Wolf nodded, and I could have sworn that a flare of flames danced in his eyes. "If my scrying's correct, he's on the hunt for another sacrifice. If we get to him in time, we may save a life tonight."

WE DECIDED TO TRAVEL TOGETHER, using one of the hunter's portal keys. Even though I told him the SF had supplied us with a dozen of them, on top of what the sentry at the Nolus palace had given us, the hunter still insisted we conserve them.

"You never know when you might need one." He waved everyone closer. "We all need to be holding hands."

"Where are we going?" Ilara asked as her fingers threaded through mine.

"He's currently in northern Canada."

"Do you mind explaining that a bit further?" Haxil frowned. "I'm afraid we are not familiar with the different lands of your realm."

"It's a country north of here. It would appear the warlock has ventured to a remote area in the Mackenzie Mountains in the Yukon. It's a tactic warlocks often use to avoid detection from the Supernatural Forces. If warlocks are able to successfully hunt an unsuspecting human in a remote area of our world, it can be weeks to months before anyone's aware of the individual's disappearance. By that time, many have been missing for so long that few clues remain. It makes it harder to track warlocks, and it's probably why this one has gone so long undetected. Most warlocks leave a path of bodies in their wakes. Their lust for power and blood can consume them, but the warlock we met seems to be able to control his bloodlust enough to stay off the radar."

I grunted, and even though the Fire Wolf had used a number of terms I was unfamiliar with, I understood his meaning. "In that case, I look forward to this."

"Do you have the looking glass?" Ilara glanced at my glamoured clothes. "We'll need to record what happens. We need every bit of evidence captured completely to show the council."

I brushed my knuckles over her cheek. "It's still safely tucked within my cloak even though you can't see it. We'll be able to record what occurs if we capture the warlock."

She breathed a sigh of relief before straightening her spine. "Then let's find him."

"Ready?" the Fire Wolf asked.

"Whenever you are," Ryder replied.

In a swirl of the portal key's magic, the land of Portland disappeared.

❄

WE REAPPEARED in an area filled with white snow and crisp air. Mountains rose all around us as thick forest covered a hillside. Trees covered in green needles, or bare save for thin branches, rose alongside us as fresh, clean air swirled around our limbs. Bird song trilled through the breeze, making this new land seem peaceful and idyllic.

"How lovely," Nish commented even though he looked a bit green from the portal transfer. He breathed deeply, soaking in the winter air. "This feels more like home."

"Indeed," I agreed. "Is the warlock near here?"

The hunter's nostrils flared just as the faint set of rot hit my senses. I stiffened.

"He is. Do you smell him?" the hunter replied.

I nodded as my guards pulled their swords free while magic began to vibrate around my mate. Wings burst from Ilara's back, and their beautiful shimmery white color blended into the snowy landscape.

The hunter inclined his head away from where we'd appeared. "Follow me. He's currently waiting within a human's cabin. My guess is that since the warlock's stationary, the cabin's owner is currently out, most likely in these woods somewhere. With any luck, we'll catch the warlock unaware."

We crept silently through the snow, our footsteps light and undetectable. Even the hunter remained silent, making me think about his earlier comment that hunting prey was his normal daily activity.

The faint rotting scent grew more potent the farther

we moved from our original location. Through the trees, just ahead from where we walked, a building emerged.

Wooden slats. A highly peaked roof. One chimney. The house was simple and rustic, similar in appearance to what I would find on the northern edges of our continent.

When we reached the end of the trees, a clearing spread before us. A small yard had been made around the cabin. The hunter kneeled, and we followed his lead, hunkering closer to the ground.

"Shall I cast an illusion over us to conceal our movements?" I asked him quietly.

"No, the warlock will be able to sense any magic used within the area. We need to attack quickly and silently without the aid of magic, at least, initially."

"Where exactly is he in there?" Ilara nodded at the building.

"My scrying showed him waiting near the fireplace. He's not trying to hide. He's simply waiting for the cabin's owner to return so he can sacrifice him."

"Will he be able to see us from here?" Sandus asked as he brushed snow from his beard. A light dusting fell from the sky, but darker clouds were moving in.

"Unlikely." The Fire Wolf pointed. "Do you see the chimney? It's on the other side of the house, and since those windows"—he indicated the ones facing us—"only show a kitchen, the living area is likely on the opposite side. We're not visible to anyone by the chimney right now."

"Which area do you suggest we enter?" I asked.

"Back door," the hunter replied readily. "As soon as he realizes how many of us are present, he'll try to escape. It's imperative that we capture him immediately and bind his hands. Following that, you can interrogate him as long as you like."

Ilara frowned. "How are we going to bind him?"

The Fire Wolf gave a sly smile. "I have something that'll do the trick."

I gave a curt nod. "All right then. When you're ready." I glanced at my mate. Her eyes were hard and determined.

Nish was grinning. The surly guard rubbed his hands. "Oh, this fight shall be good."

"Don't mind him," Ryder said to the hunter. "He's always spoiling for action."

The Fire Wolf grunted. "We have that in common then." He crouched more. "On my mark, we all enter at once through the back door. Move fast. Stay close."

Everyone nodded, and a moment of fear stole over me when I recalled the warlock's immense magic and power. My mate was storming this cabin at my side. If the warlock hurt her, if he got to her in a moment of weakness—

A push of reassurance surged through me on the bond, and then Ilara's fingers were curling around mine. "Don't underestimate me," she whispered.

I locked my jaw, my teeth grinding, but I canted my head. She was right. My mate was a warrior queen.

"Ready?" the hunter said. "Now!"

We all burst from the foliage, moving in a single line

as fast as the northern winds. Before anyone could blink, we were at the back door. With a twist of his wrist, the Fire Wolf snapped the lock, and we were inside.

The scent of wood smoke hit me, then the putrid stench of the warlock. Before we'd moved two steps, a hiss came from the other room.

"Move!" the hunter yelled.

Blood thundered in my ears, and Ilara's magic hummed around her. Fierceness echoed to me on our bond. The need for vengeance. The need for blood. A warrior's call.

On a gust of her air affinity, my mate had us all through the door and in the living area just as the warlock released a curse. The death magic sailed right for her, but Ilara ducked and spun, avoiding the hit before she crouched and launched herself at him.

We all moved just as fast, each guard circling the warlock before he could react further, and my death affinity rose and shot toward him.

But my magic hit a barrier. A Shield of some kind. It was so potent, so impenetrable . . . I'd never encountered magic like it, so vile and dark, and so incredibly monumental.

My death affinity ricocheted off it, and I sucked it back inside me before anyone got hurt.

"Get his hands!" the hunter called.

But the warlock was already pulling his arm back, and then curse after curse exploded upon us. The couch behind me caught fire. Heat blazed at my back.

Another curse exploded through the wall. Raging wind from outside whistled through my ears as the dark clouds above unleashed a storm.

Within seconds, the entire cabin was engulfed in flames as the warlock moved as fast as the wind.

It was just like in the Isalee field, except this time, he wasn't taunting us. He was utilizing every ounce of power he possessed to beat us. To *kill* us.

A sear of magic whizzed past my ear. The seven of us turned into cyclones, dodging and swiping, ripping and clawing. We all fought to pin the warlock and stop his escape, but no matter how fast any of us moved, the warlock matched our speed and countered it.

"He's going to get away!" Sandus called when the warlock abruptly shot upward, launching himself through the burning cabin's roof before disappearing into the snowy yard outside.

The hunter snarled and jumped through the roof right after him. The rest of us took flight.

Ilara sailed out of the cabin first, her beautiful white wings glimmering like the new snow spiraling through the sky.

"Ilara!" I bellowed when the warlock hurled a curse right for her.

She dipped in the air, her body automatically correcting itself as her warrior magic sang.

The warlock pulled a portal key from his pocket, but before he could activate it, the Fire Wolf tackled him to the ground. The portal key flew from the warlock's hand, disappearing into the snow, but the warlock was already back on his feet.

My guards circled him again as the hunter crouched, looking for an opening.

I threw a gust of air at him, creating a Shield at his back to prevent his escape, but the warlock only grinned and then . . . disappeared.

My eyes grew wide. I spun around, the others doing the same. All of us were on the ground except for my mate. She still hovered in the sky.

Ilara pointed. "There!"

Before I could ask what she saw, she took off, zooming through the air so fast that in a blink she was gone.

"Ilara!" I catapulted into the sky behind her, the earthly air currents picking up as more snow flew around me. Thunder cracked, and a flash of lightning sizzled near a mountain.

In the distance, I could barely make out Ilara's form since the snow blew so hard, and she was flying so fast.

I wrenched a huge amount of magic from my limbs and created a bubble of air behind us, rocketing my guards and me toward her. Beneath us, the Fire Wolf shifted into a wolf's form. My guards shot through the sky with me, and the hunter took off in a blast of speed toward where Ilara had flown.

Blood pounded through my veins as determination barreled from Ilara through our bond. *Mother Above and Below.* She wasn't going to let the warlock escape. Even if she encountered him alone.

But even though my mate was strong, capable, and just as magical as me, that warlock was the most powerful creature I'd ever encountered. He was older than her, more experienced, more savage, and he was no doubt willing to destroy her using any means necessary.

"We'll find her!" Haxil called through the wind. "She'll be okay, Nori."

The others chimed in as we raced through the air. The terrain turned into a blur beneath us. Nostrils flaring, I tried to scent her on the wind, and a flash of fur caught my attention. The Fire Wolf was running through the trees, moving just as fast beneath us.

"Does anyone see—"

A scream tore through the air, then searing pain came along the bond.

"Ilara!" I bellowed across the valley. It echoed, cracking across the snowcapped mountains as a glimpse of my mate appeared through the clouds.

She was millees ahead of us, barely visible.

Fire had ignited along one of her wings. Her beautiful white feathers were up in flames, and then my mate plummeted from the sky.

CHAPTER 13 - ILARA

Searing pain tore through my wing. Fire engulfed my feathers. *Oh Blessed Mother! I've been hit!*

I fell from the sky, the air only igniting the flames further. My entire wing had erupted from the spell the warlock had cast from below.

I frantically tried to smother the flames with my clothing, but I was tumbling too fast and too awkwardly through the air to stop it.

The tip of a tree loomed.

A huge canopy of jagged branches waited.

I hit it at full speed.

Another scream tore from me when I crashed through the snapping branches.

Fire still raged along my wing, but I called upon my fire elemental affinity and smothered the flames. Charred feathers and burned flesh remained as I fell from one branch to another, hitting each painfully hard.

I yanked a dose of my air affinity from my gut when

my thoughts finally cleared enough to do so, and it cushioned the remainder of my fall.

I landed in a crouch on the ground, wincing when my burned wing raked against the tree trunk, but at least I hadn't fallen on my back.

One glance over my shoulder confirmed that my entire wing had burned. My beautiful white feathers were gone. Black, bloody flesh stared back at me as pain radiated along my appendage.

Regret spiraled through me, but I knew I didn't have time to mourn my wing now.

Whipping my attention back to my surroundings, I searched for the warlock. Cold snow pressed against my fingertips as I stayed low to the ground. The entire forest floor was covered in white.

Where is he?

Agony hummed along my injury, but I did my best to ignore it. I knew the warlock had to be close. His curse that had hit my wing had come from directly below where I'd flown.

My gaze whipped around. Bare trees. Snow. A thick forest. Fresh air swirled around me when the breeze blew the burned stench of my flesh away.

But no warlock.

Mother Below. He's here somewhere.

I'd caught a flash of him in the distance when he'd reappeared from whatever magic had made him disappear from the cabin. He'd been hovering over the trees. As though suspended in midair even though he had no wings. He'd been waiting. Watching. It was as if he'd wanted me to follow him. As though he was leading me into a trap, which I'd blindly fallen for.

Ock.

"I'm surprised that curse didn't kill you."

My head spun toward his voice.

Nothing.

Only trees and snow.

But his dark, gravelly voice came from the bare trees. It was rough and deep, and the sound of it reminded me of the bedtime stories my mother used to tell me. About the beasts of the snow and wood, the vicious creatures who roamed our land at night and preyed upon unsuspecting children who'd fled from their beds when their naughtiness had gotten the best of them.

"Most supernaturals would have died from that blast, but it seems you're special, just as I sensed."

I crouched lower and began to creep along the ground. "Is that why you lured me out here?"

"It is. I look forward to taking your blood, then your life. It shall be decadent."

I slowly shifted on the balls of my feet before darting a small distance to the side as I searched for him. My wing dragged painfully behind me, and every touch on my scorched flesh felt as though someone was dragging a shredder down my spine.

"What are you?" he called. "All Solis fae have black wings, yet you don't."

"What an astute observation," I replied dryly. It sounded as though the warlock's voice came from everywhere and nowhere. *How is he invisible?* "But thanks to you, I now have one black wing."

He chuckled. "Ah yes, I can smell its destruction. Such a pity, but I'm sure it won't detract from the rest of your flavor. Did you know that Solis fae have the most delicious-tasting blood?" His voice came from the right. I whipped that way, but only air greeted me. "So much magic is in your system, and since I've enjoyed so many of you, it's made me the most powerful warlock on Earth." Another deep chuckle from him resonated around me. "I have no doubt your blood is going to make me invincible."

A rush of air flew past my cheek, and I ducked at the last moment, avoiding the warlock's curse. I swallowed a scream when it exploded against a tree trunk. A wolf's howl rose in the distance, and then frantic yells came from my mate and his guards.

They were searching for me, but they wouldn't know where I'd fallen. Nothing surrounded me but nameless forest, and I had no idea if Norivun's sensory affinity would allow him to find me or not. Scents dissipated too quickly on the wind, and I'd flown here at a frantic pace. Most likely, he would have to use the bond to locate me.

But I didn't call for them. Even though I was wounded, I also knew that if they all showed up now, the warlock would flee, and we'd possibly never find him again.

"Why are you hiding from me?" I positioned my back in front of a large trunk in case the warlock was behind me. I hissed in a breath when my wing scraped against the tree before it fell limply to the side. "If you're so strong, why don't you show yourself?"

The dark sorcerer laughed again. "But then this wouldn't be so fun."

I heard it before I felt it. The searing sound of another curse headed directly toward me. I closed my eyes, relying on my warrior senses to guide me in the correct direction. I spun at the last second, and the curse exploded into the tree, right where my shoulder had been. That hit wouldn't have killed me, but it would have rendered me immobile.

"You're fast. I'll give you that."

My lip curled. "Fast enough to beat you."

Another laugh came on the wind. "It would appear not, especially with that unfortunate injury of yours."

"Really? I disagree. Injuries only make me more determined." I circled the tree, flexing my charred wing and forcing it up even though the movement made me nauseous. I kept myself low to the ground again, making myself a harder target to hit as I listened carefully. "I've lived with bullies my entire life. You're no exception. I'll deal with you just like I dealt with them."

"Big words for a little girl."

"I could say the same for you. Big words for a little boy. Only little boys hide."

His snarl resonated through the air. It lasted long enough that it gave me a hint of his whereabouts, and a burst of satisfaction hummed through me that my taunt had hit its mark. *There.*

I spun on a burst of my warrior affinity and flung out my fire element. Fire arced through the air and reached the area I suspected he had hidden before I could blink.

A cry of pain erupted, and then the warlock appeared before me, whatever magic he'd been using to cloak himself gone as my fire raged around him. I increased its temperature, trapping him within a dome of flames while letting it lick his mottled gray skin. My breaths came faster when the warlock shot spells and curses at my flames, but I quickly erected a solid Shield of air outside of my fire, trapping him completely within, but each of his hits on my Shield made me shudder. Mother, he was strong.

The warlock bellowed in fury just as the prince, the hunter, and all four of his guards reached me.

Panting, they ground to a stop.

Wildness filled Norivun's eyes. "Your wing!" His aura pounded into me, and then his lip curled as he shot the warlock a murderous glare.

"I know." My rush of excitement from ensnaring the warlock dimmed as pain radiated along my wing anew. "I don't know if a healer will be able to save it or not."

"I saw you fall. I saw him hit you." The prince's fists pumped, and his jaw muscle flexed. "I'm going to *kill* him."

"Nori." I grabbed his arm. "No. We need him alive and talking. Remember?"

"But you're hurt."

"Yes, but we don't have time for that right now, and it's not a lethal blow. I'll get to a healer when we're done. Until then, we need to finish here." I locked down the agony at what had happened to my wing. I had no idea if a gifted healer could repair so much burned flesh or not, but with any luck, Murl or someone the SF knew would be able to help me when we finished. But until then, securing proof of what the king had done took precedence.

"Please," I added quietly when Norivun's expression remained torn. "I'm asking you to put our continent first right now. I'll be okay."

His jaw clenched tightly. A few moments passed as the muscles worked, but he finally gave a curt nod. "All right."

In a blink, the hunter shifted back into his human form. He was naked, but he didn't seem to care as he casually pulled on a pair of pants that he'd strapped to his leg. He must have done it before shifting while I'd been flying away. Following that, the Fire Wolf tried to push his hands through my Shield, but my air stopped him.

"Do you mind?" he asked casually.

I cocked my head but did as he asked, releasing my solid air Shield only.

"Thanks," the hunter replied just before he shot his arms through my flames and around the warlock, not even flinching under my fire.

I gaped.

The Fire Wolf whipped out a pair of blazing handcuffs from his back pocket and cuffed the warlock's wrists behind his back. Blue light blazed from the restraints.

Since Norivun had released us from his illusion masks during the fight, I nudged his attention toward the looking glass in his cloak. "Shall we use that?"

A hint of sanity rolled across Norivun's features even though he kept looking at my ruined wing. He took another deep breath, his chest heaving, before he extracted the looking glass from his cloak.

"If you don't release these flames soon, you're going to torch him," the hunter called casually.

The Fire Wolf's pragmatic reminder had me abruptly releasing my fire elemental affinity as it struck me anew that the hunter was resistant to my flames. He'd also been immune to Norivun's dragon fire, and nobody was immune to that. *What is he?* Apparently more than just a werewolf.

The hunter leaned down and sniffed while the warlock hissed in pain. "Fuck, you stink," the hunter said quietly. "Has anyone ever told you that?"

The hideous warlock's lips peeled back, and he snarled in the hunter's face. Not deterred, the Fire Wolf shoved him forward until the warlock was on his knees in the snow.

The hunter glanced through the trees, then scented the breeze. "Nobody's around for miles. I figure if you want to do an interrogation, this place is as good as any."

THE LOOKING glass hovered above us, suspended with its magic, as it recorded everything that was taking place. The blazing blue handcuffs the Fire Wolf had produced subdued the warlock's power, but it didn't stop the dark sorcerer from continually fighting against their tethering hold.

"Where did you get those?" I asked the Fire Wolf. While we had restraining devices on our continent as well, not even the Solis Guard had anything strong enough to contain one as dynamic as the warlock. "They're as powerful as Tylen's nulling ability."

The hunter shrugged. "Just something I picked up over the years."

Haxil, Ryder, Nish, and Sandus had formed a circle around the warlock, and Norivun had crouched in front of him. My wing still hurt, and a throbbing ache had set in, but I forced my attention away from it.

Concentrating, I kept my life-giving affinity ignited on the perimeter since it was my job to detect if anyone came near. So far, I hadn't sensed anything other than animals, but if a human came within millees of this area, I would know.

However, I highly doubted an unsuspecting bystander would stumble upon us. As a safeguard, Norivun had cast an illusion over us as well, hiding our sight and sound. The Supernatural Forces had been adamant we keep our activities hidden, so we weren't taking any chances.

Sweat beaded along my forehead from the pain radiating along my wing, and the Fire Wolf kept glancing at my charred flesh, then my face. I could have sworn that he wanted to say something, but he remained silent every time we made eye contact.

Norivun had shed his illusion mask entirely. Huge black wings draped down his back, and his silver hair fluttered in the breeze. Cold air blew around us, but it felt like home, and I took some comfort in that.

A strong Shield surrounded my mate, and he gazed at the warlock with a penetrating stare. Even though the hunter had placed magic-binding cuffs on the warlock, none of us were stupid enough not to add an extra precaution to protect ourselves.

"Why did you aid my father, King Novakin, when he requested your help in destroying my continent's *orem*?"

The warlock smirked.

Cocking his head, Norivun asked, "What were you given in return for your dark magic?"

When the warlock remained silent, I created a flicker of flames around him, just small enough that it burned his skin slightly.

A hiss of pain erupted from his thin gray lips, and he shot me a deadly glare.

Norivun sighed. "We can do this the painful way or the easy way."

"Why should I tell you anything?" The warlock's lips peeled back, revealing black teeth.

I released my flames, giving him a chance to speak.

Norivun arched an eyebrow. "If you care to live, you'll speak."

"You're assuming you can kill me."

A swell of Norivun's death affinity rolled out of him. The warlock's eyes widened, so briefly that I wouldn't have caught it if I wasn't standing so close.

"Even *you* are not strong enough to defy my magic with those cuffs in place." Norivun angled his head.

The warlock's throat bobbed. "I won't tell you anything unless you swear not to kill me."

The prince's jaw clenched. "Fine. I swear not to kill you."

A sly smile lifted the warlock's lips. "I don't think so, Dark Prince of the Solis Continent. I need that promise sealed in a fairy bargain if I'm to tell you anything. If I reveal what the king and I agreed upon, I leave this clearing alive when we're through."

The muscle in Norivun's jaw began to tick, but he inclined his head and stepped around the warlock. My stomach coiled when he allowed the warlock's hand to clasp his forearm. Given Norivun's curling lip and the disgust leaking through our bond, he was as repulsed as I was.

"What's your full name?" the prince asked.

Once the warlock revealed it, my mate began the bargain, stating he would not kill the warlock if he told us the truth of his involvement with the Solis king.

The warlock *tsked*. "Our bargain needs to be more thorough. I want it stated that every one of you will never be allowed to hunt me, kill me, or harm me in any way if I tell you the truth about your father."

"Nori—"

My mate cut me off with a look. "We need the truth, Ilara. If he's sealed in a fairy bargain, he can't lie to us. The gods won't allow it."

The prince stated the bargain again, adding to it that none of us in this clearing would harm the warlock in any way, for as long as we all lived, if the warlock revealed the truth.

"However, if you lie, the gods will strike you down," Norivun added at the end. "Do you accept this bargain?"

The warlock grinned and stated the prince's name before saying, "I hereby accept your bargain."

A clash of magic billowed between them, and bargain marks appeared on their wrists.

Smiling smugly, the warlock's gray skin was practically glowing with satisfaction when the prince pulled his hand free and cleansed the disgusting stench from his skin in a burst of magic.

Norivun prowled around, then crouched again in front of the warlock. "Now that you're sealed by a bargain, if you're not truthful, the gods will kill you. So tell me, why are you protecting the Solis king?"

"Because if I comply with his wishes, he gives me fae to sacrifice."

My heart jolted. *That* was how King Novakin was paying him? By giving him our fae to sacrifice? My hatred for the king strengthened a thousand fold.

Norivun's jaw worked, and his rage billowed toward me on the bond, but other than that one hint of movement on his face, he gave no other outward reaction. "In exchange for what?" he pushed.

The warlock smiled, the expression truly hideous. "In exchange for a death veil that I created in Isalee Territory, which spread throughout your land and killed all of your crops."

A flare of Norivun's magic pulsed around him, and the anger strumming from him along our bond increased even more. "And how many Solis fae sacrifices were you promised in exchange for creating that veil?"

"As many as I wanted."

Nish made a sound of disgust, and Ryder's lip curled. Haxil and Sandus's auras swelled even higher as they gazed at the warlock with pure contempt. Even the Fire Wolf reacted. The hunter's eyes flickered briefly to flames.

Norivun's nostrils flared. "So, King Novakin said you could sacrifice an *endless* amount of Solis fae as long as you complied with his wishes? Those wishes being that you created a deadly veil in our soil, which killed all of our crops, and ultimately would lead to the starvation of all of our fae?"

"Yes."

I sucked in a breath, and it took everything in me not to incinerate the warlock on the spot. We'd guessed that the king had been paying him in some way, but to hear it confirmed and to learn *how* the warlock was being paid . . .

Blessed Mother. The king had intentionally and

willingly allowed the warlock to pluck as many fae from the castle as he wanted. It was beyond appalling. It was infuriating. The king would have even allowed *my* life to be taken. If my fire affinity hadn't fended the warlock off following that disastrous date with Lord Waterline, I would have been one of his victims.

And the king had condoned that.

Muscles bunched around Norivun's shoulders as he shifted in his crouch. His hands were curled into fists so tightly, his knuckles were white. "And why did my father want all of this done? Why would he offer to you the fae he was supposed to protect in exchange for that veil?"

A dark, perverse light lit the warlock's eyes. "He wanted all of the crops to die so the Solis fae would starve. Starving, desperate fae would be more likely to comply when the king invaded the Nolus continent."

"So all of this was done—the veil, the murders—to starve the fae of our continent, so they would be more likely to support my father when he marched upon our southern neighbors and started a war?"

"Yes."

"And why did he want a war?"

The warlock shrugged, his expression turning bored. "For the same reason all powerful leaders start wars—to increase his reach, to expand his territory. The motivation is nothing new or interesting."

The prince's guards all shifted in place. Their attention was still focused on the warlock, still ready in case those cuffs failed, yet fury burned brightly in all their eyes.

The crown prince glanced up at the looking glass. "I think we have what we need."

The warlock laughed. "Which means, it's time you released me from these cuffs."

Norivun gave a curt nod to the Fire Wolf. "Do as he says."

"You know he'll go back to killing innocents, right?" the hunter said, an edge to his tone.

"A bargain was made. I must honor it."

A low snarl rumbled in the hunter's chest, but he unlocked the cuffs from around the warlock and tucked them into his back pocket.

Grinning, the warlock rubbed his wrists. My stomach clenched when a triumphant smile spread across his gray face.

"You're all fools." The warlock pulled a portal key from his pocket. "I've already planned to meet the Solis king again tonight. I shall be sacrificing a dozen fae lives at dusk, increasing my power so I can re-create that veil once more, and do you know the best thing about it?" He didn't wait for Norivun's reply before saying, "There's nothing *any* of you can do about it. The bargain protects me indefinitely from all of you."

I dropped the worried mask I'd been wearing just as Norivun and the Fire Wolf did the same.

My mate smirked. "You're right. There's nothing any of *us* can do about it, but *they,* however, can."

Norivun's head inclined toward the two dozen SF

members that appeared through the trees, hidden previously by the prince's illusion.

Particle guns buzzed as the Supernatural Forces advanced. The warlock's eyes widened a split second before hellfire rained.

CHAPTER 14 - ILARA

The bargain mark that had appeared following his deal with the warlock fizzled out of existence and disappeared from Norivun's wrist the second the warlock was dead.

The SF cleaned up the obliterated remains of the dark sorcerer. With two dozen highly trained and experienced SF members against one unsuspecting warlock, the fight had been quick and efficient. The evil sorcerer hadn't stood a chance.

"Do you feel bad for tricking him so completely?" Haxil asked the prince with a smile.

Norivun's lips curved upward. "No, not even slightly."

Haxil laughed and clapped him on the back. "Me neither."

The Fire Wolf smirked, then said to one of the SF commanders, "I'll send my bill to headquarters."

The commander dipped his head. "Wes is expecting it."

Norivun stepped closer to me and placed a hand on my back, then eyed my wing. His brows pinched together. "I'm going to ask them to give you medical help."

I scanned the SF members. They were all busy, working hard. Biting my lip, I shook my head. "No, not here. I'll wait until we reach their headquarters in Idaho. They have enough to deal with as it is."

Norivun's frown grew. "But your wing—"

"I'll be fine. My wing hasn't worsened."

The seven of us stepped away from the clearing, letting the SF finish their job. But when my wing scraped against a tree when I walked too closely to it, and I winced for what felt like the hundredth time, I began to wonder if I *should* ask for help.

Norivun grumbled and stepped closer to me.

Watching me, the Fire Wolf frowned, and I couldn't help but give him an irritated side-eye. He'd been giving me continual looks ever since they'd found me. "What?"

He shrugged, then raked a hand through his hair, and his fingers tangled in the dark locks. "Sorry, but I keep wondering why you haven't healed yourself yet."

"Healed myself?" I repeated. I cocked my head as Norivun and his four guards all paused.

The hunter waved to my wing. "Your magic turns you into an angel, right? Angels have extraordinary healing abilities, so this entire time, I couldn't help but wonder why you haven't healed your wing yet."

My eyes bugged out when a moment of clarity hit me. Bavar had said something similar earlier today. *"Angels have* extraordinary *healing power. The likes of which this world has never seen."*

My jaw dropped as the possibility of being able to fix my ruined wing slammed into me. "Do you really think *I* can heal myself?"

The Fire Wolf shrugged. "I'm assuming you can. Do you not know how?"

I shook my head. "No, I have no idea."

The hunter grunted. "Well, you should at least try. It would be a pity if you lost the ability to fly."

Norivun stepped closer to me, and his hope surged to me on our bond. "Try, my love. Take your time. You're safe here."

"He's right, Ilara. You should try," Haxil agreed.

The other three guards all voiced similar responses.

My breaths came quickly. I gazed up at my mate. They were right. I needed to try. Still, a moment of apprehension pricked my conscience. "How do I start?"

Norivun's hand drifted to my lower back. He was careful not to jar my injured wing as he began stroking me in soft, lulling motions. "Do as Matron Olsander instructed you. Mental imagery. That's how we all first learn our affinities, remember?" He stepped even closer until his alluring snow and cedar scent wrapped around me. "Close your eyes, concentrate on where your angel affinity resides within your body, and imagine it healing your wing. No harm will come from trying."

"And if I fail?"

"Then we'll find a healer, the best healer this realm has to offer. I'm sure the Fire Wolf could help us locate one if the SF can't."

The hunter crossed his arms. "No problem. I know a few witches you could contact if this doesn't work."

I took a deep breath and nodded, then did as my mate instructed, using Norivun's belief in me that strummed along our bond. The prince had always believed in me. It was time I met his confidence with my own.

Brow furrowing in determination, I let my wing fall limply, wincing slightly when the tip met the cold snow, then focused all of my attention on the dense ball of power between my shoulder blades.

Swirling, brilliant light and cold power circulated between my wings. Such *strength* and such immense purpose were held within this affinity that I had a feeling I hadn't even scratched the surface of all that it was capable of.

Closing my eyes, I concentrated on what Matron Olsander had taught me, about feeling each affinity individually.

That ball of light and coldness that nestled between my shoulder blades beckoned me. I'd never thought to try anything more with it than to unleash my wings, but now, with an unfurling sense of its potential, I tapped into it.

I stroked my newest affinity and imagined that ball of light and power unfurling like a flower in my garden. Growing, blooming, and thriving. A tingling sensation began in my back, followed by a cooling sense of numbness.

Slowly, the dense energy began to widen until its solid mass of light and iciness pulsed along my wings.

I pictured that blazing light and frigid energy curling along my injured wing, racing and dipping into each divot and turn of flesh until the skin knitted together, the blood vessels reformed, and my feathers regrew.

Fatigue swelled within me. So much energy. So much power was needed to ask this of my affinity. The depth of what this magic could do pulled at me, but I had no idea how to truly control it or wield it, so I simply let it go and didn't try to manipulate it completely. Instead, I kept imagining what I hoped it would do.

Exhaustion made me breathe heavier, and just as the last of my mental imaginings finished, I fell to the forest floor, my legs too limp to keep me upright.

Norivun kneeled beside me as a look of wonder washed over his face. "Ilara . . ."

His shock filtered to me on our bond, and I tentatively glanced behind me.

Gasping, I beheld two healthy wings, strong and filled with feathers as white as snow.

"You did it," Norivun breathed. "Bavar and the Fire Wolf are right. You can *heal*."

"That's not an illusion?" I flapped each wing, amazed when no pain accompanied the movement and equally in awe when both of my wings appeared strong and resilient. "I just did that?"

"Indeed." Norivun grinned, and his joy flowed to me along our connection.

Sandus whooped, and Nish tousled the hair on the top of my head. Haxil patted the Fire Wolf on the back, and Ryder grinned.

The Fire Wolf crossed his arms. "I thought that would work."

"You're truly an enigma, love," Sandus said affectionately.

"A powerful enigma who has so much potential." My mate pulled me close, wrapping his arms around me before whispering in my ear, "You amaze me more and more each day, my love. You truly are a warrior queen."

AFTER THE SHOCK of being healed had worn off, I relaxed my angel affinity and sucked my wings back into my body. I still couldn't fully believe that I was an angel and that I could indeed heal as one too, but such seemed to be the case.

I was also reminded of how I used to feel when I was training extensively with Matron Olsander. Learning new affinities was truly and utterly exhausting.

The SF was nearly done with their cleaning by the

time I felt strong enough to leave. "Did the looking glass capture everything?" I asked Norivun.

He showed it to me, whispering the spell to replay it. The looking glass now contained two recordings. The encounter we had within the Isalee field when we destroyed the warlock's veil, and now the warlock's bargain-bound confession about what the king had truly done as well.

It was all there.

We finally had solid proof.

"So our work here is done." I exhaled in relief.

"That it is. We may return to Solisarium now and convene with the council. Surely, after this, they will side with us and unanimously vote to remove my father."

I nodded. "Thank the Mother."

Norivun pulled out one of the portal keys to whisk us home, and I couldn't help but glance toward where this fight had started.

"You know, the only thing I feel bad about is that cabin we destroyed here." I frowned and nibbled on my bottom lip. "What's the human going to do when he returns to find his home ruined?"

The hunter shook his head. "No need to worry. The SF will take care of it. They have witches and sorcerers that specialize in fixing things like that."

My jaw dropped. "They have constructo affinities?"

"No, not the same as Solis magic, but they can repair things in a similar way, so don't sweat it," the Fire Wolf replied. "Whoever owns that cabin won't even know anything happened by the time the witches are done."

Haxil and I shared an amazed look.

"They truly do have magic wielders here, don't they?" I whispered to him. "Even if the atmosphere is magicless, not everything in this realm is."

Haxil grinned. "It would be fun to watch them work, just to compare the different types of magic."

Norivun snorted, and Ryder coughed to hide a smile. Nish, however, rolled his eyes and muttered something about how he disagreed and believed this realm to be vastly inferior to ours.

The hunter merely watched all of us with raised eyebrows before saying, "Are you all heading back to the fae lands for good?"

I smothered my curiosity and brought a fist to my chest before bowing. "Indeed. We thank you again for your assistance."

Norivun and his guards did the same, each bowing in respect.

The Fire Wolf inclined his head. "No worries. I'll be on my way back to Chicago then." He pulled his yellow crystal from his pocket, a crystal that had somehow been mined from Harrivee's floating meadows and had come to rest in the hunter's possession.

With that, he ducked into his portal and disappeared.

❄

ALONE IN THE forest with the SF members disappearing in small groups as their work was finished, I took a deep breath and thought of what the coming days would bring.

"Join hands," Norivun instructed. "It's time to return home."

Frowning, I nibbled on my lip.

"Everything all right, love?" Sandus cocked his head, his brow furrowing. He entwined his fingers with mine.

I gave a quick nod. "Yes, I'm thankful we finally have enough evidence to sway the council to our side, but I keep thinking about the bigger picture."

My mate frowned and stepped closer to me. He clasped my free hand. "What do you mean?"

The soothing feeling of his touch coursed through me. I eyed Norivun, who was watching me raptly, and once again, I got the impression that he was allowing me to lead. "I keep thinking about the Crimsonales and how they refused to act until we held firm proof of the king's treasonous activities, and I can't help but wonder how the Solis fae will react when we overthrow their beloved king."

My thoughts returned to the stop we'd made at the castle, to the queen's tower before we'd escaped following the gods' wrath. We still had that material captured within the looking glass, but we hadn't used it yet. I'd planned to also show it to the council, but now . . .

Sandus's eyebrows rose. "What are you getting at, love?"

"I'm saying that I don't think we should return to Solisarium. If we're going to successfully overthrow the king and transfer the crown to Norivun, we need not only the council on our side but our fae as well."

Norivun smiled, yet it didn't reach his eyes. "That's a fanciful wish, my love."

"It wouldn't be if they saw you for who you really are."

Nish grunted. "Exactly. They'd be fools not to accept you."

Ryder crossed his arms, and the telltale shrewd look that often covered his face appeared. "What are you proposing we do, Ilara? Speak plainly."

I took another deep breath. "I'm concerned that the Solis love King Novakin so much that they won't believe what he's really done, and I'm also worried about what will happen when we try to overthrow him. You've said before that the Crimsonales are always striving for power, right?"

The prince nodded and ran his thumb along my inner wrist. "Indeed. Michas even told me that someday he would be ruling *me*, and"—he chuckled darkly—"that conversation didn't end well."

I smirked and squeezed his hand. "So not only could we have an entire continent of angry fae questioning why we ousted the king—even if the council voted with us—but we could also have a noble family striving to seize power. The Crimsonales want to rule, and they'll only act when they know the chance of gaining more power is possible, which is the only reason they were willing to march on the Nolus, so if we return to the council now—"

"The Crimsonales will try to gain the upper hand," my mate finished for me as a dark light entered his eyes. Power swelled around him, rippling the air. "You're probably right."

Nish scowled. "Then what do we do?"

"We need more fae on our side," I replied. When Norivun's eyebrows rose, I added, "We need to show our fae who King Novakin really is, so when the time comes that we challenge his rule, they'll be behind us. And we need them to believe in you, not Lord Crimsonale." Norivun's breath hitched, so I pushed a beat of love along our bond to him. "Your father has done a magnificent job of painting you as the villain. We need that perception to change. We need the fae of our land to see you for *you*, so when we do go to the council, the Solis will be ready to accept you as their new king, and the crown will be transferred peacefully."

Ryder chuckled. "Clever, Ilara, very clever indeed. You're concerned that once the king is ousted, our continent will be wary of accepting the crown prince as their ruler after believing for decades that their beloved King Novakin has only had their best interests at heart, even though the crown is Norivun's birthright."

I nodded. "Exactly. I'm concerned they'll see this all as a coup, even if we have the council's support. Our citizens love the king, but that's only because they don't know who he really is. We need them to see his true character because if they don't, what better time will there be for the Crimsonales to make their move?"

Worry pulsed along the bond from Norivun, and I placed a hand on his cheek. I knew what he feared. I knew what his darkest concern was. Even though he'd spent winters protecting innocent fae and giving so much to those around him, he was hated, and deep down, he still believed he deserved their hate.

But he was wrong. He deserved their *love*, and I intended to prove that to him.

I ran my thumb along his jaw, the bristles from his hair scraping against my skin. "Allow me this chance to prove to our fae that my eternal husband is the fairy all of them should hope to have on the throne."

His throat bobbed in a swallow. "And if they reject me?"

"They won't. Not after they see who you really are."

"And how are we going to do that, love?" Sandus placed his hands on his hips, his fingers drumming against his tunic. "How do we gain support from an entire continent?"

"By showing them that." Ryder pointed to the looking glass. A sharp smile curved his lips. "Ilara wants the fae of our land to see who Nori really is while also revealing the king for the snake he's always been, and what better way to do that than to show them their king wanted them starved while their son sought to protect them and keep them fed?"

I glanced up at the guard, a smile blooming across my face. "Exactly."

Instead of returning to Solisarium, we mistphased back to my village. If we were going to convince any fae of who the prince really was while also showing them the king's true nature, the best place to start was with those I knew and trusted and who trusted me in return.

We reappeared in the middle of my village's main street. Snow flew through the air, and a biting wind cut into my cheeks. Norivun whipped an air Shield around us to keep the elements at bay just as a few fae from my village shrieked at our return.

"Ilara! It's Ilara Seary! She's come home, and she's brought her mate, the prince!" a child yelled, pointing at us and tugging at his mother's cloak.

My brow furrowed when villagers poured into the street, coming from shops and their homes. All of them began congratulating the prince and me on our mate bond, and not one of them looked at the prince with fear in their eyes.

"What's happened?" The familiar look and scents of home sank into my soul. I swirled around. "How do you all know that the prince is my mate?"

"Evis and Krisil are telling everyone, my dear," Callaleel, our village's primary school teacher, replied. "The whole of Mervalee Territory probably knows by now." She winked. "You know how those two are. They really get the tongues wagging."

"But how did *they* know?" I looked at Norivun, searching his face for answers.

He smirked. "The boys and I might have made a visit to your field-barn cooks before we found you with Drachu."

Ryder shrugged. "It's a long story, but it obviously worked."

"We sent my father's fae who were hunting for you off on a wild chase, and I also explained to the cooks in your field barn that you were my mate, so I was trying to protect you."

My eyebrows shot up. "That's how everyone here knows we're mated?"

Norivun grinned. "You did tell me Evis and Krisil were the biggest gossips this side of the Gielis Mountains. I figured I'd use that to my advantage."

I snorted a laugh.

Still grinning, he added, "It seems they've told everyone, and if anything, it will help our fae understand why I could never marry Georgyanna." The prince's arm curled around my waist. He dipped his head to run the tip of his nose along my neck. "All fae understand the mate bond. They'll realize I could have never married her when I had you."

My lips curled into a smile as hope filled my chest. "That was clever."

"Almost as clever as your plan."

I laughed, and tendrils of renewed hope made

determination surge through my soul. "Perhaps our endeavors *will* work, especially if they all know we're mates. Come, let's gather everyone together."

We ventured to the fields, mistphasing to them in a blink.

Rolling swells of land were covered with growing plants of various colors. Warm air swirled just above the soil. Laborers dotted the field as they tended the crops. Without Vorl, the mood throughout the field was calmer and lighter.

Gracelyn, a female who'd been born in my village and had tended the crops for hundreds of winters, was currently the interim archon of our village according to Cailis.

The female inclined her head in my direction, her expression curious as she surveyed the prince and his guards, before she bent over to assist one of the younger fae with a wheat stalk.

My heart surged. My home's thriving plants were growing and blooming amidst the field's protective cloud of *orem*. It was as it should be.

"Ock, Ilara Seary, good day to you, love!" one of the males called from the field, waving from a distance. "Your Highness." He bowed formally to Norivun before returning to his work.

Dozens of other laborers did the same, greeting me and then their crown prince.

An aching sensation cracked my chest from the way they all readily welcomed my mate. It was the exact opposite reaction to what he'd been given months ago when he'd stormed into the field barn to collect me.

Norivun threaded his fingers through mine.

"Come, we have much to do." I tugged the prince into the barn, and his guards followed.

Inside, we found Evis and Krisil, laboring over their steaming pots and kettles. I squeezed the prince again, then released him just as Evis shrieked, "Ilara!"

Krisil wiped her hands on her apron and bustled around the steaming cauldrons. "Ock, Ilara, you've finally returned home and with your handsome prince nonetheless."

Both bowed to the prince, reverence apparent upon their expressions. I started again at how readily they greeted the heir to the throne. Whatever the prince had said to them when I'd been with Drachu had definitely made an impression.

They both hugged me after the customary bows, then looked me over. Evis glanced around my shoulder and frowned. "Where's Cailis?"

"Not here, but she's safe." I squeezed her again, then clasped both of their hands. "I've returned because we have something to ask of you. Will you come with us now to the village center?"

Krisil cocked her head as she scanned the prince and his guards, her face a mask of confusion. "Of course we will, Ilara."

"That's Lady Seary," Nish corrected.

Evis covered her mouth with a laugh. "Of course, I forgot how far you've come. *Lady* Seary, we would be honored to accompany you and the prince to the village center."

Disbelief again coursed through me at how much their demeanor had changed. "Will you call the laborers too? Everyone needs to hear this. I'm counting on both of you to continue spreading the truth about the prince and also the king."

The small auras swirling around the two cooks began to buzz with anticipation. "Whatever are you talking about?" Krisil asked.

I smiled. "You'll see."

CHAPTER 15 - ILARA

It wasn't hard to gather the laborers and other villagers in the middle of our small main street. Everyone was eager to learn how I fared, to know more of Cailis, and to learn why the prince and I had returned to my home.

I smiled as reassuringly as I could as I promised all of them that Cailis was safe, but I wished so desperately that I could tell them the truth. That, not only was my sister safe and alive, but my parents and brother were too. But our visit today wasn't to divulge the truth of the haven on the Cliffs of Sarum. That would have to come later, when we knew the king couldn't get to them.

One step at a time.

"Gather round. Everyone, come on now, get closer." Nish made a swishing movement with his hands. He signaled all of the villagers to stand before me and the prince.

Haxil, Ryder, and Sandus did the same until we

had a crowd of a hundred fae, nearly all of the citizens from my home, surrounding us.

The prince placed his hands on his hips, his huge frame towering over everybody. The tips of his talons, one on each wing bone, shone like onyx in the sunlight.

I took a deep breath and gazed at the fae I'd grown up with. "I have something I need all of you to see. It's the truth of what has been happening on our continent for the past full season." My voice carried through the air as snow swirled around us. "I know you previously all believed that Prince Norivun was to be feared, but he's not who his father has made him out to be. The king has been lying to you."

Perplexed expressions shown on all of the villagers around me. Some looked to one another in confusion, others crossed their arms and waited for me to continue, but one of the villagers cocked his head, then yelled, "What are you talking about, Ilara? King Novakin has never lied to us."

Nish grumbled from behind me, and Ryder's lip curled.

The crown prince didn't move a muscle. The stoic mask he always wore had descended, and it struck me that such a mask was how he'd survived. He'd grown accustomed to wearing his emotional armor when pitted against the fae he'd so desperately tried to protect. For winters, Norivun had done everything in his power to keep them safe.

And they'd hated him in return, none of them knowing the truth.

But today, their perception would change. I would make sure of it.

Raising my voice louder, I called, "I don't expect all of you to believe me immediately. You know that Prince Norivun is my mate, so of course, I will do everything in my power to protect him. But what I'm about to show you is the *truth* of what's been going on, and it's the truth of who King Novakin really is."

I extended my hand to the prince. Slowly, he withdrew the looking glass and gave it to me.

A few mumbled in the crowd. Even though only two in my village had enough rulibs to afford a looking glass, everyone knew what they were.

I held up the magical mirror, the shiny surface reflecting the snow and sun. "Only weeks ago, we discovered the truth of what has been happening within our land. You've all heard the rumors. You've all heard that crops have been dying, our fae have been starving, and nothing's been done about it."

"Indeed we have, Ilara. It's why Tormesh and your parents died!" a male called as a look of unease filled his face when he eyed my mate. They all still believed that my mate had killed my family.

I glanced at Norivun, emotion making my voice break when I said, "The prince is not who you believe him to be. He's not evil. He doesn't have a heart of stone. He doesn't relish hurting those around him. The truth is that he's been working tirelessly to prevent innocents from dying, and he's done everything in his power to stop needless deaths." I gazed at the crowd again. A hush had descended over all of them, and I gathered my courage. My next words would condemn me as a traitor and undoubtedly seal my death if the council failed to dethrone King Novakin and if the king got me in his clutches again.

Steeling myself and knowing there was no turning back after this, I shouted, "The truth is that King Novakin is behind the poison that has spread throughout our land, killing the crops. The king has been causing dissent!"

Silence followed.

A few villagers shuffled their feet, most glancing at one another in confusion.

"Ock, that's preposterous!" a female finally yelled from the back.

A few other villagers grumbled in agreement. Some even shook their heads in disgust as though horrified that I could even claim such a thing.

I fisted my hands. Everyone was so quick to defend the king. Taking another deep breath, I worked at calming my rage before igniting the magic that rolled between my shoulder blades. I called upon my angel affinity, and my wings burst from my back in a flurry of power.

A collective gasp emitted from the crowd—a crowd that several months ago had always thought I was a defective.

I shot upward, flapping my wings until I was hovering above them all, then used my air affinity to amplify my voice even more. Through the bond, I felt

Norivun's pride, his love, and his unfailing belief in me. I latched onto his emotions so tightly it felt as though he were in the sky beside me.

I used his unwavering support to fuel my courage, then thrust my arm out in front of me and activated the looking glass's magic. "It's not preposterous. It's the truth. See for yourself."

Light burst from the looking glass before a scene was projected over the crowd. I called upon all of the looking glass's magic to portray what they needed to see, and the image projected in a huge recording in the sky.

Every villager's eyes went wide. Their jaws collectively dropped as the scene of what we'd done in Isalee began to unfold.

"The crown prince and I found the source of the deadly poison that had seeped into our land. It took all of our magic and the help of a male from the *other* realm to destroy it."

The scene shifted, showing the Fire Wolf holding the lava rock over the land before it fell into the ground, burrowing a huge hole into the soil as magic was being pulled from me, the prince, and all of his guards.

Whispering and sounds of disbelief erupted from the crowd when I swirled through the air, revealing the scene to all of them. The spider-like structure of the veil lifted, its ugly black heart rising to the surface of the soil.

Several villagers recoiled, and more than a few made the sign of the Blessed Mother. Even though the looking glass was only showing them what had occurred, it was as though they could *feel* the evil power that had stained our land.

And when the scene shifted, and the warlock appeared after the veil's heart had been destroyed, all of the villagers shouted in fright.

"What in the realm is that?" a male asked, revulsion in his voice.

"He's called a warlock." My wings continued to hold me aloft as my village watched what I was showing them. "He comes from the *other* realm. He's a male that King Novakin has been working with in secret. The king commissioned him to destroy our *orem*. It's because of this warlock's dark magic that our fields and food sources began to die."

"Why in the realm would the king do that? King Novakin has been nothing but an unfailing leader for centuries!" a female, who worked in one of the shops, called from the side.

A few muttered in agreement.

I inclined my head, nodding at their skepticism. "I initially felt the same. We've all felt the king has had our best interests at heart. He's united us. He's led us for centuries. For the most part, we've been prosperous. But in the past full season, as you all know, that's changed."

I swirled in the air again, showing them once more what had transpired in Isalee, commanding the looking glass to show them everything anew from the beginning.

Before them, the unfailing crown prince was weakened and vulnerable, but he didn't give up. He kept fighting the warlock even when our deaths seemed imminent.

I whispered the spell needed to activate the second recording, the one that showed the warlock confessing what the king had done while we'd been in Canada.

The image started anew, showing the warlock cuffed and on his knees amidst the snowy trees in the forest. It showed the prince making a bargain with the warlock, a bargain that would strike the warlock dead if the warlock lied about what he was saying.

Every villager watched with rapt attention, their expressions changing from disbelief to confusion and then to anger. And when the warlock finished confessing what had truly gone on, I knew the moment had come to accuse the king of who he really was.

"The king isn't who you believe him to be. He does not care for your safety, your well-being, or if your children go to bed hungry or sick. All he cares about is power. He hired this warlock to infuse our land with a poisonous veil. He wants to start a war, and he doesn't care how many of you die to feed his hunger for power."

A male scoffed. "You're saying the king was willing to starve us so we would want to go to war?"

I nodded. "That's exactly right."

Several shuddered when the second recording began playing again, repeating everything they'd just witnessed. A few shouts rang in the crowd when the looking glass showed the crown prince questioning the dark sorcerer. Some furrowed their brows. Others pressed their lips into tight lines and scoffed.

I flew to the other side, letting everyone glimpse the magical apparatus close-up. "Because of the poisonous veil that King Novakin demanded be created, entire crops have died. I saw firsthand the result of this dark magic. And it was only with the crown prince's determination to end the starvation upon our continent that we were able to defeat it, find this warlock, and end him too. You all know that the magic within a looking glass doesn't allow it to lie. What you've just witnessed is the *truth*, as you all know."

A few of the villagers nodded. Shock still filled most of their faces, but some began to bow toward the prince as they brought fists to their chests.

A kernel of hope alighted inside me.

Directly to my right, a young female shook her head. "But, Ilara, what you're saying is that the king has tried to kill *all* of us. Why would the king do that?"

"Because he's not who you think he is." I lifted the looking glass again, then glanced at my mate to ensure he was in agreement.

Norivun gave a curt nod.

Breaths coming faster, I showed them a third recording, but instead of the looking glass portraying the Isalee field or the forest in Canada, I showed them what we'd done on our last stop before leaving the castle. "Would a true leader who wants the best for his fae do something like this?"

The recording revealed Queen Lissandra in her chambers. Bruises covered her chest and back. Her hair hung limply, her frame thin.

The female at my right gasped. "Is that the queen?"

I nodded. "Her husband, the *king*, beats her regularly. And he has done so for over a hundred winters."

Gasps emitted through the crowd, and more than one female's hand flew to her mouth.

"But why?" someone called.

"Because he's cruel, and he uses his own wife to control his son. For full seasons, King Novakin has abused the queen if Prince Norivun didn't do as he commanded. He demanded that his son be portrayed as a tyrant and a murderer, and the prince fulfilled that role, because if he didn't, his mother was horrifically tortured."

Sounds of disgust rang from the crowd when the queen turned in the image, lifting her sleeves to reveal ugly slashes and lacerations along her arms and shoulders.

"That doesn't prove the king did it!" a male yelled from the crowd. "Anyone could have given the queen those wounds."

A few nodded in agreement, but uneasiness seeped through the crowd.

"It's the truth. Keep watching." I shone the looking glass over the crowd again, and after the queen had revealed the extent of her abuse, her eyes met the looking glass's recording.

The queen's voice rang out, clear and strong despite her physical state. "I've remained quiet for hundreds of winters, but no more. The male I'm married to, the male who sits atop the throne, is the male responsible for this.

For more winters than I can count, King Novakin has beaten me, starved me, humiliated me, and done everything in his power to keep me contained." She took a deep, shuddering breath. "Many of you know that I possess great magic, but I can no longer call forth my affinities. In a bid to control me and my children completely, the king commissioned a powerful spell to suppress my power. For dozens of winters, I haven't been able to call forth my magic, and it's been festering inside me ever since. But I'm coming forward now because it's time for his tyrannical rule to end. King Novakin is not who he seems. He's a monster, and it's time that the Solis fae of our great continent know that and put a stop to his rule."

When the image flickered out of existence, nothing but the wind whistling through the street made a sound.

My heart was beating so fast that blood thundered in my ears.

I gazed at all of the fae who'd been at my side since the day I was born. Swallowing the thickness in my throat, I stared at them imploringly. "The king used Queen Lissandra as leverage to control the crown prince. If Prince Norivun doesn't do as he commands, he abuses the prince's mother. What you just witnessed is a common state that our queen, the female we all love and cherish, resides in. Now tell me if that's truly a male you want atop the throne? A male who not only abuses his wife but will just as soon starve and abuse you if you don't do what he wants. Tell me that's not a male you want stopped."

Silence reigned, and my heart thundered so fast I felt lightheaded.

Flapping my wings more, I said, "I know all of this is coming as a shock to you, but it's important that you know the truth. It's important that *all* of the fae on our continent know what's really gone on. Prince Norivun isn't who you've been led to believe. The *king* isn't who you believe him to be either." I flung an arm toward my mate, who still stood with a carefully guarded expression.

"The king is a liar," I shouted. "Everything you've known has been a lie, but I'm pleading with all of you to consider what I'm telling you. Our continent is on the brink of war. The king wants to march on the Nolus fae and steal their land. He commissioned that warlock to create the veil within Isalee in order to drum up support for a war. He's been starving *all of you* so that you're more malleable and are able to be manipulated for his personal gain."

Several villagers glanced at one another, shock and wariness apparent in their expressions, yet I still felt their hesitance to believe everything.

"I know I'm turning everything you've ever known upside down, but you all deserve to know the truth."

"Ock . . . it's true!" Haxil all but growled as he stepped forward. "Everything Ilara is telling you is what's been happening. The prince's guards and I have witnessed *everything* she's claiming." He gestured toward Nish, Ryder, and Sandus, all of whom stood taller and gave firm nods. "For many winters, we've watched the king abuse the queen and her sons—Prince Norivun and Prince Nuwin. For *full seasons*, we've remained silent out of respect of Prince Norivun's wishes, but I cannot tell you how much I've burned for you all to know the truth. This male"—Haxil pointed at the prince, who stood unmoving beside him—"has suffered for many winters under the king's hand. We've remained silent, but no more. As Ilara said, war is coming, but now the question becomes on which side you will fight. Will you fight with a tyrant who would willingly feed you to that warlock or for a prince who's fought silently for you his entire life?" Haxil pointed at the looking glass. "And remember, *looking glasses can't lie*. Everything you just saw is true. The Isalee field. The warlock's confession, which was done under a fairy bargain, would have struck him dead if he lied. *Everything* you just witnessed is real. How can any of you not see that?"

Ryder jutted his chin up. "The true question becomes, do you wish to stay upon your land, continuing to live as you always have, or do you wish to slaughter the neighbors south of us and steal the continent that is rightfully theirs?"

Several females covered their mouths as wings ruffled around the village males.

"Because that is what will occur if King Novakin stays in power," Ryder growled.

Finally, a female in the crowd broke the quiet. She made a sound of disgust.

Then another grumbled before spitting on the ground.

And another glowered heavily before planting her hands on her hips.

Several of the males did the same.

"To abuse one's wife . . . that's despicable behavior." One of the older males crossed his arms. "Solis don't harm our females. We protect them when they can't protect themselves. Only a weak male would do such a thing."

It was on the tip of my tongue to tell them that our archon had been one of those males, but Vorl held no place in the discussion here. That was a conversation for another day.

"And to march on our neighbors to take what's theirs is also abhorrent!" another shouted.

"We've never had a problem with the Nolus." A male's brow furrowed. He was a laborer like me. I'd grown up working in the fields beside him. "I have no desire to march upon their land."

"Neither do I!" A female clutched her child closer to her. She'd been a friend of my mother's, and more than once, she'd come to our home to join us in my mother's favorite game of cards. "War brings nothing but death and destruction. It's been hundreds of winters since the territories were at war when the king united us all, but that strife was nothing like the true wars." She shuddered. "My grandmother told me what life was like during the elvish wars." Her eyes grew distant and haunted as her tiny aura buzzed. "Even though that was thousands of seasons ago, she still remembered. I have no desire to see my children starved or killed."

The prince's aura strengthened as more and more villagers voiced their desire for peace.

"Then we ask that you help us spread the word." I flapped my wings again and soared over the crowd, the looking glass on full display for all of them to see as the scenes again portrayed our battle with the warlock, the warlock's confession in Canada, and their queen's abused state. "Tell *everybody* you know what you were shown today. Tell them the truth of Prince Norivun, the vindictive scheming of the king, and the abuse that the royal family has suffered for dozens of winters under the hand of King Novakin. Help us stop the king from starting another war!"

CHAPTER 16 - NORIVUN

The fire crackled in the hearth as Ilara and I sat in front of the fireplace of her childhood home. A cracked windowpane in the kitchen allowed chilled air to seep in as the night sky shone through the glass. Wind whistled through the rafters. Everything about this house was simple and rustic. The poverty Ilara had grown up in was prevalent, yet within these wooden walls, a warrior queen had been born.

My guards had positioned themselves outside, adamant that they didn't mind the winter's cold as they fiercely protected the true Rising Queen of the Solis continent, yet I knew the real reason they'd done it was to give my mate and me a moment of privacy.

At this time, we were still on our own. Nobody from Prinavee had pursued us yet, my father likely concentrating on repairing the castle in Solisarium. But I knew that was to be short-lived and that his revenge would be coming.

Inevitably, he would send fae to hunt for us. Especially after what Ilara had done today. Soon, word would spread, and the king would learn of her actions. His plan to invade the Nolus continent and expand his reach was failing, which meant his vengeance was coming.

Ilara sat beside me, silently watching the crackling fire. Love for my mate flowed deep into my bones, and my cock stirred when I drank in her determined scent.

Even though fatigue lined her eyes, Ilara's jaw had set into a hard line of determination.

I'd never been more proud of her as when she told her fellow villagers the truth. She'd defied the king. She'd drawn a line. She'd voiced the reality of what was occurring to our fae, and all because of her love for me and her love for the citizens of the Solis continent.

Emotion made my breath hitch. I'd never been one to show how I truly felt, but when her magnificent angel wings had been flapping above us, her expression fierce, her tone defiant as she showed all of the villagers what had taken place within the Isalee field, the Canadian forest, and my mother's private chambers—I'd never felt more in awe of her.

"So what do you want to do from here?" I leaned back in my seat, letting my wings relax behind me.

She canted her head, the firelight making her ebony hair shine. "We should find Lord Crimsonale first so we can share what happened in Canada. Now that we have solid proof, he'll surely help us convince the council to overthrow your father."

My lip curled. "He'll help, but as you've pointed out, that will only likely be in an attempt to claim the throne for himself."

"Even if he does try that, he'll still help to overthrow the king. But maybe he'll surprise us. Maybe he'll do the right thing and support your ascension, and perhaps once all of this is over, and *you're* wearing the crown, maybe you and the Crimsonales can learn to put your differences aside. Michas could make a good ally."

I sighed. "While it's possible Michas would be useful as an ally, it's unlikely that we'll ever truly let go of our grievances. I'll work with them now, though, since the Crimsonales are in agreement that my father's a tyrant, but once my father's removed from power, I'm not making any promises."

Ilara rolled to her feet, then prowled toward me with liquid grace. Magic swirled around her. Her aura was so potent now, so much so that I wondered if she was even aware of it. She'd truly mastered her warrior affinity, and she was quickly learning her angel power. I admired every bit of her as she flowed closer to me. Each movement she made hummed with her fighting magic. Her steps were light, her limbs graceful.

My cock felt as though it would punch through my pants as she neared, and all thoughts of the damned Crimsonales fled.

She stopped before me and placed her hands on my knees. I drank in the heady scent pulsing from her.

I ran my hands up her thighs. Firm muscle greeted me beneath her lush softness. I smirked as my gaze dropped to her mouth. "Your parents would be scandalized if they knew I wanted to ravish their daughter in their living room."

"Do you now?" She nipped my lip before slipping her pants off and straddling me. I hissed in a breath when her bare pussy settled right over my clothed cock. "They don't need to know."

Growling, I gripped her hips and met her mouth. She kissed me passionately, our tongues entwining, our breaths mingling. She tasted of mint and snow, and her rosebud and dew scent clouded around me, going straight to my head.

One of my guards snickered from outside, and I knew they'd either heard us or scented what was about to happen.

Ilara laughed when I growled, and then I cast a solid wall of air around us, my Shield stopping any sound my mate was about to make as I pleasured her.

I pulled my cock out, then anchored her to me before lowering her onto my length. Groaning, I slid into her wet heat with ease as her softness gripped me tightly. "Gods, Ilara."

She moaned, rocking on me as her smooth sheath gripped me even harder.

All coherent thought left me.

I panted, then kissed her again as she began riding me. Every time she lifted herself up, only to fall back onto my cock, my heart pounded while creating a savage need to stamp *mine* upon her.

The possessiveness I felt for her was unparalleled.

Even our eternal marriage and mate bond hadn't quelled it. I'd been with many females over the seasons, long before my mate had even been born, but I'd never truly wanted any of them. I couldn't even remember their faces. My entire existence now centered on my mate. Her smile. Her laugh. Her fierceness. Everything about her called to me.

"You're mine," I growled as she began working my cock in earnest. I lifted her tunic, freeing one of her breasts before bringing her taut nipple to my mouth.

She gasped when I began to ravish her tits as her bouncing grew faster. "And you're mine," she breathed.

"Forever."

She bounced more, her actions growing feverish as her aroused scent grew until it bathed me in her essence. I drank in her scent, watching her head tilt back as her lips parted. A rosy hue filled her cheeks, and the firelight glinted off her black hair. With her breasts bare, her face flushed, and her bare pussy visible in front of me . . .

Fuck.

I grew even harder and began pulling her faster onto me.

Only minutes passed before she cried out in ecstasy when an orgasm ripped through her. Satisfaction barreled through me, and feeling her channel tighten as her moisture coated my cock tipped me over the edge.

I roared when she seated herself entirely on my length, rubbing my cock deep inside her as she rode the waves of her pleasure.

She clung to me the entire time and never complained as my hands gripped her hips tightly.

When the aftermath of our lovemaking calmed, I savored her scent as our panting breaths mingled.

Heart pounding, I gathered her closer to me, then leaned down and inhaled her scent. "Never in all of the winters that I've walked on this realm have I ever felt anything close to the love I feel for you, Ilara."

She tenderly brushed a lock of hair from my face, then kissed me. "My king. I love you just as fiercely. You were made for me."

I growled low in my throat before enclosing her in my embrace.

She was mine.

My eternal mate.

My warrior queen.

And one day, if it was the last thing I ever did, I would ensure she wore the crown of the Court of Winter.

"WE'LL HAVE TO BE FAST." I eyed my guards as the six of us stood outside of Ilara's childhood home. An entire day had passed in which we'd allowed ourselves to rest and our magic to recover. The night sky shone above us, the three moons visible as the galaxy created a cloudy strip against the stars. "If my father hears that we've returned to Solisarium, he'll demand Ilara's capture."

Nish sneered. "Over my dead body."

Haxil nodded and crossed his arms. "He's not getting her again, Nori. I'll go down fighting to keep that from happening, even if my life ends with a sword through my heart."

"I as well," Ryder said with a gleam in his eye. "He's not taking her."

"We'll keep our queen safe, my prince." Sandus's nostrils flared, and he clapped me on the back. "We won't fail you or her again."

"None of you failed us." Ilara's wings spread out behind her, blending into the winter landscape as the wind howled. "You were doing as your prince commanded when the king forced me into the dungeon, as what we both wanted. The king would have shaved your wings or had all of your heads if you'd defied him in the throne room."

Ilara's worry pulsed toward me on the bond as she stood at my side. She'd never been one to ask others to sacrifice themselves for her, but she also didn't grasp how much of an impact her journey had made on my guards and those who'd been with her along the way.

It was obvious yesterday that the fae in her village loved her. And all four of my guards were now fiercely loyal to her. Servants in the castle were as well.

According to Balbus, Daiseeum had asked about her daily, usually multiple times per day, when she'd been locked in the dungeon. Patrice and Haisley had been just as involved, and I'd even heard Murl had inquired about her well-being.

Even when I'd been locked within my chambers for

three days, I'd heard the mutterings among the staff. Their anger and discontent at what had been done to Ilara had floated through the halls. Everyone had stated it wasn't justice. It was cruelty.

"Ready?" I asked my mate and guards.

They all nodded.

In a blur of mist and shadows, air and wind, we all disappeared as we ventured back to the castle—back to the heart of it all.

Back to where our destinies would ultimately be decided.

CHAPTER 17 - ILARA

We mistphased to the wing where archons and nobles stayed while they were at court, to the same area we'd been at previously when we'd confronted Michas in his private chambers.

When we reappeared, my jaw dropped at what surrounded us. As before, the hall lay in ruins. Cracked stone. Shattered windows. Dust on everything.

"Blessed Mother. The castle still isn't repaired?" I asked in a hushed tone.

Norivun shook his head. "This will likely take weeks to fully fix. The castle has never sustained damage like this before, and we only have so many constructo fae on staff."

"Serves the bastard king right." Nish sneered.

The other guards chuckled, then muttered the same sentiment.

We strode toward Michas's door. All of us had

agreed that it was best to go to Michas first and request that he retrieve his father. It was too dangerous to be lurking around the castle openly looking for Lord Crimsonale. Even if Norivun's illusion Shielded us, masking our sight and sound, it wouldn't stop anyone's awareness if they bumped into us.

We stopped at the young lord's door, and after two knocks, the young Crimsonale opened it wide. Michas's brow furrowed in confusion, but when Norivun pushed past him, the young lord shrieked.

It was only when we were safely inside, with the door locked behind us, that Norivun dispelled his illusion Shield.

When we appeared before him as though from thin air, Michas immediately glowered. "I wondered when I'd see you next."

The prince smirked. "Miss me?"

The young lord seethed, then hissed under his breath, "Are you crazy? The king is looking for you. *All* of you."

"Tell us something we don't know," Nish replied in a bored tone.

"What are you doing back here?" Michas glared at the prince as Norivun pulled the looking glass from its concealment.

"Bringing proof as promised. The proof *you* demanded," Norivun replied. "Where's your father?"

Michas shrugged. "My guess would be in his chambers."

Norivun nodded toward the looking glass. "We now

have solid evidence that implicates the king. It's important that Lord Crimsonale see this. Fetch him. Now."

When Michas's eyes narrowed, and he opened his mouth to argue, I laid a hand on his arm. My mate growled the second I made contact with the male, but I didn't let his possessiveness deter me.

"Please, Michas." I gazed up at him imploringly. "We wouldn't be here risking our lives if we didn't have enough information to firmly sway the entire council to our side, but we still need your help."

Michas's expression softened for the merest moment before he gave Norivun an irritated side-eye. He finally nodded. "Stay here. Don't leave, and don't make a sound. The king has ordered every single castle guard to arrest you the second any of you are spotted."

Ryder's jaw clenched, making his angular features look even sharper than usual. "They could certainly try."

"Just . . . stay here." Michas raked a hand through his silvery-white hair, then grabbed his dinner jacket. He was still dressed, but it was obvious he'd been in for the night. His undershirt was unbuttoned at the throat, and only socks covered his feet. A flickering fire filled the hearth. Close to the fireplace, an open book and a half-drunk glass of wine waited on a table. Beside it was a chair with a thick blanket draped over it.

We'd obviously interrupted a quiet evening for him.

"Sorry to, uh, intrude on your solitude," I said awkwardly.

Some of the tension radiating from Michas lessened. "It's fine. You just caught me unaware." He stuffed his feet into loafers, then flung his jacket on, the slits fluttering around his wings. After buttoning it, he smoothed his hair and stepped to the door. "I'll be back soon."

Michas made a move to leave, but Norivun grabbed his arm. "Don't betray us. If you return with the castle guard, I'll end you."

Michas ripped his arm free. "Save the threats for your father. I'm part of the reason we're all in this mess. Once that comes to light, I'll end up in the dungeons just like the rest of you if this ends badly."

"Or the executioner's block." Nish snickered.

"Nish," Haxil growled. "Don't."

"Be quick," Norivun added.

Michas bowed mockingly. "As you wish, my prince."

He slipped out the door and closed it quietly behind him.

Nish sighed as Sandus and Ryder began to prowl the room's perimeter. Frequent bursts of their magic clouded around them, and I could only guess they were searching for hidden enchantments or covert listening charms.

The energy in the room swelled with every passing moment. Seconds ticked by before the two finally stopped.

"We're clear," Ryder said to Norivun.

My mate dipped his head. "Thank you."

Nish flipped the book over near the fire, then

grinned when he saw the title. "Look at this, Haxil. It's your favorite novel."

A small smile curved my lips when I saw it. *Of Fae and Might.*

I waved to the book, then looked at Norivun. "See? Michas isn't that bad. Anybody with decent taste in books is worth a second chance."

Norivun's wings rippled, and he grumbled something under his breath. Nish returned the book to the page it'd been on before prowling to the window and subtly peeking through the curtains.

The other guards all positioned themselves at various points in the chamber. Their movements were so practiced, so automatic.

I cocked my head. "How long have you all been guarding the prince?"

Sandus shrugged from the corner near the door. "It's been so many seasons I've lost count."

"Three of us have been with him for eighty-seven seasons." Ryder peeked out the window on the other side of the room from Nish, then moved away from the glass. "Except for Haxil. He joined us thirty seasons ago."

"Should we be concerned that you know those numbers so precisely, Ryder?" Haxil joked.

Ryder snickered, then tapped his head. "It's not my fault if I'm the most intelligent one here."

Nish gave him his pinky finger while Sandus barked out a laugh.

A smile parted my lips, and I asked Norivun, "Is that so? Did you used to only have three guards?"

Norivun looked down, his easy smile vanishing. "Not quite," he said quietly.

"There've always been four guards, Ilara, but we lost a male just over thirty winters ago. His name was Lichen." Sandus rubbed his beard as the fire crackled. "An attempt was made on Nori's life. It was a pretty brutal attack, and —" He shrugged. "'Tis the life of a guard. We all knew what we signed up for when we took this position."

The room grew quiet, only the snapping fire making a sound.

I placed my hands on Norivun's waist. "I'm sorry. I didn't know."

He shrugged. "That night is when I got the scar on my abdomen that you're always eyeing." Norivun trailed a finger along the side of his stomach, and my heart broke when he took a deep breath. Outwardly, his features barely changed, yet his sorrow strummed toward me on our bond. *Blessed Mother.* He was so practiced at controlling his facial expressions.

"I'm sorry," I said again quietly. I'd been curious about that scar since I'd first seen it. Now, I wished I'd never asked.

He kissed me on the forehead. "It was a long time ago. That night we made a mistake. We were too exposed. Too relaxed. We haven't made that mistake since."

Nish grunted. "And we won't ever again."

Ryder inclined his head. "But now we have this old bastard with us." Ryder patted Haxil's shoulder. "He thinks he keeps us in line."

"Thinks?" Haxil chuckled. "I *do* keep you in line. It's like working with wee babes half the time."

"Just because you were a commander in the Solis Guard doesn't mean you're the commander here," Nish replied with a smirk. "It took twenty seasons for that message to fully sink into him."

Haxil slugged him in the arm. "Not my fault that you were all children when I joined you and still are."

"Children?" Sandus arched an eyebrow. "I'd rather be a child than a cantankerous old bastard like you."

Haxil snorted. "Cantankerous . . . when has that word ever been used to describe me?"

Norivun watched their good-natured bantering, a smile finally returning to his lips, and not for the first time, I felt the love and loyalty that existed among the five of them. I could only imagine what they'd all seen and gone through together. Their deep bond was unmistakable.

"How old are all of you?" I asked, knowing the question wasn't entirely proper, but I figured at this stage, we were well past propriety.

"Haxil's the oldest. Nearly a grandpa at two hundred and sixty-two winters." Ryder threw Haxil a wink.

"They're all just pups, Ilara," Haxil chimed in. "Ryder's a hundred and eighty, Nish a hundred and ninety-three even though he acts younger than you, and

Sandus is a hundred and seventy-one." He tapped his head and eyed Ryder. "See, my friend? It's not just you who can keep numbers straight in one's mind."

Ryder snorted.

So they *were* all young, just as I'd always assumed. "In other words, the only true pup in your group is the prince," I teased.

Since Norivun had turned a hundred winters this season, he'd been subjected to the Rising Queen Trial as demanded by his father, but even a hundred winters was still so young. It was commonly agreed that most males didn't reach their prime until five hundred winters, and then it was a very slow decline until our end came around two thousand winters.

My mate chuckled, and the earlier darkness I'd sensed in him lightened even more.

"And what about you?" Nish thumped me on the back after throwing Haxil his pinky finger. "A wee babe at only twenty-four winters. You're practically a child, Ilara."

I rolled my eyes and slugged him.

Nish grabbed his shoulder, mocking an injury, and everyone began to laugh.

We were all still chuckling when the lock sounded at the door. Our laughter stopped, and each guard went into a defensive position, hands on their swords, as I crouched in a fighter's stance.

The prince inhaled. "There's three fae."

Nish swore under his breath, and the guards' grips

on their swords tightened even more just as Michas opened the door.

But no guards were present. Behind Michas stood his father, Lord Crimsonale, and Taberitha Wormiful. They all shuffled into the room, then shut the door with a flourish and engaged the lock.

Nish growled, his gaze accusing when he addressed Michas. "What's *she* doing here?"

Lady Wormiful, the archon of Kroravee Territory, sneered at Nish down her long nose. "Quiet, guard. You have no authority here."

A rumble of Norivun's power filled the room, but it was subtle enough that nobody outside of our immediate area would be able to sense it. "Careful, Taberitha. He's with me."

"And that's supposed to be a threat?" She scoffed, and her wings flexed slightly. "All of you are fugitives now. Even your blood won't save you, Prince Norivun, if the king gets his hands on you. You defied his command to marry the lovely Georgyanna, and now rumors are circulating that you're spreading word about his character. His patience has run out. He's ordered you to be arrested on sight."

"So the day has finally come." Norivun shrugged. "I knew it would happen sooner or later."

"Did she really just call Georgyanna, *lovely*?" Nish asked Ryder.

"I thought I was hearing things," Ryder replied flippantly even though his gaze remained sharp, and his muscles taut.

"Norivun and I are eternally wed." I held up my hand, showing the Kroravee archon the silver marking on my finger. "He's my *mate*. Surely, of all fae, you can understand the bond we share. He could never have married Georgyanna."

Lady Wormiful's eyes widened just as Lord Crimsonale muttered a sound of surprise.

"So it's true, he's your eternal husband?" The older lord shook his head. "Nuwin told me, but I didn't know if I should believe it."

Taberitha's gaze stayed glued on my finger, her throat bobbing when she swallowed. For the briefest moment, she looked at her hand, at the same mark on her finger.

I still recalled when I'd seen that mark on her. The afternoon I'd joined Nuwin at a council meeting following the balance beam incident in which Georgyanna had tried to murder me. Lord Thisslewater from the Dresher Islands had been present, and while Taberitha had been sipping a cup of tea, the light had caught on the silvery ink.

"Surely, you understand that this was the only outcome Norivun and I would have ever allowed. All fae understand how sacred a mate bond is, and considering you also have such a bond, can you really tell me you would have agreed to marry anyone other than your mate?" I stared at her, waiting for her response.

Her chest rose quickly before she ran her thumb over the eternal mark on her finger. "I'm sorry. I didn't know," she finally said quietly. "I could have never married anyone other than my wife. Gysabelle's my light." A soft smile spread across Taberitha's face, and for the first time, she looked like a female in love, not a conniving evil serpent.

My gut clenched, and hope surged through me. If Taberitha Wormiful, of all fae, could understand why the prince and I had done what we had, then there was hope that others would also sympathize with our plight.

"Many still don't know that Ilara's my mate and we're eternally wed," Norivun's deep tone cut through the room as he eyed the Crimsonales. "That's probably to my father's advantage right now. Our fae are only going to see that we defied the king. They won't under-stand why we did it."

Michas nodded and placed his hands on his hips. "It would work in your favor to have the knowledge spread that you're fated mates who have eternally wed. It's the one bond that even the most cynical Solis would have a difficult time arguing against."

"We've realized that as well." Norivun replied.

Lord Crimsonale cut his son a sharp look, a gesture that wasn't lost on Norivun either. A rumble of my mate's irritation flowed through our bond.

Because if rumors were already spreading about the king's character, then it was possible the Crimsonales would also know that Norivun and I were actively working to clear his name and mine.

I could only hope that the fae from my village were spreading the word at this exact moment. We needed to win the fae over on our continent, and hopefully the

CROWNS OF ICE

mate bond we shared would help those who'd been against us understand why we'd defied the king, especially after they learned of the king's treachery.

"But enough of all of that." Lord Crimsonale puffed his chest up. "Michas tells me you have something to show us."

"We do." Norivun pulled the looking glass out again. "You were right to be suspicious when you heard my father that night in the hall, speaking with that strange male who had the pungent scent. This was who he was meeting with."

Norivun angled the looking glass so Lord Crimsonale, Michas, and Lady Wormiful could all see it clearly, then he activated its magic, and the scenes played out of what we'd done in Isalee before switching to the scene in Canada.

Gasps and words of shock came from all three of them. When it finished, Norivun whispered the spell that returned the recording to the beginning. Then he played all of it again but at a slower pace.

"What's pulsing in the soil?" Lord Crimsonale asked when the black writhing heart of the warlock's spell appeared at the ground's surface.

"Dark magic," I replied. "What you're seeing is what was killing the crops. A veil had spread throughout the land, beneath the soil, suppressing the *orem*. It's why nothing could grow anymore. But it wasn't because the gods had forgotten us. The *orem* was still being replenished, but it was being suppressed."

Lord Crimsonale seethed. "So the king *is* ultimately behind this, just as we suspected."

"Indeed," Norivun replied.

The older lord shook his head. "That means he's been playing all of us for fools." The scene changed to show the warlock kneeling before us in Canada. "The king knew all along that our concerns were valid, and he was only pretending that our land would eventually be fine."

"Exactly," I nodded.

Taberitha shuddered when the warlock's face was revealed in more detail at the slower pace. "How hideous. What is it?"

"A dark sorcerer from the *other* realm." Norivun's brow furrowed. "We believe my father hired him to create that poisonous veil. This is who Lord Crimsonale scented last season when he overheard the king speaking at night. It's a long story, but we found the dark spell the warlock used to create a veil of death to suppress the *orem,* and then, with the help of the male you see here"—he pointed at the Fire Wolf—"we were able to destroy that veil and eventually capture the warlock for authorities in the *other* realm to kill."

"And this warlock originates from the *other* realm? That's where he's been hiding all along?" Lord Crimsonale glowered as he studied the hunter.

"Correct," Norivun replied.

"Disgraceful!" Lord Crimsonale's cheeks turned ruddy, and his jowls jiggled. The archon's fire affinity heated his skin and warmed the air around him. "To purposefully cause our fae to starve and be harmed . . ." He shook his head. "There are many atrocious things your father has done over the seasons, Prince Norivun, but this is unforgivable."

My eyes narrowed at his righteous rant. "That may be true, but don't you agree that it's also disgraceful to burn a servant for tripping?"

Lord Crimsonale scowled. "What are you talking about?"

"I think you know." I stepped closer to him, meeting his gaze unflinchingly. "Starving our fae is atrocious and worthy of time spent in the dungeons, and then lying about it and purposefully pushing for a war is reprehensible. I'm in agreement with you on that. But purposefully burning a servant who accidentally ripped your clothing is also disdainful."

The older lord cocked his head. "Are you implying something, Lady Seary?"

"I'm not implying. I know what you did." Months ago, Daiseeum had told me of Lord Crimsonale burning a servant who made an innocent mistake. That burn had left a gruesome scar on the young servant that not even Murl had been able to heal.

Lord Crimsonale's nostrils flared as Nish said dryly, "She's calling you out, Lord Crimsonale. Isn't it obvious? Our queen is saying your acts aren't much better than the king's."

"She's not our queen yet," Michas snapped, just as Taberitha cut Nish a sharp glare and exclaimed, "Quiet, you!"

"His name's Nish," I said to Lady Wormiful. "Not *you*. And you're right, Michas. I'm not the queen, but that doesn't mean I'm not going to stand up for our fae."

Norivun's lips curved up.

Michas sighed and rolled his eyes. "All right, let's get back to what the king's done. We can discuss other atrocities"—he cut me an aggrieved look—"another time."

I inclined my head even though Lord Crimsonale now looked like he wanted to burn me.

"Don't be thinking that I'll be spending any time in the dungeons, Lady Seary." Lord Crimsonale adjusted his jacket. "I'm merely an archon who's trying to right what's been wronged on our continent."

Norivun's guards all shook their heads and made disgusted sounds, but I reined in my sharp retort. The Osaravee archon would likely never take responsibility for what he'd done, but right now, we all needed to find common ground and work together even if the two archons present made my skin crawl.

Norivun canted his head toward the looking glass. "The council needs to see this."

Lady Wormiful nodded. "That they do."

"As well as the fae of our land," I added. "We need all of the fae on our continent to know what the king did."

"Yes, that too," Norivun replied.

"So how do we share this with everyone?" I asked. "How do we spread the truth about what the king's done?" While I knew my villagers would undoubtedly help, it wouldn't be enough. There were too few of them.

"I shall be in charge of that." Lord Crimsonale's chin lifted. "Hand that over. I shall keep it safe and ensure everyone who needs to see it does." He held his hand out for the looking glass.

Norivun put it behind his back. "I'm not giving this to you. It's the only proof we have of what my father's done."

"Are you saying you don't trust me?" Lord Crimsonale scoffed.

Norivun's eyes narrowed. "I'm not a fool."

"Prince Norivun," Michas said in an irritated tone. "You came to us for help, yet you're now unwilling to let us help you."

I shared an apprehensive look with my mate before asking the Crimsonales, "What are you proposing?"

Michas eyed his father, and an unspoken exchange took place between them.

Michas nodded subtly, and then said, "My father and I have contacts throughout the continent. There have been small factions at work for some time that no longer believe King Novakin is who should be ruling this land."

My eyes widened. It was as I'd suspected. The Crimsonales were actively involved in a treasonous movement to dethrone the king.

Norivun's jaw worked as he eyed them suspiciously. "How long has this been going on?"

The Crimsonales again shared a look before the older of the two replied, "That's irrelevant."

"Hardly," Norivun growled. "If you want us to trust you, then you must also trust us. How long has such a movement been occurring?"

"Five full seasons," Michas replied.

His father huffed at him, but the younger of the two shrugged. It wasn't lost on me that Lord Crimsonale had risen to his territory archon status five winters ago.

"Prince Norivun wants the king dethroned too," Michas said quietly to his father. "And with all of us working together . . ."

"Fine." Lord Crimsonale's cheeks reddened again when he held his hand out a second time. "I can create copies of the looking glass and disperse them."

But Norivun shook his head. "As much as I'd like to trust you, I don't believe you won't attempt to alter this."

My eyes widened even more. I hadn't considered that possibility, and given the growing anger on the older lord's face, I had a feeling that was exactly what he'd planned to do. Magic rumbled in my gut even though altering looking-glass magic was impossible. He couldn't have changed any of the actual scenes—the looking glass's magic wouldn't allow it—but he could have played certain scenes only. Whatever he had planned, it was possible that it could have portrayed us in a bad light.

"You conniving, evil—"

Norivun held a hand up, stopping Nish's rant. "I'm

keeping this," the prince growled, "but I'll create copies. Your job is to disperse them to your factions."

Lord Crimsonale's nostrils flared, and his entire body was practically vibrating. Lady Wormiful planted her hands on her hips, then rolled her eyes and made a sound of disgust. "Leave it, Gregorian. The prince won't be dissuaded. It's more important that we work to dethrone the king right now."

I started at hearing Lord Crimsonale's given name.

The older lord smoothed his hair back and huffed again.

"She's right, Father." Michas glared at the crown prince but then said softly to the Osaravee archon, "One step at a time. King Novakin needs to be removed. Now is the time to make that happen. We can worry about our land's ruler after that occurs."

"But *he'll* be the next king if King Novakin is dethroned," Lord Crimsonale hissed as he waved at my mate.

My magic stirred again inside me. Knowing that these three were working to remove King Novakin from power was one thing, but to also have it confirmed that they wanted *all* of the Achul family removed was where I drew the line.

The crown prince had given his life to the fae of this land, even if they hated him, and even if they believed him the villain. The truth was, Norivun was far from the evil ruler here, and my mate deserved to sit atop the throne if that was what he wished.

But I kept my lips closed as the three came to their

own decision. I knew if the older lord agreed with our final plan, he was more likely to stick to it, but if we forced it upon him, the fragile truce between us would crumble.

Lady Wormiful and Michas didn't budge, and after a few more exchanges, Lord Crimsonale glowered but said, "Fine. I'll disperse copies to our contacts."

Norivun held out his arm. "Shall we seal it in a bargain?"

Lord Crimsonale's eyes flashed. "Did I not just promise to give you aid?"

"You did, but a sealed bargain will ensure all parties involved hold their word."

The older lord's nostrils flared, but when Michas nudged him, he held out his arm. "Fine," he snapped.

Prince Norivun cocked his head, moments ticking by as he thought. He finally gripped the Osaravee archon's forearm. "Lord Gregorian Crimsonale, baron of Highsteer Castle, councilor on the king's council, and son and archon of Osaravee Territory, I hereby agree to a bargain that ensures myself, Lady Ilara Seary, my four personal guards—Haxil, Ryder, Nish, and Sandus—you, Lord Michas Crimsonale, and Lady Taberitha Wormiful all will work together in good faith to dethrone King Novakin of the Solis continent. I shall create replicas of the looking glass, the original of which I'll keep in my possession, and you shall distribute the unedited replicas that I created to the informants of your known factions. You, Lord Michas Crimsonale, and Lady Taberitha Wormiful will all provide knowledge of every faction that exists so that all parties will stay informed. During the time the nine of us work together to dethrone King Novakin, none of us will betray one another, and we shall only speak truthfully and plainly if necessary information comes to light regarding King Novakin's activities. Once King Novakin is dethroned, our bargain will end. I hereby end the terms of our agreement. Do you accept this bargain?"

Nish smirked, and Lord Crimsonale's lips pressed into a tight line. By adding Michas and Lady Wormiful to the bargain, Norivun truly had tied the older lord's hands. Now, none of them could betray us unless they were willing to let Gregorian suffer from the gods' wrath, and we'd all seen how that went when the king had locked me in the dungeon.

Reluctantly, Lord Crimsonale tightened his hold on the prince's forearm. "Prince Norivun Deema Melustral Achul, first son of the king, Bringer of Darkness, Death Master of the continent, son of Prinavee Territory, and crown prince and heir to the Winter Court's throne, I hereby accept your bargain."

A clash of magic billowed around them, and the bargain's mark seared into their inner wrists. Both marks glowed brightly, depicting a king's crown, before the marks disappeared.

The prince lowered his arm, and Lord Crimsonale smoothed his lapels.

A king's crown. I knew those marks hadn't been chosen at random. The gods' marks always meant something, and I could only assume that was because both males coveted the throne.

Michas clapped his father on the back as Lady Wormiful fingered her eternal mark again before glancing briefly at me, her look guarded yet pensive.

Lord Crimsonale stood taller, puffing his chest out. "All right, Prince Norivun. Now that we're sealed before the gods and goddesses, none of us can betray one another." His teeth ground together, but then he gave a curt nod. "Let's get to work."

CHAPTER 18 - NORIVUN

F ollowing our sealed bargain, we agreed upon meeting in four days' time. It would take that long to produce replicas of the looking glass for Lord Crimsonale, Michas, and Lady Wormiful to distribute. If we worked fast.

"We shall see you then." Lord Crimsonale swept his cape over his shoulder with a flourish as Lady Wormiful sneered down her nose at Nish.

Michas saw them out, then closed the door behind them.

"We'll let you get back to your evening now." Ilara waved toward his book and wine. "Are you enjoying *Of Fae and Might*?"

Michas's eyebrows rose. Scratching his head, he replied, "Surprisingly, yes."

"Just wait until you get to the scene when Lady Furyful confronts Sir Risserton." Haxil grinned, then waggled his eyebrows.

Michas canted his head, and Ilara smothered a smile.

"We won't reveal anything," my mate added, "but keep reading, and let me know what you think when you finish."

Michas nodded, and I gave Ilara a side-eye.

She shrugged unapologetically. "What? Maybe we'll form a book club when this is all over. You never know."

Nish laughed as I rolled my eyes, but I couldn't stop the tug of my lips. The confidence and swagger that had bloomed in my mate over the last few months still took me by surprise at times.

I planted a kiss on her temple, and her roses and dew scent flooded my senses. "Before we start any book clubs, let's work on removing my father from power."

She bowed, and her long dark hair draped over her shoulders. "Of course, my prince."

"Mind if I get back to my wine and reading now?" Michas asked.

"By all means, Lord Crimsonale. We'll get out of your hair." Nish waved the six of us together.

I activated my mistphasing magic, and the realm disappeared around us.

WE RETREATED to the inn near the Nolus border, the same inn we'd used previously when I'd been weakened and had to recharge my magic.

We tucked into our chambers for the night, and Ilara slipped out of her tunic. She stood only in her underthings, and the firelight caught on her feathered wings and ebony hair. Gods, she was beautiful.

She eyed me curiously. "Why didn't you just make a bargain with Lord Crimsonale that stated he couldn't alter the looking glass's scenes and have him create replicas? For us to create copies won't be easy."

"No, it won't be." My shirt caught on my wings when I took it off, and Ilara's gaze crawled over my shoulders and chest. A surge of pride worked through me when her scent grew muskier. "And true, I could have included that in our bargain and had him do the work, but then Lord Crimsonale would have also taken credit for stirring the unrest. The less involved he is in all of this, the better."

She nibbled on her lower lip as a frown marred her features. "I didn't consider that."

"Which is why two minds working together are better than one." I prowled toward her, unable to resist the curve of her back and the swell of her hips. I ran my hands over her, loving her dips and smooth flesh.

Her breath hitched, and her wings relaxed more, draping down her back as I growled and leaned in to kiss her. "But enough of him and what lies ahead. I would like to take my wife to bed."

Her frown disappeared, and a smile ghosted her lips.

I scooped her up and kissed her in the same beat. Her scent flooded me, possessing me, owning me. It took everything in me not to ravish her right then and there, and when I laid her on the bed and stared at the beautiful creature that was my eternal mate, I wondered what I'd done in this realm and the next to deserve the pure joy that was radiating through me.

WE SPENT the next two days gathering the supplies needed to make copies of the looking glass. It wasn't easy. Looking glass could only be forged from sand and rock found on the tip of Alshee, the tallest peak in the Gielis mountain range. And once a looking glass was crafted, it had to be spelled using ancient magic that only a fairy with a truth affinity could weave.

Thankfully, we happened to know a fairy with a truth affinity.

"Do you need help carrying them?" Ilara asked as we were about to depart for the Cliffs of Sarum.

"I'll manage." I tucked the six newly forged looking glasses into my cloak. Silver metal frames glinted around them, and their long handles made holding them easy. Their shiny surfaces were currently smooth, only appearing as a normal mirror, but once they were spelled, they could be used to communicate with someone from far away or used to record events as we'd done.

Those who could afford looking glasses often had memories stored in them of meaningful times or events. However, they'd been known to appear in the supernatural courts a time or two when criminal activity was caught in action.

"One looking glass for each territory." I stowed them deeper into my cloak. "Are you sure Cailis can bespell them?"

Ilara wrung her hands, and then forced a smile. "She's a quick study. I'm sure she can do it as long as we provide the spell that's needed."

"We have a backup plan, right?" Nish asked from the corner of our inn room. My guards were staying behind, but that didn't mean they were any less involved in what we were doing.

I cocked an eyebrow. "Do you know of any other fae with a truth affinity that we can trust to dethrone the king?"

Nish sighed. "Good point. So no backup plan then."

"Cailis can do it." Ryder crossed his arms. "I've seen enough of your sister to know that she's fearless and doesn't give up."

"And who does that remind you of?" Sadness asked with a nod in Ilara's direction.

Haxil laughed. "Exactly. With the Seary girls helping us, we'll be all right."

Ilara glanced up at me, her blue eyes shining with apprehension, but beneath that lay a fierceness that had been born in her when her warrior affinity had manifested. "Ready?"

I pulled her toward me as magic flowed along my limbs. Now that plans were finally in motion to remove my father, an aching need to destroy every part of him fired through me.

"Yes, my love. Let's go see your family."

ILARA and I mistphased to the Cliffs of Sarum, leaving my guards behind so they could enjoy a much deserved break. Cold pelting snow hit Ilara and me from every angle the second we reappeared. I formed a thin area of high pressure beneath us, creating a solid bubble for us to stand upon. The snow was so deep now that we would easily sink to our waists without the aid of magic.

Winter had truly set in, bringing with it non-surviv-able temperatures. Those with a fire affinity to keep their blood and limbs heated could survive in this area until their magic tapped out, but everyone else would perish within hours if they were exposed.

The glistening, enchanted ice cliffs rose before us as my mate created a warm pocket of air around us, cutting off the wind and stinging snow. The cliffs' magic made them glisten like jagged spears, a rainbow of colors appearing in them when the light hit them just right. Other times, they appeared like blue razors, sawing and cleaving their way through our frozen land.

I still remembered the first time I'd ventured here, having to bring Balbus with me to navigate them. Only the locals knew the intricacies of this land. But even though Balbus was a son of Harrivee, he'd spent hundreds of winters on the Cliffs of Sarum in his younger days. He knew the intricacies of the cliffs nearly as well as those born on the northern tip of Isalee. Without my loyal servant aiding me, I never could have created this refuge. Of course, Balbus had no idea why I'd brought him here. Only my guards knew of this oasis, but my faithful servant had helped save the fae trapped within these cliffs, even if he didn't know it.

"You'll need to rest after this." Ilara touched my arm as the wind howled outside of my magic.

The contact sent a rumble of pleasure through me. Every time she touched me, I longed for more.

My wings tightened at my back, and I let my magic build along my limbs. "I'll rest until tomorrow."

She nodded as I drew upon my magic to cleave through the veil hiding the fae within. The veil shimmered before us, and I pumped my hands into fists. My illusion was so thick surrounding the hidden village that it felt as though I was trying to hack through twenty feet of solid steel.

I called upon more of my affinity, heating and rolling it through me, and my illusion magic began to shimmer.

A moment passed before my illusion parted, revealing the hidden city within. Ilara and I stepped through the barrier, and my wards gripped both of us. After the magic detected that neither of us was a threat, we were released.

Breathing heavily, I sucked in air as I let my magic calm. *Ock.* I would never get used to the feeling of growing so depleted so quickly as I did every time I visited here.

"Ah, the prince and Lady Seary have come!" a female yelled.

The fae who spotted us grinned and waved in our direction. A few ran up to me and began asking what had been occurring in the outside realm. While I knew everyone here was grateful to be alive, I also knew that this existence wasn't fulfilling. None of them could leave. All of them were trapped here. It was the lesser of two evils, but it was evil nonetheless.

"Troubling events are occurring in Solisarium right now," I answered truthfully.

The female's lips downturned.

"We're hoping to free you all soon," Ilara added, and that fierceness lit her eyes that I loved so much. "We're working to dethrone the king."

Gasps followed, and the female to our left brought a hand to her chest. "But how? How in the realm will you take down King Novakin?"

My mate looked to me to respond, and through our bond I could feel her hesitancy. She wanted to provide the citizens here with hope, but she didn't know how much to reveal.

"There are others working against my father as well. Factions have formed, and a rebellion is on the horizon." I stood taller, lifting my wings more. "His end is coming."

I didn't add that my end could be coming just as fast. While I would go down fighting against my father,

I wasn't foolish enough to believe that it would be easy. In all likelihood, some of us wouldn't survive.

I locked down that fear as far as it would go. So far, I'd managed to keep my darkest thoughts from bleeding through the mate bond to Ilara. She was under enough stress as it was. I wouldn't add to her anxieties.

"When will this happen, my prince?" one of the females asked.

"Soon," was all I replied before I nudged my mate toward her family's temporary home.

We passed the familiar shops, gardens, and decorative fountains on our way to their single lane. Their house sat at the end of a narrow street, and Ilara burst through the door.

All four of her family members were there, and they jumped to standing when we appeared in their living area.

"Ilara! Prince Norivun!" Her mother beamed. "How lovely that you've come for a visit."

Ilara's smile faltered.

Her father glanced between the two of us, then stepped toward her mother. He slipped an arm around her shoulders and drew her close. "I don't think they're here just for a visit, my love." He kissed her on the temple.

Farahn's grin faded.

"What's gone wrong now?" Cailis tossed the book she was reading to the side. She plopped her hands on her hips and gazed at both of us shrewdly.

"Have we been discovered?" her brother, Tormesh, asked. His hands fisted and wings flexed.

"No, nothing like that," Ilara said in a hurry. She began to pick at her fingernails. "But we're here because we need your help, Cailis."

"Oh?" Her sister cocked her head, then said in a rush, "Of course, whatever you need."

I withdrew the six new looking glasses from my cloak along with the original that contained the recording of what had occurred. Cailis's eyebrows drew together. "Are those mirrors or looking glasses?"

"They're currently mirrors forged with looking-glass material, other than this one." I jostled the one with the recordings. "We need you to create these six into spelled looking glasses. And then we need you to transfer what's recorded on this one"—I indicated the original looking glass again—"to the new ones."

Cailis's jaw dropped. "You want me to—" She shook her head. "But I've never done anything like that."

Ilara pulled a piece of parchment from her pocket that held the ancient spell her sister would need to weave. "I know, but we need somebody with a truth affinity to do this, and we don't know anyone else we can trust. But I know you can do it, Cailis. Your affinity is above average. You should be able to."

Her sister paled. "Mother Below."

Tormesh came up behind Cailis and clapped her on the back, right between her wings. "You've been saying all week that you wanted to help the cause. Now's your chance."

"The cause?" I raised my eyebrows.

Ilara's father gestured outside their home. "Cailis has told everybody here the truth about the king. They all know what he's done to the queen. And if they didn't already hate him for ordering their executions, knowing that he's abused your mother, you, and Prince Nuwin your entire lives, and then his despicable plot to starve our fae . . ." His cheeks flushed as his magic grew around him. "Everybody wants to help bring the king down."

A rush of disbelief flowed toward me on the bond. Ilara turned wide eyes upon me, then gripped my hand. "What better fae to help spread the word about what King Novakin's truly like than the fae here?" She spread her arm wide, waving toward the hidden village. "With Crimsonale's factions showing everybody what happened in the Isalee field and Canada, the fae from my village spreading the word about our mate bond and eternal marriage and the king, *and* those here telling everyone what you're truly like and what your father ordered to happen to them . . ." She let her words hang as a surge of her hope billowed toward me. "Let the fae here help."

"Wait a minute." Tormesh held up a hand. "Did you just say *eternal marriage?*"

Ilara turned scarlet, and her mother gasped.

"Ilara Seary!" she proclaimed. "You didn't! You didn't get married without us!" She rushed toward her daughter and grabbed her hand. A shriek emitted from her when she saw the silver ink on Ilara's finger. Just as fast, she snatched my hand and studied the mark on my finger. "They did! They got married! And eternally wed, nonetheless."

Her mother fell in a heap on the couch, and I gave her father an apprehensive look. Ilara rushed toward her while Cailis gaped and Tormesh began to laugh.

"Cheeky, so cheeky," her brother said. "Just wait till Birnee and Finley hear that they weren't invited to the wedding either."

"I'm sorry, Mother. I'm so sorry, but we had to. You don't understand what the king was demanding of me." Ilara began to tell the story, but her mother stopped her, cupping her face between her palms.

"I know, sweet girl. Your sister told me the king demanded you be married to an awful pedophile. I'm relieved you found a way out of it, but to miss your wedding . . ."

Tears filled her eyes, and Ilara's father crouched beside her. "Oh, Farahn." He curled an arm around her shoulders and drew her close. "It's not the end of the realm. We knew as mates they would be together no matter what."

"But to miss their wedding—"

"Shh." He hushed her and pulled her close. "At least she's not married to that vile lord from Isalee. 'Tis all right."

I gripped Ilara's shoulders from behind, and she leaned into me. Slipping my arms around her waist, I crouched behind her and pressed a kiss to her neck before whispering, "We'll have a proper celebration when this is all over, and your family, friends, and anyone you desire within this realm will be invited."

Ilara gripped my arms and squeezed, yet guilt still racked her along our bond.

Cailis sighed. "Mother, don't fret, please. We have bigger things to worry about right now, like how in the realm I'm going to bespell six looking glasses."

Farahn dabbed at her eyes and eventually nodded. "You're right. It's just that . . ." She shook her head. "No, you're right. That's what's important right now. What matters most is dethroning the king, and like Ilara implied, we all want to help make that occur."

My brows drew together. "You do understand that you'd all be put in danger. If my father knew that any of the fae here were still alive, he'd—"

"We know the risk." Her mother brushed off her father's arm and stood, her chin lifting. "We had a village meeting last night, and every fairy here is in agreement. We want to help, my prince. We don't want to hide behind you anymore while you face the king alone. Free us. Let us tell all of the Solis citizens of our great nation's son, and the truth of the current king who sits upon the throne. That male has a heart of evil while his son possesses a heart of gold."

Ilara's grip on my arms tightened, and her love for me surged through our bond. For a moment, I couldn't speak. My throat grew thick as my mate's entire family gazed at me with determination and resolve written upon their features.

"Anybody caught by my father's guards will be executed on sight," I said softly, hoping they understood exactly what they were requesting.

Her father's throat bobbed in a swallow. "We know."

I pressed a kiss to Ilara's temple and released her. Standing, my hands pumped into fists. "It's possible he'll torture some of you to learn where you've been all this time."

Tormesh's wings flexed. "We're not afraid, my prince, and we're not naïve. We know the risks we're taking."

Ilara took a deep breath. Similar fears were running through the bond from her, but the strength of where she'd inherited her character was shining in this room. Her family might have been poor, they might have only been field laborers and been looked down upon by the nobles of the Winter Court, but etched into all of their faces was the core of strength that our great nation had been forged upon. Here, within this room, was what the Solis spoke of when they boasted of our infallible courage.

I took a deep breath. Magic vibrated along my limbs. "All right, if you're sure. I won't stop any of you from fighting. But those who do not want to partake may remain here—safe and hidden."

Once word got out where all of these fae had been hiding, my father would hunt for them. But my illusions were strong, my wards thick.

I could only pray to the Blessed Mother that my magic was enough to keep them safe.

IT TOOK Cailis fifty-three attempts before she was able to successfully turn one of the mirrors into a looking glass and then transfer the recording to it.

But she'd done it, just as Ilara said she would.

Cailis breathed heavily, her aura pounding from her with determination as a grin streaked across her face. "It worked!"

Tormesh whooped, and Ilara's mother and father clapped.

I watched in amazement as a scene from the Isalee field, then Canada, played before us. Who would have thought that a young laboring female from Mervalee had the wit and character to pull off such a feat. It only made me wonder how many other fae on our great continent were also capable of so much more than what their lives had asked of them.

"Well done, sister." Ilara squeezed her in a hug.

The scene continued to play in the looking glass, and we all watched as it showed us with the Fire Wolf destroying the veil and then battling the warlock and ultimately tricking him into confessing.

"Your children are truly remarkable," I commented to her parents as Cailis reached for the second mirror.

"That they are," Farahn agreed. Pride shone in her eyes.

Ilara gazed up at me impishly. The teasing light that entered her eyes was like a punch to my gut. *Blessed Mother, this female could control me with only a look.*

"I told you she could do it." Ilara bumped her arm playfully against mine.

I laughed. "You weren't wrong."

Tormesh scratched his chin, then dug into his pocket. "How many rulibs do I owe you?" he asked Ilara.

"Just one." She held out her palm, and glowing satisfaction burst across her cheeks. "But I believe that's the third time you've lost against me in the past two winters."

Tormesh rolled his eyes. "Yeah, yeah, don't rub it in." He shook his head and grumbled, "You would think my faked death would have made you forget those bets."

Ilara snorted. "As if death could stop me from rubbing your nose in a loss."

Her father put a hand to his forehead and sighed before shaking his head.

"Are they always this competitive?" I asked her parents.

Her mother sighed. "Always."

Her father placed his hands on his hips. "You should see how they are when Birnee and Finley get involved. They place bets on everything, especially when it's the females against the males."

I crossed my arms and couldn't help but think of my guards as I watched my mate with her siblings. A similar comradery existed between the five of us.

Cocking my head, I contemplated what dynamic would develop between my guards and the Seary family if we were lucky enough to survive what was to come and be allowed to live a normal existence together.

A grin split my face when I imagined my mother and Nuwin being added to the mix. One thing I knew, family holidays would definitely be interesting.

BY EVENING, we had all six looking glasses ready to deliver to Lord Crimsonale. Ilara's family joined us as we left their tiny home to gather the fae of the hidden village.

Some of the fae here had been trapped within these icy walls for over twenty full seasons. Others had only been here months. Regardless, some were itching to be free, while just as many had accepted their new way of life.

Whatever the case, every single fairy here would be given the choice of what they wanted to do. They could join us in our uprising against the king, or they could stay here, behind my protected wards, while continuing to live in peace.

All I knew was that I would not make that choice for any of them.

"Gather round!" Tormesh yelled.

Fae shuffled out of houses and from the small shops and gardens dotting this veiled city. When everyone was present—all one hundred and seventeen of them—I hopped onto a stone wall so I could better see their faces.

Ilara stayed on the ground, at my side, her black hair shining like obsidian against all of the silver and white-haired fairies.

"I've been told you're all aware of the dissent growing within our land," I said in a raised voice that carried through the air, echoing off the ice walls.

Several nodded. Others voiced their agreement.

"I've also been told that you know my father was ultimately behind our crops dying."

Lips curled, and a few fae spat into the snow at their feet.

"Down with King Novakin!" One of the males raised his fist into the air and began pumping it.

Others joined in, their chants echoing his.

All of the fae here knew of my father's true nature. He'd ordered all of their executions even though they were entirely innocent of any wrongdoings. None of them had deserved death. Not one.

I raised my hands, letting my wings flex slightly as I quieted the roar growing from the crowd. "It's important that you understand that by leaving this hidden village, your lives will be at risk."

"We know. We're tired of hiding, my prince." A female raised her voice above the others and jutted her chin up. "All of us are incredibly thankful for what you've done for us, but it's time that we fight with you versus letting you fight for us alone."

"Ock, Norleen's right!" one of the males agreed.

"Our fae need to know the truth about you, Your Highness. It's time that bastard on the throne was revealed for who he truly is."

Their energy and fervor rose again as magic began to simmer in the air. Their auras strummed steadily around us. I could practically taste their need for vengeance and freedom.

"Anybody who chooses to stay here will not be judged." I looked as many of them in the eye as I could. "I created this village to keep you safe. You may continue to stay here and remain unharmed if you wish. I'll continue bringing supplies as they're needed. Nobody will be forced to leave these walls unless they choose to."

All of the villagers looked to one another, some dipping their heads in obvious embarrassment.

A low growl rumbled in my chest. "Again, *nobody* will be shamed or forced to leave these walls if they choose not to."

"I would like to, my prince, but my daughter . . ." Ellosy, a female fae around my mother's age, waved a hand toward the young girl at her side who wasn't more than eight winters if I remembered correctly. "I can't leave her."

I nodded in agreement. My father had ordered Ellosy's execution when he'd learned that she was telling other fae working in the kitchens of the dying crops. On the night I'd whisked her away, she begged me to bring her daughter with her. Her husband had died the winter prior, falling through the ice in a pond near their home when he'd been trying to catch enough fish to feed his family. After his drowning, her daughter didn't have anyone other than her, so I'd allowed her to bring the child, knowing that tearing them apart would destroy both of them.

"Nobody expects you to leave your child behind while you put yourself at risk." Ilara jumped onto the wall beside me and threaded her fingers through mine. The contact sent a tingle all the way to my soul.

Her love pushed toward me, and then in a rush of magic, her white feathers burst from her back. A collective gasp emitted from the town. Her beautiful feathered appendages glimmered like freshly fallen snow. "Those of us who have enough magic to fight the king and don't have young children that we need to protect will fight in the name of those who stay behind. We're united in our cause, and united we will remain."

"Indeed, Lady Seary!" Several males raised their fists.

"We stand united!" others shouted.

Ilara raised her fist as well, her expression fierce, her demeanor defiant.

Pride surged through me at the magnificent display that my mate portrayed. Her parents gazed up at her in equal awe, her brother and sister looking speechless.

I knew they'd seen glimpses of the female that Ilara was to become, that they'd always known on some level the inner strength their daughter and sister carried, but in this moment, the power of her magic and resilience of her character were shining for the entire realm to see.

More fists raised in the air as shouts of victory began.

"To the new king and queen!" a female yelled, her eyes upon me and my mate.

"To the new king and queen!" another joined in.

"King Norivun and Queen Ilara! King Norivun and Queen Ilara!"

Ilara smiled up at me while the villagers' energy soared around us. Her warrior affinity hummed, the strength and feel of it practically bursting from her skin as her angel wings shined.

A burning intensity began to consume me at what the future held. More and more were standing against my father. More and more were willing to fight, and the female at my side—the mate that the gods had blessed me with—was ready to lead them into battle.

N orivun and I collected his guards to help us mistphase all of the fae. Even with the prince and I transporting four to five fae at a time while his guards mistphased one after another until their magic grew too low, it was painstakingly slow, especially since I did most of the relocating.

Norivun needed to conserve his magic to weave his illusion around the small village and reseal the wards once more, so most of the work fell to me.

Moving my family and then leaving them was one of the hardest things I'd ever done. Even though I'd never been more proud of them for wanting to help, fear also bled into my heart. They were no longer protected by Norivun's refuge, but we needed as many fae as possible spreading the word about my mate's true character and the king's evil heart.

We'd secured a room for them at a busy inn within Coolisbar. Nobody knew them there, yet once my family started speaking throughout the city and then moved on to the surrounding villages, their identities would be revealed, and their locations whispered among those forever loyal to the king.

"Stay safe." I hugged each of them closely, my limbs trembling when I let them go.

Tormesh created a fireball in his hand and lobbed it into the air. "We may not have as much magic as you, but that doesn't mean we can't hold our own. Don't worry about us. We'll stay safe."

"We'll meet up in two weeks' time?" I asked.

"Indeed, little Lara." My father pulled me into another fierce hug. "We shall see you soon."

"Remember, if the king's guards come, do everything in your power to fight them." I gripped my mother's hands so tightly my knuckles turned white. "If Norivun or I hear that you've been taken, we'll do everything in our power to save you."

I swallowed the lump in my throat. It was so thick I could no longer speak. Tears threatened to fill my eyes, so I blinked rapidly.

"Oh, Lara." Cailis wrapped me in a hug, and then my parents did the same. Tormesh hugged me last, folding me between his massive arms as he gave me a big squeeze.

"We'll keep our wits about us," Cailis whispered.

I gave a firm nod and with our farewells complete, I waved one last time before mistphasing back to the Cliffs of Sarum to gather the remaining fae.

✳

BY THE TIME NORIVUN, his guards, and I finished, I was so tired and so depleted that I could barely stand.

I'd mistphased dozens of times, transporting more fae at once than I ever had before. It took all of my training and everything Matron Olsander had taught me of mistphasing magic to achieve such a feat.

Still, I'd never pushed my mistphasing magic like this before, and I was at my limit when we finally relocated the last fae.

When Norivun and I returned to the inn, our bodies reformed slowly, so slowly that a moment of fear rang through me. The moment we were solid, both of us collapsed on the bed, breathing heavily.

Just as the mattress bounced beneath me, my magic ran completely dry. I groaned. *Everything* in my body ached.

"Ock, do you need a healer?" Nish was beside me before I could blink, his expression feral.

I somehow managed to wave a hand, but I was too tired to speak.

Norivun's and my eyes closed simultaneously, and our magic was so drained that the bond between us was barely palpable.

Sleep stole me away, and dreams of fear, burning, and death plagued me throughout the night, but so did images of love, hope, and resilience.

Come tomorrow, all of the rebellion forces would be

at work throughout the continent after the Crimsonale's factions received their looking glasses.

Which meant that once our magic returned, the time had come to tell the council.

THE NEXT DAY, the guards delivered the looking glasses. Even though Norivun and I had slept over sixteen hours, both of us were still too weak to attempt mistphasing, and his guards had conserved enough of their strength to be able to continue their guarding duties. Consequently, Haxil and Sandus left to meet with Lord Crimsonale and Lady Wormiful while Norivun and I stayed in the inn.

When they returned, they confirmed that the rebellion was firmly in action.

"You need more food." Nish scowled as he gazed at the tray between my mate and me on the bed. It only contained a thin broth and several slices of forest bread.

Food was growing scarcer on the continent, and this inn was no exception. Even though we'd destroyed the warlock's veil, and the *orem* was thriving again, it would still take time for the crops to grow and fields to be harvested.

"We'll be all right." I tried to reassure him, but inside my magic was only a whisper of its potential. We were still far too depleted.

Norivun threaded his fingers through mine and squeezed. His massive frame needed even more nourishment than mine, but he'd still insisted that I take half of everything.

Ryder growled. "Nish is right. You need more sustenance. At this rate, it'll take a week for you two to fully recover unless you have more food. Come on, Nish. We're going hunting."

Before the prince or I could reply, the two departed, leaving Sandus and Haxil to guard us. They both crossed their arms, their wings tucked in tight as they positioned themselves at the exit and entry points of the room.

"Close your eyes again," Sandus called over his shoulder. "Best to rest until they return. We need you two in top shape if we're going to take on the king."

NISH AND RYDER had returned by nightfall with a brommel stag draped over Ryder's shoulders. I didn't even want to know how many millees they'd traveled to find it since such a stag could run like the wind. Most fae were never able to catch one, their arrows falling short each time they shot. I figured their warrior affinities were the only reason they'd been able to hunt one.

With the help of the inn's chef, they butchered the animal and cooked entire platters of meat for the prince and I to consume before giving the rest to the hungry villagers.

The dense meat, along with the bread, finally replenished our stores, and three days later, Norivun and I were finally recovered from the exhausting efforts we'd made on the Cliffs of Sarum.

"All right then?" Nish clapped me on the back as magic vibrated strongly in my gut.

I smiled, my first true smile since we'd left the Cliffs of Sarum. My affinities flowed hotly inside me as my mate bond with the prince billowed and writhed. "Yes, let's go."

CHAPTER 20 - NORIVUN

We mistphased back to Solisarium and reappeared in my warded bedroom chambers. The second our bodies materialized, a shriek reached my ears.

"Oh, my prince! You're back." Balbus ran toward us, his eyes wide as worry pulsed from him in waves.

I could have sworn he was trying to tell me something without speaking, and then I sensed why he was so fearful at the same time everyone else did.

All four guards reached for their swords, and Ilara's warrior affinity heated around her.

Wings flexing, I swung around.

A pair of Lochen green eyes gazed at us from the couch near my fireplace.

My eyes flashed wide. After all that had happened, I'd completely forgotten about the other problem we were still dealing with.

And it looked as though that problem had come to us.

"Greetings, Your Highness and Princess," Drachu said mockingly, his voice a low purr. "I knew you'd all eventually return."

"How did you get in?" I asked in a deadly cold voice. I inhaled, scenting the room. Tylen wasn't here. Not yet, at least.

"My prince, I'm sorry. Please forgive me." Balbus wrung his hands. Wispy hairs on his head fluttered in the breeze billowing through the room from my air element. I was barely controlling my affinities, I was so furious.

"What happened?" I snapped.

Balbus trembled and began sobbing. "The Lochen king stayed very close to my side when I entered your chamber. The close proximity somehow got him through your wards and allowed him to enter."

"Don't blame your servant." Drachu waved a hand, then prowled to his feet. "I found where his wife lived. It was either the servant let me enter through the secret door you created for them, or I kill her." He shrugged as though murdering my most faithful servant's wife was par for the course.

"I'm so sorry." A sob shook Balbus's chest. "He has Marcina locked in his chambers. If I didn't let him try to enter with me, he was going to—"

"It's all right." My nostrils flared, but I didn't blame Balbus. In all honesty, I was surprised my father hadn't tried something similar over the seasons when I hadn't been falling in line fast enough. Drachu certainly hadn't wasted any time, but the bastard was tricky. He must have been watching closely enough to learn that my wards apparently wouldn't detect him if he plastered himself so closely to my servant.

"What do you want?" I asked the Lochen king just as a new scent entered the room.

Fuck. Tylen crept through my servant's door. With Balbus's wife in tow nonetheless.

"Marcina!" Balbus stumbled toward her, and Tylen released her into the servant's arms. They both started crying, their fear potent enough to taste.

Drachu beckoned his son closer as Marcina clung to Balbus. My mate hissed, and all of my guards unsheathed their swords. The Lochen king's gaze grew wary.

I created a solid Shield of air around us, but with Tylen's magic, it wouldn't hold if he touched it. "Again, what do you want?"

"I think that's obvious," Drachu finally replied when Tylen was safely at his side. "I. Want. My. Pendant." His lips thinned, and his eyes flashed.

My dragon snarled within, and I bared my teeth. "No. You'll never control my mate again."

Drachu hissed. "I won't give up until it's mine."

My death affinity undulated out of me. I wrapped it tightly around the king's soul, and his throat bobbed in a swallow. "I won't either. Perhaps I should just end you right now and be done with all of this."

Tylen made a move toward me, but Sandus and

Ryder were there before the Lochen prince had taken a full step. Swords pressed into his neck and abdomen. The weapon's reach gave my guards an advantage. They were over an arm's length away from the null's touch.

"Never again, fish boy." Ryder bared his teeth and pressed his blade more into Tylen's throat. A trickle of blood welled at its tip.

Tylen seethed but took a step back.

I smirked. "My guards have spent over a hundred seasons honing their warrior abilities. Do you really think they don't train without the aid of magic?" Tylen's eyes narrowed, so I added, "Even if you touched them, they could still kill you. Just try it. Push them and see what happens even with your nulling magic swimming through their veins."

Sandus grinned darkly as Nish's eyes took on that manic gleam every time he was in a fight. Only Haxil's expression remained unchanged, the seasoned warrior in him patiently waiting for the perfect strike.

The agitation in Drachu's scent grew, but he waved a hand at Tylen, and his son returned to his side.

Drachu's dark hair flickered in the firelight as Ilara and my guards positioned themselves around the Lochen traitors. The basic warrior tactic wasn't lost on me. Their affinities had them all moving in sync, just waiting to pounce.

As if sensing the same, Drachu cocked his head. "Killing me would start a war with our kind."

I strengthened my hold on his soul. "Perhaps, but then my eternal mate would be safe."

Drachu's eyes widened for the briefest second.

I held up my hand, showing him the faint silver mark. "That's right. We're now eternally bound. You should know that I will do *anything* to protect her, including starting a war with you seafaring fae."

Drachu's throat bobbed again. Other than that subtle response, he showed nothing, yet a sour stench of fear rose from him. It grew more potent with every breath.

Taking a step closer to him, I let my dragon flash in my eyes, morphing them into reptilian slits as my tone deepened. "I'd rather go to battle with the Lochen for the next millennia than allow you to *ever* touch her again."

Ilara's shoulders drew back. "You won't win, Drachu. We won't back down." Her expression hardened.

Silence reigned in the room. Even Balbus and his wife had grown quiet.

My guards still held their swords up, and their warrior affinities hummed thickly around them. They were a storm cloud just waiting to be unleashed.

Drachu regarded all of us with a calculating assessment. He first looked at me, then Ilara, and last my guards. With each second that passed, his scent grew more potent.

Finally, he sighed, then lifted his shoulders. A broad smile stretched across his face as he held his hands up.

"I can see that perhaps I made a mistake when I tethered your wife to me."

I took another step closer to him, stopping just before my air Shield. "You did. I will hunt you to the ends of the realm if you try to take anything from her again. Mark my word. You will *never* rest. You will *never* be free of me. I will end you if you try to hurt Ilara again, and I'll make it painful, exquisitely slow, and I will relish every second of it."

"Have you ever seen the Death Master take his time with someone?" Haxil said nonchalantly from my side. "'Tis truly gruesome."

Drachu's nostrils flared.

"Father," Tylen said in a low tone. "This is growing weary." The Lochen prince, indeed, looked fatigued. Even though it'd been days since we'd left, I had no idea what other deeds his father was demanding of him.

"Strike a deal," Tylen urged. "Release Ilara's power in exchange for the pendant, and let's be done with this and done with them. Our kingdom is strong. We don't need her magic, and I miss the sea."

I cocked my head but held Drachu's challenging glare.

Lip curling, the Lochen king finally broke eye contact. "Fine. I'll release your mate's diamond from my pendant only if you give my pendant back to me and never take it from me again." He held out his arm. "I'll seal it with a bargain."

My lips curved. "Deal."

Our hands curled around one another's forearms. My aura rose. Magic rumbled along my limbs.

Drachu's voice rang through my room, dripping with annoyance. "Prince Norivun Deema Melustral Achul, first son of the king, Bringer of Darkness, Death Master of the Solis continent, son of Prinavee Territory, and crown prince and heir to the Winter Court's throne, I hereby agree to a bargain that ensures all of Ilara Seary's magic and affinities are released from the pendant I wore that commanded her power. I agree to never again command your mate or tether her to me. In return, you shall give me my undamaged pendant that you stole from my kingdom and never attempt to steal it from me again. I hereby end the terms of our agreement. Do you accept this bargain?"

I licked my lips. The wording was simple and concise. I didn't see any loopholes in it, but Drachu was clever. If there was one, he'd find a way to take advantage of it. So I added, "In addition to the above terms, I shall also add that if either bargainer doesn't uphold their end, a death chosen by the other will immediately follow."

Drachu's eyes widened when my meaning hit him. *That's right. I'll torture you for full seasons before I fully spill your blood if you betray me.* "Do you agree to the amendment?"

"I agree," Drachu replied, albeit a tad warily.

Squeezing his arm harder, I said, "In that case, King Drachu, leader of the Lochen fae, commander and ruler of the fae lands' seas, I hereby accept your bargain."

A clash of magic clanged around us as another mark burned into my skin. An image of a diamond appeared on my inner wrist as a trident spear burned into Drachu's flesh.

The Lochen king stood straighter, his dark hair framing his face. "Now that that's done, we shall venture to the Adrall Temple and finish this bargain and be done with one another once and for all."

"You've certainly gotten in the habit of making fairy bargains, my prince," Ryder said to me under his breath. We were leading Balbus and Marcina out of my chambers while Ilara and my other three guards kept an eye on Drachu and his son.

I released a breath through my teeth. "It's a habit I intend to break as soon as my father is dead."

Ryder grinned wolfishly, and the planes and angles of his face sharpened.

"My prince," Balbus said when he reached the door. "I'm so sorry . . . I wish that I had—" He twisted his hands, shaking his head.

"You have nothing to fear," I said quietly to him. Balbus had been manipulated and had done what any mated male fairy would have done in such circumstances.

"Oh, my prince." Another sob shook his chest. "I feel most dreadful. I've let you down. In a moment of weakness, I allowed that horrid—"

"It's all right, Balbus. I shall rework my wards to prohibit such an event from occurring again."

Balbus dabbed at his eyes as his wife clung to him.

"Take the rest of the day off. I shall see you on the morrow."

"Yes, my prince." He bowed deeply, and the self-loathing rising in his scent was enough affirmation of his good intentions that I knew punishing him would serve no purpose. "I shall find a way to make this up to you."

With that, he and his wife departed, leaving me and Ryder alone as we prowled back to my living area. We passed the small music room attached to my chambers along the way. I eyed the piano wistfully and wondered if there would ever be a day where I could play and not have something horrible looming over my head.

I ducked into my closet to retrieve the pendant from my safe. Ryder stood watch by the door, and when the necklace was safely stowed deep within my pocket, we joined the others.

Everyone waited in my living area. And despite knowing that we needed to speak with the Crimsonales, learn what had become of the factions, see just how far word had spread about the truth of the Solis king, and speak to the council, my mate's safety was paramount.

"Ready?" I asked my mate and guards. When they all nodded, I inclined my head to Drachu who'd already pulled out a portal key. "We'll follow you."

※

WE REAPPEARED on the top of a mountain on an island just north of the Lochen continent. Colorful leaves coated the island's plants, not one speck of snow or frost anywhere.

A fierce wind whipped the air around us, and hundreds of feet below, the ocean crashed against a pale sandy beach. The breeze was warm and salty, and a clear pale-green sky stretched above us.

Drachu and Tylen regarded us from near the stairs.

"Back to the warmth, I see," Nish said on a low growl.

Haxil widened his stance.

"Cheer up, Nishy," Sandus called. "If this truly ends here, we'll be on the Solis continent at the heart of winter for the foreseeable future."

"This ends here, or Drachu's life is mine." My lip curled, and I stuffed my hand into my pocket, firmly grasping hold of the pendant.

Ilara stood stiffly at my side. She grew even more rigid when Drachu and his son walked toward us, but my mate's gaze never left Drachu. I had a feeling that if she didn't fear the repercussions, she would have burned the king out of existence right here and now with her fire elemental affinity.

"Priestess Genoova?" Drachu called toward the temple rising from the mountain's peak.

Positioned above us, the Adrall Temple waited. White stone stairs rose from the mountaintop. They were made of the same pearly rock as the temple. Air swirled through the open, circular design. Its domed ceiling and freestanding pillars allowed all of us a clear view of the temple's interior.

Magic rumbled inside me. It was here that my mate had met a god and experienced the depth of Drachu's ambition.

All of my guards kept their swords up. At the top of the stairs, the priestess appeared. Her eyes widened when she beheld us, yet her scent reeked of contempt. Ilara had told me of this female, how Priestess Genoova had played the part of a gentle fairy, yet my mate had seen enough to know that the snake had relished taking her magic.

"Come." Drachu beckoned the priestess closer. "We have something to rectify with the crown prince, and I have need of your expertise again."

"My king?" she said, her voice light and innocent sounding.

Drachu just growled and waved her down the stairs.

She descended the steps slowly, her pace wary. Like all Lochen fae, the priestess had startling green eyes. Dark hair, a shade lighter than my mate's, hung in ringlets to her shoulders. The sunlight shone off her umber-brown skin, then caught on the pendant hanging from her neck. Like Drachu, she also wore a necklace with shells and gems, but unlike the fae king, there wasn't a central stone throbbing with light.

"Where's my pendant?" Drachu demanded of me when the priestess reached us.

I pulled it from my pocket and dangled it from my fingers. "Here."

The sunlight flashed on the green stone, and Drachu's features sharpened with feral need.

Ilara narrowed her eyes at the priestess and then Drachu. "Will returning my magic to me involve asking God Zorifel for help again?"

"No," Drachu replied. "Genoova will be able to conduct the ceremony without summoning any gods or goddesses."

Genoova brought a hand to her throat. "My king? Are you sure that you no longer want her tethered to you?"

"I'm sure," he replied in a clipped tone. "In exchange for removing Ilara's magic from my pendant, the prince has agreed to return it to me. We're sealed by a bargain. I must comply."

The priestess dipped her head. "Of course, my king, if that is what you wish."

"I shall remind you," I growled softly to him. "Should you fail to uphold your end of our bargain, your immediate surrender to me will follow."

"I'm aware," Drachu all but snarled in return.

Priestess Genoova eyed me cautiously. "If you would all follow me."

"Not him." I nodded toward Tylen. "He stays down here."

Drachu smirked. "Are you afraid of my son?"

I bared my teeth. "Hardly, but he stays here."

Drachu scoffed. "Very well."

The priestess's chest rose and fell quickly with each breath, and the contempt I'd detected from her scent morphed into fear as she climbed the stairs. All of us followed, except for Tylen.

At the top, my guards positioned themselves around the circular design, and Genoova waved toward two divots on the floor.

"Stand there, Ilara, as you did last time."

Ilara stalked toward the temple's center, her aura rising. Agitation oozed from my wife's pores, making the dragon inside me writhe and snarl.

"The necklace, please." Genoova held her hand out to me with trembling fingers.

I leaned down and said quietly, "If you fail to return all of my mate's power to her, and if you keep any bit of it for yourself or anybody else, I shall filet the skin from your bones inch by inch, and then I'll call a healer, have you fully healed, before I do it all again. You shall suffer for winters under my brutality if you even think of betraying us."

She paled, and her eyes whipped to mine. A sour stench rose from her so violently that I was surprised she wasn't wetting herself.

"Yes, my prince." She dipped into a hasty curtsy, and the second I dangled the pendant over her palm, she grasped it in a trembling grip and scurried away.

"Was that necessary?" Drachu asked me in a mocking tone. "Priestess Genoova is a gentle creature."

Ilara's lip curled. "I disagree. She was more than happy to see me suffer under your command."

The priestess's steps slowed as she approached my mate.

"And," I added with an arched eyebrow, "considering the priestess is loyal to you, yes, it was necessary." I didn't put it past Drachu to try and find a way around the bargain, and Genoova tethering Ilara's power to her, instead of the king, seemed the easiest option.

The Lochen king scoffed.

Genoova placed the pendant between the divots my mate stood on. She straightened, again putting distance between them. "Close your eyes and open your mind. Like last time."

Ilara's nostrils flared, but she did as the female asked.

Genoova began to chant in the Lochen tongue, an ancient one from the sounds of it. Her chants grew stronger and faster until air was whipping through the temple, and sand was flying from the steps below.

Ilara's hair lifted from her shoulders as a void seemed to fall around her, and if she hadn't appeared so calm and so focused, I would have been ripping her out of that magically spiraling tornado.

The priestess's chants grew louder until a thunderbolt of magic cracked the air around us.

In a brilliant flash of light, the pendant sitting between Ilara's feet exploded with power. When the blinding magic dissipated, Drachu's necklace remained, along with the huge diamond that held my mate's magical essence.

Drachu strode forward and snatched his pendant

off the ground before I could blink. He secured it around his neck, his eyes shining with victory before he pulled a portal key from his pocket.

The diamond that had burned into my skin from our bargain flared and then fizzled out of existence, just as a similar flash came from Drachu's arm.

A relieved breath left me. Our bargain was fulfilled, and the only way that could happen would be if Ilara was no longer tethered to that necklace or the Lochen king.

"Our bargain is complete. This pendant is mine, and you can never take it again." Drachu laughed and nodded toward the diamond. "Have fun trying to extract your mate's magic from that."

What?

I roared and flew toward the Lochen king, but in a whisper of the portal key's magic, he and his son disappeared from the realm just as my arms enclosed empty air.

CHAPTER 21 - ILARA

"What did Drachu mean by that?" Norivun snarled at Genoova.

I snatched the diamond off the floor. The gemstone was large and heavy and throbbed with magic. Its power felt familiar and beckoning, and without even looking at it, I knew this diamond held *my* power. Yet it was still within the gemstone. It wasn't back in me.

Curling my fingers around it, I brought the diamond to my chest. Anger fired through me as the priestess twisted her hands. I shot a glare toward the bottom of the stairs, but Tylen and his father were truly both gone.

The tricky bastards had both escaped the second the bargain was completed.

"Why isn't my magic back inside me?" I demanded of the priestess.

A sob rose in her chest, and she looked at Norivun

with petrified eyes. "I'm sorry, my lady and my prince. I can't extract your magic from that diamond. I could only remove it from Drachu's pendant. Only divine magic can place it back inside you." She sobbed louder and clutched her necklace. "Please, I'm sorry, but it's true. There's nothing more I can do."

"Divine power." I shook my head. "Then summon God Zorifel again. Ask him to do it."

"I can't, my lady. I'm sorry. The gods grow angry when the day's end draws near, and I would need to prepare myself to make such a request. It requires much magic. It can take weeks for a priestess to harness what's needed to make such an attempt."

My nostrils flared, and I stalked toward her. "Are you telling me that Drachu had prepared you for my arrival *weeks* before I actually showed up?"

She nodded hastily. "Yes, my lady. He knew you were coming."

"Fucking tyrant," Norivun snarled.

I kicked the stone pillar, and since a huge dose of my warrior affinity had gone into it, the stone cracked slightly.

"So we have to wait weeks until you could even try to remove Ilara's affinities from that gem, if you don't disappear on us too." Norivun shook his head, his anger rising as it thrummed toward me on our bond. "I knew he would do something deceitful."

"I'm sorry." Large teardrops rolled down Genoova's cheeks, but I didn't fall for her fake contrition. The female had been too eager to deceive me when I first met her. "Truly. There's nothing I can do at the moment. All I can recommend is that you keep that diamond safely stored somewhere so it never falls into the wrong hands."

Hissing, I swung away from her. This was no different than before, when we'd also tried to hide Drachu's pendant. Either way, I was still vulnerable. If the king or some other nefarious individual were to possess this gem and harness it, I would once again be at their mercy.

"Fucking Lochen." Nish spat on the ground.

All of Norivun's guards seethed while their wings flexed. Fierce anger and irritation wafted in their auras, creating a potent storm of affinities around them.

Tension radiated down my spine, and my wings lifted. "Is there any other way to extract my magic?"

"No, my lady. Like I said, you need divine power to do it."

Divine power. I cocked my head. "Wait, I have a divine affinity, and so does Norivun." I took a step closer to the priestess. She immediately retreated two steps back. "What is needed of divine powers to extract my magic?"

"The stone must be destroyed. Once it is, the magic will be released and return to its rightful owner."

Forehead furrowing, I recalled how God Zorifel had destroyed the veil encapsulating my power. He'd ripped it right out of me. Something similar was apparently needed to destroy this diamond.

"Will dragon fire destroy it?" I asked.

Genoova raised her shoulders. "It's possible. Dragons are divine creatures of the underworld."

"My love?" I held the diamond out for him. "Would you try?"

A savage light lit his eyes. "Gladly."

Norivun gave me the looking glass to keep safe, and then he instructed all of us to stand as far back from the temple as possible. All four of his guards, the priestess, and I retreated down the steps and to the edge of the mountain. Warm wind flowed across my back even though the sun hung low in the sky. We positioned ourselves just behind a large boulder, near the cliff's edge.

I peeked over the top of the rock barrier. Norivun stayed in the center of the temple. He grinned wickedly, his eyes trained on me. "This one's for you, my love!"

In a flash of affinity magic that was so strong it whipped the hair from around my face and reverberated through my bones, Norivun disappeared in a blinding light, only to reappear a second later in his massive dragon form.

His dragon was so large that he ripped right through the domed temple. The roof flew upward. Crumbling rock and pillars tumbled down the mountainside in a massive rockslide. Almost everything hit the sandy beach at once in a horrific crash of jagged stones. But the rocks didn't stop there. They tumbled into the ocean, causing huge waves to rise.

The domed ceiling landed last. It plunged into the water at least a millee from the shore, yet its splash was enough to make my jaw drop.

Genoova screamed and brought her hands to her mouth. New tears formed in her eyes. Her beautiful temple had become nothing more than a pile of ruins.

Nish gave the priestess a mocking wink. "Next time your king brings a request to you that hurts my king or queen, remember this moment. Remember what happens when you cross the Death Master."

A sob shook her chest, and her face paled until she was as white as the sand below.

For a moment, I felt pity for the priestess, but then I remembered how eager she'd been to trick me when I'd come to this temple. She'd never tried to warn me or had even been fully honest with what they had planned. Of course, that wasn't surprising. She was loyal to the Lochen.

But Norivun was right to remind her of what happened when anyone crossed us. Jaw locking, I returned my attention to my mate.

Norivun's giant dragon maw opened, and a roll of fire gathered in his throat. The heat of it was enough to singe one's eyebrows off even though he hadn't released his flames.

"Stay behind this rock," I instructed, then created a solid Shield of air around us.

Norivun glanced our way, his reptilian eyes narrowing to slits.

"We're safe, my prince!" Sandus called.

Norivun swung his massive head back to the diamond. A rush of flames shot from him. His fire was so thick that it consumed the entire circular remains of the temple. Scorching flames burned the mountaintop. Intense heat rose from his fire. It was so hot that it could have melted glass.

And then a fluttering sense of awareness began to creep over me.

"Stop!" I shouted.

The prince abruptly released his fire, and my eyes widened when I beheld nothing but a simple rock where the diamond had once been. Norivun had let his fire burn long enough that a crater had formed where the diamond had lain. Everything around it was charred to black bits, ruined beyond recognition. The once beautiful white stone temple had turned into black melted rock.

But at the center of the crater lay the simple pebble that Drachu had used to channel my power. It remained untouched. It was the only thing unaffected by the fire.

And the diamond was gone.

Norivun had destroyed it.

I felt my magic flying toward me on the wind, like the whispered call of an old friend. I sang to it internally, sensing it as it barreled through the air from the obliterated gemstone.

The missing piece of my magic hit me like a lightning bolt. My arms flew out, and my breath rushed out of me. Heat tingled along my fingertips before my magic barreled toward my center.

My core throbbed when the returning essence that I hadn't even realized had been missing molded within me once more, and when all of my magic was finally fully seated back inside me, I opened my eyes and grinned.

I felt whole. Complete.

Norivun stared down at us from the top of the charred mountaintop, back in his fae form. He was dressed, an illusion covering his naked body since his real clothes lay in charred tatters around him.

"Did it work?" he asked as a strum of worry drifted toward me on our bond.

"Yes," I grinned. "It worked!"

We left Genoova on the mountaintop. She'd collapsed to her hands and knees, crying and wailing over the destruction we'd left behind. Another twinge of guilt bit me when I saw how broken she appeared, but then I recalled how she and Drachu had betrayed me.

Norivun clasped my hand. Leaning down, he whispered just before our mistphasing magic swept around us, "You're right not to feel guilty. You are a queen now. Queens do not show mercy to their enemies, not when those enemies sought to destroy them."

I nodded and firmly shoved any remaining guilt away.

Norivun was right. If he and I were to one day rule the Solis continent with crowns of ice, an icy heart was needed at times when difficult decisions were to be made.

With one last look at the priestess and ruined temple, we all disappeared from the mountain as mist and shadows sucked us away.

We reappeared in Norivun's chambers. A fire crackled in the hearth, and despite being told to take the rest of the day off, Balbus was there. He was fussing and fixing everything even though nothing appeared out of order.

The second the six of us materialized from thin air, he straightened by the fireplace, then dipped into a deep bow. "Your Highness."

All of us were filthy. Soot from the mountaintop covered us since none of us had bothered to clean it with our magic yet, and since Norivun's clothes were a constructed illusion and nothing more, his bare skin met my fingertips when I reached for him.

"We're finally done with Drachu," I whispered.

He pulled me to him, his wings snapping out around us as he held me close.

Every path my fingers traveled met hard, unyielding muscle. I gripped him tightly, savagely. For once, something had gone our way.

He growled low in his throat, then angled his attention to his guards. "We'll retire for the night. I'd like to spend some time with my wife. Mistphase to your chambers to ensure no one sees you, and when you get there, stay behind your wards and have the servants bring you food and drink. If word gets out that we're back, my father will likely try to drag all of us to the dungeons, although without Tylen's nulling magic, he'd have a Mother of a time trying." Norivun eyed his servant. "Balbus, I trust that you'll instruct Patrice and Haisley to see to their needs?"

"Indeed!" Balbus bowed again, his large belly pushing against his top. "And, my prince, once again, I want to tell you how sorry I—"

"It's all right." The prince held up his hand. "It's well and truly behind us now. You won't be seeing Drachu again, and I don't blame you for doing as he demanded. How's Marcina?"

"She's fine, my prince. She's recovering at home. Our daughter and son are with her while I returned to ensure that dastardly king's scent was cleansed from your room." He shuddered, and when I inhaled, I didn't detect any of Drachu's lingering fragrance tainting the air.

The prince's lips curved. "You know me too well, Balbus."

"I do try, my prince. Your comfort and well-being are of my utmost concern."

My heart softened as I watched Balbus. Everything about him was earnest, and he truly seemed devastated by what had happened.

"It's all worked out for the best," I told him and gave him a comforting smile.

Balbus dipped his head again. "Please do not hesitate to call if there's anything you need."

I stayed in Norivun's arms as he said to his guards, "We'll reconvene in the morning when the council meets at eight."

"Are you sure that you don't want to go to them now?" Ryder raised his eyebrows.

"No. I'd rather we catch them unaware when they're all present. And since no one knows we're back yet, my father won't have time to prepare anything in his defense. Mistphase here at eight, and we'll travel together to the council chambers."

All four dipped their heads and said simultaneously, "Yes, my prince."

ONCE EVERYONE HAD LEFT, Norivun went to the fire to stoke it more.

Roaring flames soon filled the room. He shed his illusion, and his naked form flickered in the firelight. His giant black wings flexed slightly before he drew them in, and in a burst of cleansing magic, his skin wiped clean.

My attention traveled over his broad shoulders, strong chest, and toned waist. He had two scars on his abdomen now. One from an attempted assassination many winters prior along with the horizontal scar that the snowgum had inflicted on him a few months ago. Neither detracted from his allure.

He was so beautiful, a sculpted masterpiece of bone and flesh, and my primed body quickened in response.

My mate inhaled and arched an eyebrow. "Like what you see?" A sly, arrogant tilt curved his lips.

Breaths coming faster, all I could manage was a nod.

He prowled closer to me, his steps silent and purposeful.

I backed up until I met the bedpost. Already, arousal was tightening my belly.

His cock curved, his erection growing. When he reached me, he leaned down and inhaled my scent.

Desire unfurled in my belly, but I managed to say, "Aren't you worried about your father discovering that we're here?"

He shook his head, and his breath was a whisper against my skin. "My wards won't allow it. Besides, my father has been tormenting me for more winters than I can count. If I lived in fear of him every second, I would never get a moment's peace."

My lips thinned at the reminder of how horrific his father had been to him, but then my mate's hands drifted to my hips. He pulled me closer and began to press soft kisses along my neck.

"This is what I need right now." He growled low in his throat. "You. With me. Naked."

"But you're the only one naked."

He chuckled. "I can certainly fix that."

In a flurry of magic, his power ripped the clothes from my body. I sucked in a shriek as the strength of his affinity wrapped around me.

The firelight lit my skin, dipping over my curves and smooth flesh. My breasts peaked, and my husband rumbled low in his throat as his cock swelled even more.

"That's better." His hands trailed along my bare back, and I called upon my angel affinity. White feathers burst from my skin in a flash of power.

Another low growl vibrated his chest. "Are you wanting me to do something with your wings, my love?" He trailed a finger suggestively along one of the tips.

I gasped, and a shiver tingled all the way to my toes. "Perhaps."

"So sensitive. Exquisitely so." He pulled me closer until his erection nestled against my abdomen. I twined my fingers along his rounded shoulders, digging my nails into his muscles when his scent clouded around me.

Cedar and snow flooded my senses, commanding all of my attention.

His lips trailed up my neck, then he pressed kisses along my jaw. I turned my head until our mouths met.

He kissed me softly, then his tongue flicked out and ran along my lower lip.

I opened to him, and another growl worked up his throat before he began kissing me in earnest.

In a flash, he hoisted me up and had my legs wrapped around his waist. All the while, my mouth never left his as he pushed my back firmly against the bedpost.

My wings spread out, white feathers drifting along my peripheral vision. Head tilting back, my hair spilled down my back and along the post.

He nestled my center right over his length. "You are my queen." His cock pierced my entrance, the tip of him sliding inside. "I will worship your body until the day I die." He slowly guided me down on top of him, and the sensation of his thick erection entering me was so commanding that I lost all coherent thought.

I clung to him, soft mewling noises working up my throat.

He began kissing me in earnest while sliding his cock inside me inch by inch.

And when I was fully seated on top of him, so full from his thick length, he ran a hand along my winged feathers while his other gripped my hip. Pushing me against the bed post more, he pulled out only enough to thrust back in. And then he did it again. And again.

Each of his movements was in tandem with his strokes along my wings.

My breaths became shallow and frantic. His tempo increased, his cock slamming into me while his fingers remained as gentle as the wind along my feathers. A lick of his air affinity swirled around my clit, and I gasped when he stroked me in every sensitive area he could command.

His air continually stroked me teasingly while his cock filled and stretched me until I felt so full I wanted to scream my release.

He growled. "That's it, my love."

My wings snapped out when the simultaneous sensations of his mouth, air affinity, and teasing fingers along my feathers brought me to a fevered pitch.

The fire roared at Norivun's back, and desire heated his eyes while a dark smile spread his lips. "Ride my cock and scream my name."

My walls clamped tightly around him as his tempo increased. Slapping sounds filled the room as his fingers continued their onslaught along my feathers while his air affinity swirled relentlessly around my clit.

He shoved me hard against the post with each thrust, and the bed squeaked and heaved. And when he leaned down and bit my mating mark, right on my shoulder, while threading his entire hand around my feathered wings, I came undone.

"Norivun!" His name tumbled from my lips when my climax peaked. Wave after wave of pleasure ripped through me, but he continued his relentless thrusts while stroking my feathers, and his affinity . . . *Mother Below.* The male was a sorcerer.

My orgasm went on and on, and my mate's low growl of satisfaction only heightened my experience.

It was only when the final ripple of my climax was reached and my pleasure completed, that he laid me back on the bed, working me up the mattress until his magnificent body stood at the bed's end. He was still inside me, our bodies were still joined, and his erection was as hard as Isalee steel even though I was completely spent.

Desire heated his eyes as his wings spread wide. He leaned over me, and I ran a finger along one of the leathery membranes, getting a shudder out of him.

"My king. My love. My mate." I lifted my hips, and he sank even more inside me.

Hissing in a breath, he squeezed his eyes closed, and I wrapped my hands around his hips and began to move him within me.

A low snarl worked up his throat, and his eyes flashed wide as lust strained his features. He picked up his tempo, slapping against me so hard that I grabbed the headboard to keep me in place.

And with each thrust, my body responded more. He ran his thumb over my clit, his lips curving in a devilish smile when I panted.

"Scream for me again," he commanded.

And when he tilted his hips, driving his cock to scrape against that deep spot within me, I came again, hurtling toward the peak as his roar filled the room.

And when our bodies finally calmed and cooled enough for our panting to abate, he stroked a finger along my temple before cupping my jaw.

"I'll love you for eternity, Ilara. You're mine. Mine to love. Mine to fuck. Mine to keep."

"And you're mine, husband. Forever."

We fell asleep in a tangle of wings and limbs, and despite tomorrow looming over us, despite knowing that it was all about to come to a head, for this one night we let the stars call to our souls and let the mating bond soothe our nerves.

For this one night, everything was perfect.

CHAPTER 22 - NORIVUN

My guards arrived promptly at eight. All of them wore clean tunics, black leggings, and tall boots. Ryder's hair looked freshly washed, and Nish was even smiling.

I arched an eyebrow. "I take it you're all hoping to make a good impression on the council?"

Nish ran a hand through his shorn hair and snickered. "Are you saying I'm looking good, my prince?"

Like my guards, Ilara wore her usual tunic and leggings. She'd been continually picking at her fingernails since we'd awoken, but for once her hands relaxed, and she bit back a smile. "You all look positively dashing."

Nish preened like an overinflated hen while Sandus gave a cocky grin.

"We should get moving." The weight of what today would bring began to sink heavily on my shoulders. I already had the looking glass in my pocket, but I checked it again just to ensure the recording was still complete.

Ilara laid her hand on my arm, and I realized I hadn't masked my worry in our bond. "They'll see exactly who the king is after this."

My jaw worked, but I nodded. My entire life had been leading to this moment.

I entwined my fingers with my mate's. Ilara's hand was so small and delicate feeling, yet strength vibrated beneath her palm.

"Join hands," I instructed everyone.

The six of us created a circle, and I called upon my mistphasing magic to transport all of us to the council chambers.

But just as we were about to disappear, my door burst open.

All of my guards had their swords out, snarls on their faces the second the door cracked. Fire engulfed Ilara's hand, her arm pulled back with a fireball ready to throw.

But it was only Nuwin.

"Brother!" Nuwin called. "Thank the gods! Balbus told me you were back." He flew toward me on a gust of his air affinity. Wild eyes met mine.

"What's wrong?" Ilara asked, immediately relinquishing her fire.

"It's Mother, I mean the queen. I'm afraid—" Nuwin's throat rolled in a swallow. "I'm afraid she's not going to pull through this one. Father beat her so badly last night that I fear her end has come."

BLOOD POUNDED through my veins when we materialized just outside of my mother's tower door.

The only other time I'd felt fear like this before was during Ilara's final test, when Georgyanna had buried her alive while using every single affinity in her arsenal against my mate.

In a blink, I was through my mother's door and flying up the tower steps on a gust of air.

Nuwin and Ilara were right behind me, activating their air elements in the same manner as my guards ran faster than the wind, their affinities blurring their legs.

I burst through the top door, my stomach in my throat.

The large tower chamber spread before me. Dim winter sunlight poured in through the windows. A cold fireplace lay vacant in the room. No servants were about, and my mother lay on her bed listlessly, her body bruised and broken, her wings slashed. Blood covered her. Everywhere.

My lungs seized.

"Mumma." In another gust of air, I was at her side.

Her chest rose shallowly, her breaths rattling. I leaned closer to her to listen, and the telltale sound hit me.

Death wheezes. It was what the Solis Guard called them when a soldier was close to entering the afterlife.

"No," I whispered just as a choked gasp came from Ilara.

Given the horrific sounds, my mother's lungs were filling with fluid, her ribs likely broken and her innards bleeding. Nuwin was right. Her death was imminent.

"We have to take her to Murl." Ilara grasped my arm, her nails biting into me. "*Now.*"

"We can't," Nuwin whispered. Tears choked his words.

"What do you mean, *we can't?*" Ilara snarled.

Nuwin's eyes dimmed even more. "Our mother was forced into a fairy bargain by our father many winters ago. If she seeks a castle healer after my father's beatings, she forfeits her life."

"What?" Ilara yelled.

A howl of rage worked up my throat, battering against my insides, demanding to be let free. The need for vengeance against my father's brutality ate me up until I could barely breathe.

But killing the king wouldn't save my mother.

Hands vibrating, I clasped them tightly to stop from tearing the realm apart and forced myself to stay at my mother's side. I wouldn't leave her on her deathbed.

Ilara slumped beside me, her expression bewildered. "I don't understand."

Nuwin's wings slackened, drooping down his back. "The king forced it on her, saying if she didn't agree to the bargain, he'd beat Nori and me too every time he beat her, but if she agreed, he'd spare us from his hand, so she made the bargain to protect us. We were only children at the time."

I drew in a ragged breath and cupped my mother's

hand in my own. Her skin was cool and dry. Blood caked the back of both of her hands. Even there, my father hadn't spared her. Lacerations littered her body, ugly cuts carved into her flesh. They were done brutally. Ruthlessly.

I wanted to rage. Wanted to roar. Wanted to burn the realm.

But I couldn't.

"Mother?" I whispered.

No response.

"Mother?" I said louder.

Nuwin kneeled at my side. "She's unconscious and has been since I found her this morning."

"That fucking tyrant!" I bolted to a stand, my wings spreading as magic heated my blood.

All four of my guards gazed at me sympathetically, yet the sharp scent of their anger and need for revenge wafted around them.

"There has to be a way to save her." Ilara wrung her hands.

I met her gaze, then shook my head. "There isn't."

My guards positioned themselves around the room, guarding me, guarding us. Even here, in this horrific moment, they didn't relax. But the potent scent of the sea—the salty tinge that conveyed sorrow and remorse—swirled around them.

All four of them had seen what my mother had endured over the seasons. They knew of their queen's true nature, her resilience in the eye of my father's storm. My mother was my light. My father, my dark abyss. Where the male who sired me clouded the room in ugly menace and raging storm clouds, she brightened it with soothing words and rays of hope.

"But he can't kill her!" Ilara sobbed as she kneeled by the queen. Black hair cascaded down her back, the same shade as my mother's. Wildness grew in Ilara's eyes. She laid a gentle hand on my mother's shoulder. "Queen Lissandra?"

But my mother didn't move. Didn't speak.

A tightness squeezed my chest, so tight it was nearly unbearable. I couldn't breathe. Couldn't do this. *How did I let this happen?*

"No." Ilara wiped at her eyes. "I lost a mother once. I'm not losing another one."

"Ilara," I said, my voice rough. "Nuwin's right. If we take her to a healer following my father's beating, the bargain will kill her. There's no win in this situation."

But Ilara only shook her head, a million emotions fleeting across her features before her gaze whipped up and her eyes widened. "What if we don't take her to a healer? What if *I* heal her?"

My eyebrows snapped together.

Nuwin shook his head. "How could you heal her?"

"I have an angel affinity, and I recently learned it can also heal. Maybe I can call it forth again. Maybe I can save the queen."

"Would the bargain allow it?" I asked my brother.

Nuwin shrugged, and his mouth slackened. "The bargain stated she could never seek a healer after Father punished her. He wanted her to feel the pain he'd inflicted, but . . . Ilara's not technically a healer."

"No, she's an angel," Haxil agreed from the corner of the room. "That's different."

I faced my mate and gripped her shoulders, searching her expression. "Do you think you can do it?"

Her wings burst from her back in an explosion of power. White feathers spread wide on each side of her as her magic hummed around her. "I can try. I've never healed somebody else. I don't know what it entails, but we have to try, right?" Tears filled her eyes. "Not trying means she dies."

Nuwin nodded emphatically.

"But I'm not sure what to do." Ilara's wings snapped back in tight until her feathers were a plume along her back. "Nuwin, can you seek Matron Olsander? Maybe with her helping me, I can do this."

"I'll travel as fast as the northern winds." In a flash of mistphasing magic, Nuwin was gone.

Ilara breathed heavily, and through the bond, her fear and determination flowed simultaneously.

I laid a hand on her lower back, my palm heating her tunic. "Even if you fail, it won't be your fault. My mother's going to die no matter what in this state. Please understand any outcome that isn't favorable won't be because of you."

Ilara's vivid violet eyes, transformed within her affinity, met mine. Her lips thinned, the steel within her character shining upon her expression. "I won't fail."

THE SHOCKED LOOK on Matron Olsander's face when she appeared in the queen's tower at Nuwin's side would have made me laugh if the circumstances weren't so grave.

"Blessed Mother Above and Below," she breathed, bringing a hand to her chest when she saw both me and Ilara. "Trouble's arrived." She rushed to us and embraced me, then my mate, a bewildered expression covering her face when she beheld Ilara's wings.

"Thank the Mother you're here," Ilara sputtered. "I'm so glad Nuwin found you."

"Indeed he did." Matron Olsander gazed upon my mother, and her breath sucked in. She brought a hand to her mouth, then lowered it and balled it at her side. Her lips tightened into a thin line. "Nuwin told me what happened to the queen. So, it's true? The king abuses her?"

"He does." Nuwin's hands were fisted when he stuffed them into his pockets. "He has for many, many winters."

Matron Olsander brought a hand to her chest again. "Blessed Mother. I'd heard the talk in the capital. I just couldn't believe it, though. I've never seen an inkling of such abuse during my time within these walls."

Ilara and I exchanged a look over the tutor's white-haired head. If word had already reached the capital's citizens of my father and what he'd done, our plan was working. But what good would that do if I couldn't even protect my own mother?

"Can you help me heal her?" Ilara pleaded. Her wings extended, and she nodded over her shoulder. "You were right about my affinities. I've birthed two more."

"Two?" Matron Olsander laid a hand on Ilara's chest and closed her eyes. She gasped, and her eyes flew open. "Armarus Above! You indeed do have more affinities!"

"My wings are from an angel affinity." Ilara waved toward her violet eyes. "My irises also change color when it manifests, and a Nolus fairy told us it was the mark of an angel. He also informed us that angels have extraordinary healing abilities, and I want to try to heal the queen, but I need your help. I've never done this before."

"A divine affinity, just like the prince." Matron Olsander clucked her tongue. "Fitting, I suppose, since you're mates. But I've never worked with an angel affinity. I shall do my best to help you learn it."

"We must. It's the only way we can save her." Ilara pulled her tutor to the bed's edge. My mother's breathing had grown even shallower, her complexion now sallow. "Help me, please. She's dying."

Matron Olsander rolled up her sleeves. "I can see that she is. All right, Ilara. Let's do our best."

CHAPTER 23 - ILARA

I kneeled at the queen's side, Matron Olsander right beside me. My tutor's affinity dipped into my body, scouring through my veins and feeling along my magic.

"It seems that your angel affinity resides here." Her affinity swirled around the knotted light and dark power between my shoulder blades. Frowning, she added, "It feels immense yet tightly balled. You'll need to coax it out. Let it unfurl within you. Do you feel this here?"

It felt as though a phantom finger brushed against a side of that cold power and blinding light. "Yes."

"This seems to be where you need to pull. It's almost like a ball of yarn, coiled very, *very* tightly. Mother Below, I've never encountered such dense power, but tug here and see what happens."

I closed my eyes and did as she said, and slowly, it felt as though a stream of light began to untangle within me, uncurling until it was like a meteor streaking across the sky. I tried to zoom it toward the queen, tried to coax it to heal her. But I didn't know how.

Light continued to unravel from the dense ball until it blazed and unwound and barreled down my arms, toward my hands, and then . . .

My hands shone with white light, and a stinging pain followed. I gasped but didn't try to coil the light back inside me.

"Yes, that's it." Matron Olsander shifted closer, her brow furrowing as her magic continued to prod within me. "This darkness *here* seems to be the opposite of the light. Do you sense how it's colder?"

I nodded, biting back a yelp because the light felt like fire, except unlike my fire affinity, the pain was agonizing.

"Are you in pain?" she asked, forehead furrowing.

All I could manage was a nod.

"What does it feel like?"

"Burning . . . stinging pain." I gasped. "My hands and arms feel on fire."

"How odd. Magic shouldn't be painful if utilized correctly." Her affinity again brushed inside me. "Perhaps these powers need to work in tandem." Matron Olsander guided my concentration back to the heart of my affinity. "Usually, when an affinity has multiple facets, it means that they must work together. This sensation feels cold, does it not?"

I nodded. Sweat beaded my upper lip, but I didn't cry out again.

"Call the cold forth *here*. See what happens."

I did as she instructed, letting the magic work on its own after gentle prodding from me at my tutor's guidance. This was so different from when I'd healed my wing. Then, I'd simply coaxed my affinity, and it had seemed to know what to do, but now, when I was trying to heal another, I needed this power to leave my body, and I still had no idea how to do that.

But if my tutor thought I needed the coldness to ease this burning agony, I wasn't going to argue.

As soon as I coaxed the darkness out, soothing coolness barreled down my arms, chasing the light that burned like wildfire.

I sighed deeply. "That helps immensely."

Norivun and Nuwin both shifted at my side. Their auras pulsed around them, and I knew that each second I practiced with my tutor was another second the queen was dying.

"What do you think I need to do now?" Light still blazed from my hands, and I had no idea if that was good or not. "Sir Fieldstone insisted that angel powers can heal anything."

Matron Olsander's brow furrowed. "Are you able to extend these powers in tandem out of your hands? If this affinity can heal, common sense tells me you'll need to engulf the queen with it."

"I was thinking the same, but . . . how?" More sweat beaded on my brow.

"Mental imagery, Ilara, similar to when you learned your Outlets. Urge it forward, picture it leaving your body and entering the queen."

Heart pounding, I sucked in a breath and beckoned the light and dark to my fingertips. I pictured my affinity flowing from my hands and sinking into the queen. In my mind, Norivun's mother grew covered with healing light.

Someone gasped.

I opened my eyes and swallowed a yelp of surprise. Golden light glowed around Queen Lissandra, and my hands had lit up like stars. Biting my lip, I concentrated harder and pushed with everything I had.

My light and dark affinity shot into the queen in rivers of power. Everywhere it touched, my affinity encountered bleeding blood vessels, broken bones, and pain . . . so much pain.

"I can feel her injuries!" I nearly shouted in excitement.

"What are you doing to sense it?"

More light and dark barreled out of me, flowing as though they knew what needed to be done, and I wondered if this was, in fact, like when I'd healed my wing, that this affinity intrinsically knew what to do, and it didn't take much guidance from me. "It seems to be flowing on its own."

My tutor nodded. "This affinity may work independently of you. It's a rare trait in affinities, but I've seen it before. Are you commanding it at all?"

"Other than my initial push, not really."

"Then it would indeed seem as though it works on its own." Matron Olsander's magic tugged slightly on mine, like a gentle hand prying my fingertips off my power.

I released my iron grip on the sensation between my shoulder blades.

She gave me an encouraging smile. "That's it. Allow it to heal. Let the magic do what it's innately trying to accomplish."

I loosened my mouth, letting my lips fall slack. Mind and body opening, I allowed the light and dark spilling from my fingertips to chase through the queen, healing every cut that it passed, knitting every blood vessel that had burst, soothing all of her aches and pains, and mending every single broken bone.

Unleashed, the light barreled through her, healing in heat. The dark chased it, dousing the fiery pain away in cold.

When my affinity reached the queen's lungs, it siphoned the blood and liquid away, clearing her lungs of that horrible rattling sound.

And as my power worked, I fell into a state of deep relaxation, my mind and magic nearly disconnected from my body.

"That's it, Ilara. Allow it to do what feels natural."

My tutor's voice sounded far away, as though from another land. I sank deeper into my affinity, letting it take over, yet I still sensed what was happening. And when the queen felt mended and nearly whole, I began to rouse and was about to attempt to pull my magic back inside of me, returning it to that chasm between my shoulder blades, when I encountered something dark.

Something sinister. It was buried so deeply within the queen that I almost missed it.

Ugly webbing spread out deep inside her. Hidden so completely within Lissandra's structure that I'd almost missed it.

Frowning, I prodded my angel affinity along it. It felt . . . malevolent. Evil. Just a whisper of it caused me to shudder because it felt *wrong*.

Shivering, I wanted to retreat, but whatever that sensation was, I had a feeling it shouldn't be there. I dove my affinity deeper inside the queen.

The brush of a memory, of what I'd felt inside *me* not too long ago, feathered along my mind.

And then it hit me.

What I was feeling in the queen was the same magic that had caged my power after the warlock's veil of death had attacked me in the Isalee field.

It was the same evil spell that the warlock had used to suppress the *orem*. And given what I was feeling and what Norivun had told me about the king creating a chamber to tether the queen's abilities . . .

A crash of understanding barreled through me, and it all began to make sense.

The king had been working with the warlock for *full seasons*. King Novakin had possibly called upon the warlock to assist him whenever he wanted nefarious magic applied, and somehow, the warlock had used that same dark spell to cage the queen's power in whatever chamber he and the king had created.

Mother Below. I'd stumbled upon the dark spell the

king had cast upon the queen all of those winters ago, the spell that had suppressed her affinities within her, locking them down until she was unable to access them.

And I now knew how he'd done it.

Seething, my lips peeled back. Burning determination slid through me, and I concentrated all of my affinity on that horrible dark veil. It prickled against my touch, writhing and coiling like a deadly serpent ensnaring the queen's power and stifling her magic.

"I call upon your strength, God Zorifel," I whispered. "Please help me."

And then I violently unleashed my affinity once more, screaming from the onslaught as blinding light shot out of me, diving deeper into the queen, encapsulating the warlock's dark power that resided within her, and a war among benevolence and evil raged between my light and the warlock's dark.

But I was stronger now. Not as vulnerable as I'd been when I'd first encountered the warlock's veil. I had the power of an angel, the divine realm at my back, heightening my magic and surpassing what the warlock's spell had endeavored to destroy.

The warlock's magic bucked against me, coiling tighter around the queen's caged power, but I forced my light to spread out, heating it with each breath until it set the veil of death alight, burning and cleaving its way through the putrid netting.

I burned and burned. Divine fire raged around the warlock's spell, singeing and destroying every single bit of its essence.

A sound came from the queen. A gasp of surprise. A stifled breath.

But I didn't stop. I called upon everything I had until I'd completely destroyed the evil magic that resided within her, consuming every last speck of the black magic until nothing was left but smoke and ash.

Gasping, I stumbled back, my affinity sucking back inside me so quickly that a wave of dizziness swept over me.

Norivun caught me, holding me up just as the queen bolted upright in bed.

My eyes drooped, and my chest heaved. My angel affinity spiraled back inside me, coiling into that dense power of light and dark before nestling between my shoulder blades once more.

"My love?" Norivun said softly.

I gulped in deep breaths. The destruction of the queen's caged power happened so quickly that my head spun. I swayed despite Norivun's grip.

The prince's strong arms wrapped around my waist, and he held me close. The scent of cedar and snow enclosed me.

"By the realms, Ilara, you did it," he exclaimed, his words thick. "You *did* it."

I lifted my head to see pride shining in Matron Olsander's expression, but more than that greeted me.

Queen Lissandra sat up in bed, her eyes wide open, her body glowing with health, her wings whole and strong. Black hair, vibrant and shiny, hung down her back as straight as an arrow.

Tears filled her eyes. "Ilara," she whispered. "You sweet girl. I can't believe it, you—" The queen stumbled to a stand. Laughter spilled from her lips. She embraced me, and a wave of tiredness dashed through me again, but I hugged her tightly in return.

"Ilara." She grinned. "Oh, Ilara, you *saved* me."

Magic stole over me as she gripped me tighter, and then something brushed against my Shield. A kind hand, a gentle touch. Frowning, I lowered my Shield slightly.

The queen's voice whispered in my mind, *"Thank you, my sweet darling. Thank you!"*

I stumbled back, my eyes widening. The queen's grin stretched wide before the feel of her psychic affinity withdrew.

"Mother?" Norivun said, his head cocking. Hope billowed from him along our bond.

Nuwin dashed to the queen's side, and he whooped in delight. "Mother, your aura, it's the way it used to be!"

"It is." An explosion of magic barreled out of the queen. Young children danced at our sides. Flowers twisted along her chamber's ceiling. Grass sprouted from the stone floors as petals drifted in the air, landing on the queen's bed, rug, and chairs. Everywhere was vibrant light, bright sunshine, and peals of laughter.

I gasped. "Is this an illusion?"

The queen clasped my hands. "Yes, Ilara darling. It's *my* illusion. This is how I feel right now. Because of you, because of what you just did. I'm *free*."

The queen laughed again. Joy spilled from her lips as she twirled in a circle. She clasped my hands and pulled me with her. Our midnight hair shone in the lights while rose petals kissed our cheeks before fluttering to the floor.

I laughed with her, and we twirled and twirled, doing endless circles until my stomach hurt from laughing so hard, and my head spun with dizziness.

And when we stopped, the queen's skirts rustled along the floor before she gripped me again. She hugged me so tightly my breath stopped. "Thank *you*, you beautiful, amazing, brave girl."

Norivun and Nuwin grabbed both of us in a hug simultaneously until the room was overflowing with tears of laughter, shouts of joy, and endless illusions dancing across our vision.

And in that moment, it truly hit me what I'd done. The queen was free—the spell created by the warlock that had been placed on her many winters ago was finally broken. I'd burned it away, using my divine light, just as God Zorifel had ripped the warlock's ugly magic from me with his masterful touch.

And the same feeling that had engulfed me when I'd seen my parents whole and alive, hiding within the refuge on the Cliffs of Sarum, filled me anew. A sense of peace flowed through me, settling something deep inside me.

No matter what happened from here, no matter what fate the gods deemed necessary for me, I would have this. This moment. This heartbeat of hope and love. This victory.

I saved the queen.

And right now, I was bursting with happiness.

NORIVUN AND NUWIN were hesitant to leave their mother's side, but an hour had passed since Nuwin had burst into his brother's chambers. The council meeting was already well underway, and each moment that we delayed was only another moment for King Novakin to prepare.

"We must go, but we'll come back later today." Norivun gave his mother another long hug.

"I'll stay at her side." Nuwin positioned himself by the queen. "If Father returns, he'll have to get through me before he hurts her again. I'm done letting him abuse her, even if it means he kills me instead."

"Nuwin," the queen said, her hand laying on his shoulder. "I will *never* let him hurt you. I'm not weak anymore."

"You've suffered enough, Mother. I'm just ashamed that I didn't take a stand against him sooner." Nuwin's wings rippled, and a new expression morphed upon his face, an expression I'd never seen before. A savageness emerged, a mask his brother often wore, but the younger prince had never appeared so formidable.

"I shall stay as well." Matron Olsander's rotund figure

stood tall. Squaring her shoulders, she added, "If the king returns, I will bear witness to any abuse he tries to inflict on her, and if he's been hiding this kind of despicable behavior for winters—as the rumors have been stating—then he's unlikely to strike her if I refuse to leave her side."

"Thank you." Norivun dipped his head at her and Nuwin, then hugged his mother again. "I've never been happier."

The queen smiled, her lips curving in genuine excitement. "I feel wonderful, just like I used to feel, and all because of your darling mate."

Her finger traced along my jaw, and her psychic affinity brushed against my Shield again. I lowered it once more.

"Now, my darling Rising Queen, go claim your throne."

Norivun, his four guards, and I mistphased to outside the council chambers, appearing just shy of the arched doors. Two guards stood at attendance, one on each side. When the crown prince and I materialized only feet away from them, their wings flexed, and they reached for their swords.

But Haxil and Sandus already had blades to their throats before the guards' hands hit their sword hilts.

"If you want to keep your tongue, you'll leave that weapon where it is," Sandus hissed.

"Same goes for you." Haxil shoved his guard against the wall and arched an eyebrow. "Ryder?"

Ryder withdrew a thin rope from his leggings, and in a blurred move, both guards were bound by their wrists and ankles. Nish pulled several cloths from his pockets and gagged their mouths. When completed, a light mist of magic fell over them, and they disappeared under the prince's illusion.

Stunned, my jaw dropped. "Considering how quickly that just happened, I'm guessing this is something you've all done before?"

The prince smirked, and a dark light entered his eyes. "What did I say to you all of those months ago, that it's not my fault if you're unaware of my talents?"

I snorted despite what waited for us beyond the doors ahead.

"Let's just hope your talents keep all of us in one piece, my prince." I nodded toward the chambers. "So, are we just going to burst through them and confront the council?"

"Do you see any other way?" my mate replied.

I shook my head, and he bowed, then held out his arm, gesturing to the door. "My queen? After you."

CHAPTER 24 - NORIVUN

I gathered a gust of my air affinity and blew it through the council doors. The frame splintered at the hinges, and the doors crashed open against the stone walls within.

"He does enjoy making an entrance, doesn't he?" Nish snickered under his breath.

Ryder snorted.

Shrieks of surprise and fear echoed in the council chambers as my mate and I strode past the ruined doors.

King Novakin sat at the end of the table near the far wall. He pushed to a stand, as did all of the other territory archons. The king's wings extended past his broad shoulders, their black membranes turning translucent in the light. Everyone's auras soared.

"What is the meaning of this?" Lord Woodsbury, the archon of Isalee Territory, called.

"I knew you would be returning sooner or later."

My father's icy gaze met mine. He bared his teeth. "Guards? Seize them."

"I think not." Sandus shot in front of me as Nish, Ryder, and Haxil fanned out around us. All of them held their swords up. Tempered warrior affinities hummed around them. Magic curled through the air, swirling around their limbs.

Ilara's pulse fluttered in her neck. Despite her fear flowing through our bond, she held firm, not once showing an ounce of submission toward my father.

My lip curled, and the urge to rip my father to shreds unfurled within me. "We've come to join the meeting, Your Majesty." My words dripped with mocking sarcasm.

King Novakin's face mottled, and his hands fisted. "You've committed treason by plotting against me. Because of that, you will both be placed in the dungeons until I determine what to do next with your insubordination." My father pointed his finger at my guards. "Stand down. *Now*."

Ryder shook his head, his cheekbones as sharp as glass in the fairy lights. "I think not. We serve the one and only true king of the Solis continent, not the vile leech that sits upon the throne."

The king's breath sucked in, and Lady Busselbee paled.

"Your Majesty," the Mervalee Territory archon twirled toward him in a swirl of silk skirts. "What in all the realms is happening? He's the crown prince. You can't possibly mean to—"

"Silence!" the king roared.

My father's guards still surrounded us, their swords still raised as my guards faced them. It would be bloodshed if battle ensued. My father's guards were just as deadly as my own, which meant death would likely be dealt to both sides.

I swallowed the pang of fear that threatened to creep up my throat. I'd known death was inevitable if I were to challenge my father, so I chose my next words carefully. "I've only come today to show the council something. I have no wish for bloodshed." I withdrew the looking glass from my pocket. "I shall willingly venture to the dungeons after it airs if that's what the council wishes."

Lord Crimsonale and Lady Wormiful shared a veiled look before the Osaravee archon puffed out his chest. "What is it you bring, Prince Norivun?"

"Something I believe the council will be interested in." I held the looking glass up.

My father's eyes narrowed. "Why do you have a looking glass?"

"How about I show you?" Before he could utter a response, I waved my hand over the glass and whispered the spell to activate it.

The looking glass's magic flared, and an image blazed to life, projecting onto the ceiling of the domed council chamber.

Every councilor's gaze shot up as the scene from Isalee began to unfold.

"What is the meaning of this?" the king roared. "Guards! Stop him!"

But when his guards tried to move in, mine met them just as fast until they were playing a game of cat and mouse, dancing around one another as each tried to best the other and find an opening. But it was enough of a distraction to keep the recording going.

The Isalee scene lengthened, showing us first destroying the veil and then the warlock appearing before our battle ensued.

"Norivun!" the king growled. "You'll regret this."

I smirked. "I doubt it."

Each of the councilors' attention remained fixated on the scene.

"Dear gods, what is that *thing*?" Lady Busselbee recoiled when the image showed a close-up of the warlock with his gray skin and web of crimson veins.

The king's eyes widened, his cheeks turning ruddy. All of the archons remained transfixed. Several gasped. More than one hand flew to a mouth.

And when that Isalee scene ended, it switched to our encounter in Canada. The looking glass showed our capture of the warlock, then our bargain, and finally the dark sorcerer on his hands and knees as I began speaking to him.

And finally, his confession.

Shocked silence filled the room.

"Is that in the *other* realm?" Lord Pinebeer, the Harrivee archon, gaped.

"That's enough, Norivun." My father's jaw

pumped. He strode toward me, his aura dark and swelling. His air affinity whipped toward my hand as though he hoped to dispel the looking glass, but my Shield held firm. "Guards!" he barked again. "Stop this!"

But when they again tried to maneuver themselves past my guards, I yelled, "Stand firm!"

My guards didn't relent. King Novakin's guards looked to my father for direction. My death affinity shot out of me, punching right through their protective Shields until it wrapped around all of their souls.

I let my dragon rise, my irises turning to slits as my voice deepened. "Unless you wish to die right here and now, you'll do as *I* say. Not him."

Throat bobbing, the guard nearest me retreated a step, getting a hiss of victory out of Ryder.

My father's face was so red now he resembled a boiled turnip, but he remained frozen when my affinity squeezed his soul too.

"You wouldn't dare," he hissed under his breath.

My lips curled into a malicious smile. "Try me."

The spectacle with the warlock continued to unfold from the looking glass. The councilors' jaws dropped even more with each second that passed.

"You'll regret this," the king said again in a whisper so low that I knew only I had heard him. "By the way, have you seen your mother?"

Ilara's breath sucked in, and she seethed at the king. "We have, in fact. We found her at death's door this morning, and we were told *you* were the cause of that."

The king's lip curled. "My son knows what happens when he disobeys me."

"She was nearly dead when we found her." My hands curled into fists, and the urge to annihilate him burned through me. "Did you know that?"

My father shrugged. "I know that I was particularly displeased when I visited her last night. I heard some troubling rumors have been circulating through the capital."

"They're not rumors. They're true. You're a coward," Ilara spat.

The king's head whipped back as though he'd been slapped.

Fire flared on Ilara's hands. "Only a coward would cage a female's magic because he's afraid of her strength."

My father's brows drew together in a sharp line.

My nostrils flared, and my eyes narrowed to slits. "That's right, Your Majesty. My eternal mate knows *everything* about you."

The king took another step closer to me but stopped short when my death affinity dug deeper, piercing into him like demon claws on the edge of shredding his soul.

Fuming, my father ground his teeth. "You know what happens when you disobey me, Norivun, yet you still choose to defy me."

"I don't understand." Lady Busselbee's question interrupted us. A frown marred her features. "This looking glass is showing a scene from the *other* realm, and it appears that *thing* is accusing you of starving all of our fae, Your Majesty. But how could that possibly be true? Surely you would never do such a thing?"

My father waved his hand dismissively. In a blink, his guileless mask fell into place. "Lies, all of it. As usual, my son is making a spectacle of himself. You know what he's like. He's a monster, and right now, he's apparently looking for a good show as a way to distract from the fact that he and his mate have committed treason."

"But he made a fairy bargain with that creature." Lady Busselbee pointed at the image. "If he's lying, then why didn't the bargain strike the creature dead?"

The king's jaw muscle began to tick. "That's enough, Lady Busselbee."

Her wings ruffled. "Excuse me?"

The scenes from the looking glass ended, and for a moment nobody spoke, but then Lord Crimsonale called, "My king? I agree with Lady Busselbee. These recordings are most disturbing. And they are from *a looking glass*, which means they are true events that took place. What have you to say for it? This looks like evidence that *you* are involved in the diminishing *orem*."

"I've heard similar accusations." Lady Wormiful sneered at the king down her long nose. "Just yesterday, several of my territory's archons came to me with concerns about your involvement in the state of our continent. Apparently, this isn't the only looking glass that contains very disturbing revelations about your actions. They also reported about a dark web of black magic that had been in an Isalee field, which is exactly what that looking glass shows. How do you explain all of this, Your Majesty?"

Her biting accusation had just enough malice behind it that her meaning was clear, while at the same time, the Kroravee archon portrayed the picture of an eager territory leader who only wanted to seek the truth. She truly was a snake, and a complete master at manipulation.

My father's nostrils flared. "I am the *king* of the Solis continent. I do not have to explain myself to you or anyone else."

Ilara's chest heaved, and magic shimmered around her, but she'd gained enough control of her temper that the fire that'd flared around her hands disappeared.

"All of your concerns about the king are valid." Her bold statement rang through the room. Digging her nails into her palms, she took a step closer to my father. "King Novakin, you ordered the death of my family for speaking the truth of what was happening on our continent. You treated them as though they were traitors, but the only traitor in this room is *you*. You enlisted the help of that warlock in exchange for innocent fae to be fed to him. You had that warlock create the veil of death that sank deep within our land and destroyed all of the crops. You created all of this dissent simply because you wanted to gain support for an invasion on our peaceful southerly neighbors, and all because you wanted to extend your territory for your own personal ambition. And not once did you care what it did to our fae. The only tyrant in this room is you. The only fairy in this room that belongs in the dungeons is *you*."

Silence reigned following Ilara's accusations.

Pride surged through me. *Gods, she's magnificent.*

"Your Majesty, what do you have to say for yourself?" Lord Crimsonale raised his eyebrows. "These are very egregious actions that you're being accused of."

My father's hands pumped into fists, but he ignored the Osaravee archon. Small blood vessels burst under the king's skin, causing his cheeks to grow even redder. "I should have killed you when I had the chance," he whispered to Ilara.

Snarling, I stepped around my mate and placed myself between her and the king.

"Archons of the Solis territories," I roared. "I ask you to listen to my plea. As you have seen, we have proof that the king of the Solis continent has committed treason upon our land and our fae. He has sought to starve our citizens. He commissioned the help of a dark magical creature from the *other* realm in order to accomplish such a task. He is responsible for the murder of dozens of innocent fae within this very castle in order to fuel his self-serving ambition. And he did all of this simply to gain support for an invasion of the Nolus continent. All he wants is to expand his power at the cost of our fae. He does not care for the well-being of you or this continent's children. He is not fit to rule this land. Therefore, I am enacting an ancient accord. I hereby challenge the king of the Solis continent for the right to his throne. Do I have your support?"

I replayed the looking-glass recording again. All of the archons looked from it, to their king, then to me.

Veins swelled in my father's neck. "I'll torture your mother the next time I see her." The king's whispered comment flowed to my ears, and my ears only on his affinity. "I'll do it slowly. Weeks, no, *months* of pain because of what you've done here today."

"You'll never touch her again," I snarled.

The king's eyes bulged when my affinity stabbed into his soul. His chest rose in sharp breaths, and his eyes began to roll back in his head.

"Norivun. *Stop*." My mate's hand on my arm broke through the bloodlust that threatened to consume me. Her life-giving affinity curled around my power, stroking it gently and extracting its claws. "We need the council on our side. If you murder the king right now, all hope will be lost. Don't."

Her quiet plea and the push of her love along our bond doused the darkness inside me. The fury that had clouded my vision dissipated. I latched onto her love, her goodness, her kindness. She was my light.

Her life-giving affinity wrapped around my death more, caressing it. Soothing it.

I softened the hold on my father, and the king sucked in a breath.

"This is madness. All of this! These accusations are preposterous, and look who they're coming from." Lord Woodsbury shot an accusing finger at my mate. "That female was supposed to marry my son, yet she defied the king and married the prince. What is this treachery you bring to us now, Lady Seary? If anyone should be thrown in the dungeons here, it's *you*, not the king."

"Are you denying what you're seeing with your own eyes?" Lord Crimsonale shot his hand toward the scenes portrayed from the looking glass, still streaming across the domed ceiling since I'd commanded it to repeat. "You can see for yourself that the prince made a fairy bargain. If that creature was lying, the gods would have struck him dead."

"How do we all know this isn't just a trick, Gregorian?" Lord Woodsbury placed his hands on his hips and waved at the looking-glass image. "How do you know all of this isn't an illusion? Perhaps the prince is working with strange creatures from the *other* realm, and it's not the king at all who's behind this."

"That is something my son would do." The king nodded. Tension rolled through the air as we both stood toe to toe.

"I'm not lying," I somehow managed to hiss through my teeth. "And what you're seeing *isn't* an illusion. I'll make a fairy bargain with you right here and right now declaring it so. If I'm lying, the gods may strike me down." I arched an eyebrow at Lord Woodsbury. "What you're seeing is the truth. The king is behind the missing fae within this castle. He knowingly and willingly put every single Solis citizen at risk by what he's done to our crops. So would you like to make a bargain, Lord Woodsbury? Would you like to be tethered to me by the gods for your inability to believe what a *looking glass* is showing you?"

"You know the truth of the magic of looking glass-es," Lord Pinebeer said quietly to him. "There's a reason only fae with a truth affinity can forge them. Stop being so foolish, Lord Woodsbury."

The Isalee Territory archon's chest puffed up as he straightened his lapels. "I . . . I do not need to make a bargain with you, Prince Norivun."

"So it's settled then?" Lady Wormiful's eyebrow arched. "We're all in agreement that what we're seeing is true, as troubling as it is?"

Everyone's attention darted around. The territory leaders assessed each and every archon in the room. Wariness floated through the air.

"This is most concerning." Lady Busselbee finally said, breaking the quiet. She shook her head and brought a hand to her chest. "But it does shed some light on other things I've heard. There have been some disturbing whisperings among the citizens this week. They're also saying that Prince Norivun didn't kill dozens of fae who came to this castle with concerns about the crops. Instead, they're saying that he protected them. Safeguarded them."

"It's true." I kept my wings in tight. The king's eyes narrowed in my direction. "My father ordered all of their deaths yet made me look like the tyrant who wanted it so. But I refused to kill them. They were all innocent fae who were concerned about the state of our land. My father wanted *me* portrayed as the villain, so he ordered me to execute them, but I didn't. I hid them instead, and now, they've come out of hiding and are speaking the truth."

My father paled and stumbled back.

I pointed a finger at King Novakin. "The true villain here is *him*, not me."

"That's enough. All of you." The king's chest heaved. "You are threatening to break the peace of our land, Norivun. This time, you've gone too far. You've left me with no choice but to execute my own son."

Gasps sounded throughout the room.

My head dropped back in a sharp bark of laughter. "You couldn't kill me if you tried."

"Perhaps not, but what if I killed her?" In a flash, the king was next to my mate with a knife to her neck.

Ilara yelped in surprise just as the king drove a dagger right through her throat.

CHAPTER 25 - ILARA

B lood filled my throat, and then I was falling,
crashing to the ground as screams rang through
the air.

"Ilara!" Norivun's arms enclosed me before I hit the
floor. Blood gushed from my neck. His hands pressed
against my throat, terror coating his eyes.

The king let out a harsh laugh as my blood spurted
out of me.

The crown prince bellowed in fury, then his death
affinity speared the king. But the king vanished in a
blink of mistphasing magic.

Norivun's roar echoed in the room.

A gurgling sound filled my mouth. I tried to speak.
Tried to tell him that I loved him and always would, but
my body was growing so cold, and I couldn't whisper a
word.

"Heal yourself, Ilara. Please!" His hands worked to

stanch the blood flow as his four guards battled the king's guards before they raced for the door.

Other voices yelled and screamed, but I couldn't discern what they were saying.

My entire focus was on the male hovering above me. There was so much I had wanted to do with him in this lifetime. So many things I would never get to experience at his side.

"No! Don't even fucking think it. I can't live without you!" His hand tightened over my wound. Blackness coated the edge of my vision. "Heal yourself, my love. Use your angel affinity."

A huge push of his power barreled toward me on the bond. It was enough to snap me out of the darkness that wanted to consume me.

A force of his air shot into my mouth and tunneled through the blood pooling in my throat. My mate's air affinity filled my lungs as desperation skated over his face. "For me. Stay alive, for *me*," he begged.

A tingle of magic burned in my gut. I called upon both my life-giving affinity and my angel power simultaneously. Heat roared through my veins. I concentrated on bringing all of my magic to the puncture wound that had severed the thick blood vessel in my neck. My life-giving affinity spiraled up from my belly, and my angel magic uncoiled from between my shoulder blades. But the blackness still wanted to consume me, and I knew it would have if Norivun's air affinity wasn't keeping me alive.

I concentrated harder, doing my best to push the

darkness away. Magic, light, cold power . . . It all blended together and clouded around my throat.

"How is that possible?" a voice whispered from across the room.

"Is she healing herself?" a female hissed.

"Mother Above and Below, have you ever seen such a thing?"

Strength began to flow into me as my dual powers worked simultaneously to knit together the skin and blood vessels in my neck while keeping my soul tethered to my body. With each second that passed, the hope and relief flowing from Norivun into me increased.

"Yes, that's it. Keep working, my love," he whispered.

"She's going to be all right, my prince." Haxil's gruff tone filled my ears. All four of his guards appeared in my line of sight.

"The bastard got away," Nish said quietly to my mate.

"So did his guards." Sandus's worried eyes met mine. "Well done, Ilara. You're a true warrior."

"He's right." Ryder nodded in encouragement. "I never thought in all of my life that I would witness such an event. You're extraordinary, Ilara."

I breathed in on my own, and my mate's air affinity slowly retreated from my lungs. White feathers lay on the floor behind me as my angel affinity hummed and finished sealing the puncture wound the king had inflicted upon me.

"By the gods." Lady Wormiful brought a hand to her chest. "I thought she was going to die."

"And by the hand of our king, nonetheless." Lord Crimsonale bowed in Norivun's direction. "Crown Prince, you have my full support in challenging the king to the throne."

"And you have mine." Lady Wormiful bowed too.

Lady Busselbee's complexion was ashen, and shock filled her eyes. "Never in my life had I thought to witness such vulgarity as I did today. Prince Norivun, if what the villagers are saying is true about how you saved innocents and shielded them from the king's actions, and that you and Lady Seary have been working tirelessly behind the king's back to discover what has truly been going on with our continent, then you have my blessing as well."

Lord Pinebeer followed, uttering his support.

The only one who balked was Lord Woodsbury. He sneered at us from across the room. I slowly sat up and fingered my neck. Whole, intact skin greeted my fingertips. I swallowed, waiting for pain to follow, but it felt normal.

"You're fully healed, love." Sandus patted my shoulder. "You are an enigma, Ilara Seary, daughter of Mervalee Territory. But by the gods, am I glad you are."

Nish blinked rapidly, and I gave him a small smile.

"Are those tears you're shedding for me?" I asked, surprise filling me that my voice wasn't even hoarse.

Nish's head snapped back, and he ran a finger near his eye. "What? Of course not. Warriors don't cry."

Norivun huffed a soft, relieved laugh before helping me to my feet. The six of us faced the last territory archon who had yet to give his support.

"Lord Woodsbury? What say you of my challenge to the king?" Norivun leveled him with a heavy stare.

The archon's throat bobbed, and his wings ruffled. "But she was supposed to marry—"

"She's my eternal mate," the prince snarled. "She was to marry nobody but me."

Lady Wormiful's eternal mark flashed silver in the fairy lights when she held her hand up. She seethed at the Isalee archon. "Really, Alestair. Enough of your sniveling about that dastardly son of yours. They're eternal mates."

Lord Woodsbury's cheeks puffed out. "Excuse me? Are you accusing my son—"

"Oh, shut up, Alestair!" Lady Wormiful countered. "Everybody knows that Arcane's a pedophile and abuser. The only one in denial about it is you. So stop your condescending demands and put your pride away. We have bigger things to worry about right now than your family's marital alliances. Support the prince against the tyrant on the throne. If the looking glass's revelations against the king didn't convince you, then surely the king's behavior against Lady Seary did? Prince Norivun is right. The king's a murderer. He is no longer worthy of wearing the Solis crown."

Lord Woodsbury sneered. But after Lady Busselbee and Lord Pinebeer also voiced their support of my mate, he finally sighed. "All right. Fine. I also support you, Prince Norivun."

My mate bowed. "Thank you, councilors."

"So what now?" Ryder asked.

Norivun straightened. "Now we find my father, and we bring justice to our land."

CHAPTER 26 - NORIVUN

"How are we going to find the king?" Ilara peered up at me, her affinity-transformed violet eyes shining brightly.

My heart still thundered at how close I'd come to losing her. "I don't know, but if we enlist the help of a fairy with a tracking affinity, we'll likely locate him within—"

An explosion rocked the ground, and the windows shuddered in their panes.

"Mother Below!" Lady Busselbee flew to the window, and her mouth dropped open. "It's the king!"

On a gust of my air affinity, all four of my guards, Ilara, and I were at the window, peering down into the huge courtyard.

"Blessed Mother." My hands pumped into fists.

The king stood at the front of the courtyard, his four guards flanking his sides as the entirety of the castle guard stood at his back. Swords were drawn. Wings flexed as the guards wore their battle armor. While Ilara had been attacked and we'd subsequently been arguing with territory archons, my father had been readying soldiers who were still loyal to him.

I bared my teeth in a hiss. "He dies now." But before I could even call upon my death affinity, my father disappeared in another flash of mistphasing magic.

Yet his commanded soldiers remained.

"He's ordered them to kill us right here and now." Haxil's chest rose rapidly, and his grip tightened on his sword.

"It's because nobody outside of this chamber knows that the council has supported your challenge." Lady Wormiful pointed to the looking glass stored back in my pocket. "The king knew that he needed to act before the council could speak against him. None of them know that he's been removed from power!"

"And we're not ready to fight him." Lord Crimsonale's gaze shot my way. "The factions are still in their territories. Those that are willing to stand at our sides won't get here in time, even if Taberitha and I mistphase to them now."

"But we have to try." Lady Wormiful grabbed his sleeve. "We can't allow the king's reign to continue."

"What in all the realms?" Lord Woodsbury shouted from across the room. "Are you telling me that the three of you have been *conspiring* against the king?"

Lord Pinebeer and Lady Busselbee shared shocked expressions.

Lord Woodsbury bustled from around the table, his eyes flashing. "You all belong in the dungeons. Every single one of you. I'll have you—" His words abruptly stopped.

With fisted hands, Ilara's air affinity barreled out of her, right toward the Isalee archon.

"You're right," my mate said to Lord Crimsonale and Lady Wormiful. Lord Woodsbury gaped like a fish out of water as Ilara robbed his breath. "We haven't a moment to lose. Go now. We'll try to hold the king off in the courtyard."

Gregorian and Taberitha gave sharp nods before disappearing in a blast of mistphasing power.

Lord Woodsbury fell to the ground, clawing at his throat. A whisper of magic fluttered around my mate when she released her affinity.

The Isalee archon gasped and heaved, then sucked in air and coughed. Fear shone in his eyes when Ilara again fixated her attention on him. She could have killed him, but she hadn't.

I prowled closer, then knelt at his side. "My wife's heart is softer than mine, but if you defy the council's ruling and interfere in any way again, I won't hesitate a second before ending you."

Lord Woodsbury curled in on himself and shook his head. "I'm sorry, my prince."

A yell came through the windows, then the sound of stomping feet.

"Norivun, he's ordered them to storm the castle," Ilara called. "We must act. Now!"

My pulse raced as the reality of what waited ahead
hit me. I could kill half of the soldiers in the courtyard
below with my death affinity. It would tire me greatly
and likely render me weakened in a continued fight, but
if I had to, I would.

I joined them at the window, already calling upon
my magic to mistphase all of us.

"We can't best them without you killing them.
There's too many." Ryder's eyes narrowed, and I had no
doubt his calculating mind was already running
through an analysis of what losses were about to
unfold. "But we can stall them until the factions
arrive."

"We must get to the king." I searched for my father,
but the coward was hiding. "I can end this here and
now with my death affinity if I kill him. Without their
king commanding them, the castle guard will falter."

"But the bastard's hiding." Nish sneered.

"Join hands," I called. The sheer number of guards
below would likely still harm us to some degree, but
between my affinities and Ilara's, along with my guards'
skills, we could hold them off for at least some time
without blood being spilled. And by the gods, I didn't
want their deaths on my conscience. They were soldiers
who were merely doing as they'd been commanded.
They didn't deserve to die for that.

But my father did, wherever he was.

"He's planned something." I swung toward my
guards, and my mistphasing magic rose. "He's always
ready, always two steps ahead of me. Whatever's

waiting for us in that courtyard, be ready. We won't get a second chance."

They all nodded curtly, and I could only hope that the afterlife wouldn't be greeting all of us come sundown.

CHAPTER 27 - NORIVUN

We reappeared in the courtyard below as rumbling clouds formed overhead. The entirety of the castle guard and just as many Solis Guard soldiers waited before us, only steps from the main door.

Young faces stared back at me. Wings flexed. Magic stirred. An undercurrent of energy emanated from the thousand fae lined up before us.

So this was what my father had on hand. Trained fae ready to do his bidding at a moment's notice. I'd expected nothing less.

"Your lives don't need to end today!" I roared across the courtyard.

Only their deathly silence answered me, but those in the front glanced at one another with puckered brows.

"I don't want to kill—"

The king abruptly appeared again, standing at the

front of the line. His eyes shone with malice. "I wondered how long it would take for you to get here. I half-expected you to turn tail and run."

I immediately shot my death affinity toward him, but when it reached his form, it engulfed nothing. I sneered. He was projecting himself magically from wherever he hid. Figured.

I scoffed. "Still the coward, I see."

"Hardly. I'm merely prepared," his magical illusion replied.

"We're done running, Father, and your reign ends today."

"Did you hear that?" The projected king threw his head back and smirked. "It's exactly as I told all of you. The Death Master seeks to murder me and claim the throne as his own."

The soldiers' expressions at the front of the line hardened.

The king's projection raised his arm. "Guards!"

The projection lowered his arm, and a flurry of arrows, hundreds if not thousands, flew from the back of the soldiers and sailed through the air toward us.

Ilara, my guards, and I all instinctively ducked as Ilara cast a large air Shield around us.

She winced when hundreds of arrowheads hit her Shield, but her fierce determination barreled toward me on our bond. I squeezed her hand while the arrows rained down. She gripped me tightly, but even though defiance shone in her eyes, through our bond, I felt her fatigue. She was already weakened from healing the queen and herself. Her magic wasn't fully charged.

Snarling, the mate bond sang like a siren's song inside me.

The second the arrows stopped, I shot my death affinity out of me, wrapping it around hundreds of guards who stood before us.

Their eyes bulged, but the projected king only snickered.

"I figured that would be your first move." Before I could contemplate what my father was going to do, a vial appeared hurtling through the air.

It smashed to the ground before I could stop it, and a plume of misted magic rose around us.

"Get back!" I shouted. I flung us away on a gust of air, but I wasn't fast enough. A trace of poisoned mist coasted over my skin. The scent and feel of it made my insides quiver.

Tylen's nulling magic.

"Drachu was kind enough to allow my potion masters to formulate a few elixirs with Tylen's assistance." My father's voice rang through the air, and this voice was *his*. It came from far away, near the castle wall. "I have a few more of those just waiting to make your acquaintance."

"Spread out!" I yelled to my guards.

None of them hesitated before blurring away, putting as much distance between us as they could. Distance was the only thing that would save us from that poisoned mist if my father truly held more vials just waiting to be unleashed.

Already, I felt my affinities dimming. They weren't gone, but they felt weakened. Whatever the mist was, it wasn't as potent as being directly touched by Tylen, but with enough of it in our systems, it could render us vulnerable.

"Don't let that mist touch any of you!"

"Norivun," Ilara called. "He's in the back somewhere."

"I know. I heard him too."

But before any of us could locate him, the cannons boomed in the distance. Blazing fireballs burst from the tips of the castle wall, its offensive magic unleashing. Except instead of those cannons pointing outward, they'd been swung toward the courtyard.

Toward us.

Screams erupted from inside the castle as servants and other fae appeared at the windows, faces plastered to the panes. Horror filled all of their expressions.

The cannonballs sailed toward us, and Ilara flung her hands up. Her fire element blazed from her palms as she met the fiery cannonballs midair.

The cannonballs exploded in a dazzling display of power.

But another poisoned vial was already careening through the air.

"Ilara, watch out!" I caught the vial on a gust of air a second before it hit the ground beside her. My air pulled it toward me, and my hand closed around the intact vial as another burst of magic erupted from the castle.

Swords clashed, the sound ringing through the air. Castle soldiers were directly engaging my four guards. I tried to keep my hold on their souls, but the nulling mist was strong enough that I couldn't keep my grip.

Released, the soldiers near me fled and headed toward Haxil, Ryder, Nish, and Sandus.

They were trying to weaken us, pluck off the lesser magical beings first while they worked to erode my and Ilara's magic with weapons and potions.

"Norivun! Duck and roll!" Ilara yelled.

I didn't pause to question her warning. I crouched at her command and tumbled to the right just as more offensive magic unleashed. Nettings of crackling blue magic, coming from the ground behind me, tried to ensnare me. I rolled again, my wing nearly catching on a statue near the stair's bottom as the netting grabbed toward where I'd been standing only a second prior.

Ilara blurred out of the way a moment before a net would have captured her, my guards doing the same as their warrior abilities moved them as fast as the wind.

My father's commanding roar came from behind the soldiers near the far wall, and before I could take a breath, hundreds of arrows shot into the sky again.

"We have to get to him!" I yelled to my mate.

More sizzling blue nets zapped up from the ground as we dodged and dipped out of the way to avoid the offensive tactics of the castle's magic erupting in its full capacity.

KRISTA STREET

"Don't allow it to touch you!" I called to Ilara.

If any of those nets grazed our skin, the encapsulating magic would momentarily smother our affinities, rendering us vulnerable.

"Kill him!" my father again roared from the back.

Despite the scent of fear filling the air, the castle guard marched forward, weapons raised. Magic rumbled along my limbs, vibrating through the remains of that nulling mist, and I wrenched on my death affinity. I shot it toward the soldiers, regret hitting me so quickly that I tasted it.

"I'm sorry," I called to them.

But just as my affinity ensnared half of the castle's guard, Ilara's life-giving affinity formed a wall, a protective barrier around the soldiers, halting their demise.

"No," she called, and then on a gust of air, she was at my side. The entire time we continued to dodge the blue nets. "We're not killing them. Not yet! There has to be another way."

A rush of relief barreled through me. I hadn't wanted to murder innocents today, and my mate had just taken that decision away for me.

The guards that I'd held within my deathly grip for that brief second stumbled. The scent of their fear swam potently through the air. Most quickly recovered, but instead of attacking again, several gazed at one another with bewildered expressions.

"Did she just stop him from killing us?" one of the guards asked another. His grip on his sword slackened.

"She did! We do not wish to kill any of you!" I

❄ 318 ❄

shouted. "The king is lying to you. We just showed all of the councilors in the council chambers the truth of what's been happening on our continent, and an ancient accord has been enacted. The king has been removed from power!"

Before I could blink, Ilara had the looking glass out of my pocket. She whispered the words to activate its spell. Light blazed out of it, competing with the lightning cracking in the sky. Thunder boomed a second later. A fairy with a storm affinity was wielding their magic, no doubt at my father's command.

The image from the land of Canada glowed in the air, and a glimpse of my father appeared in the distance. He was atop the castle wall, near the main gate.

"I see him," I called to my mate.

The guards at the front of the line glanced upward. They watched the projected image of the warlock. Brows furrowing, they glanced back at one another, then to their king behind them. The confusion swimming through the air grew more potent with every breath I inhaled.

"Should we mistphase to him?" Ilara asked.

"We could, but I bet my life he'll have another surprise waiting for us if we try."

"We need everyone to see this." She nodded toward the recording blazing in the sky.

I gave a curt nod. "Stay here. Keep yourself protected, and keep that running. I'll go for my father."

I rushed forward, using the guards' momentary distraction to break through their wall.

But before I got halfway across the yard, the king roared from the safety of the wall. "*Kill* him!"

My jaw ground together, and I shot the remaining distance toward him on a gust of air. My guards were right at my back, Ilara holding her ground as she kept the looking glass's image running. A glance over my shoulder showed she'd formed a solid Shield of air and fire around herself. The recording kept going.

But just when I tried to mistphase to where my father stood, a zap of magic hit me, stalling my affinity.

I fell to the ground, my guards landing at my side.

"Stop hiding you coward!" I roared.

The castle guard, now behind me, all swirled around. I cast an illusion of dozens of masked fae holding swords and axes at my back, and the guards backed up.

"Mother Below! Where did they come from?" one of the soldiers shouted.

"Is it the prince's illusion, or are they real?" another called.

But I'd created enough of a distraction to buy me time. I searched for my father again, but the bastard had disappeared, hiding once more.

"My prince!"

I spun around just as Nish's warning reached my ears.

An arrow hit me in the shoulder.

I flew back, clutching the wound. Blood spread through my tunic, then a shout of laughter came from the wall. My father stood off to the side, holding a bow and arrow, no longer hiding.

I ripped the arrow out of my shoulder, wincing slightly, but then another arrow flung from his weapon, but I erected an air Shield around myself at the last moment, knocking it off to the side.

Growling, I called upon my air affinity to fly me toward him, but a sudden wave of dizziness hit me as more inclement weather rumbled in the sky. Lightning zigzagged through the air, hitting the ground only feet away.

A sizzling pit formed where it had landed.

I flew backward as a flash of light appeared in front of me. Then I was peering up into the eyes of God Zorifel.

The god towered over me, rising twenty feet into the air.

"Blessed Mother!" I stumbled back, my heart throbbing at the impossibility of what I was seeing.

"Do you feel the peteesium swimming through your blood, Norivun?" my father taunted.

A dragon abruptly appeared next to God Zorifel, then a dozen beheaded children just behind the divine creature.

Peteesium. "No!" I whispered as more hallucinations appeared before me. The arrow my father had hit me with had been dipped in a powerful hallucinogenic potion that could be created from an enchanted flower.

Air rushed around me, then the sound of steel meeting steel. My guards had surrounded me again.

Ilara screamed from the front of the courtyard. I felt her fear along our bond. She knew I'd been hit.

I swung my magic out, but dozens of fearsome creatures, gods and goddesses, and hundreds of soldiers stared back at me. I didn't know what was real and what was imaginary.

"My prince, behind you!" Sandus called.

My death affinity shot out of me as I swung toward the threat, but a young girl stood there. Wide blue eyes. Black hair. A wingless back. It was a child of Ilara's coloring. My child. *My daughter.*

For a moment, I couldn't move. I gazed at the girl that could one day be mine.

"Nori!" Ryder knocked me to the side, and the sound of a sword cutting through the air whistled past my ear.

My guard grunted, and a sickening sense of dread hit me. He'd been struck.

"Ryder?" I strengthened my air Shield to cover us more and tried to dispel the hallucinations, but when I opened my eyes, the morphing figures remained.

"Where is he?" I roared, not trusting myself to fight anyone in case I accidentally killed my guards or Ilara.

More grunts and yells sounded. My guards swung and thrashed as the gods, goddesses, dragons, and beheaded children came at us alongside the castle guard.

My guards' movements blurred. They took down soldiers, gods, and children alike while my mind continued to play tricks on me while dizziness made me sway.

Ilara screamed, and my head whipped in her direction. *Gods no, don't let that be real.*

Castle guards surrounded my mate. Ilara was fighting magnificently, her warrior affinity humming around her as she moved with liquid grace toward me, no longer burrowed under her protective Shield as she fought her way to my side.

But there were so many guards. So many had surrounded her. She cut them down. Quickly. Efficiently. A warrior queen in action, but for each guard that fell, another took their place.

"Ilara?" I called questioningly.

Burning determination hummed through our bond.

Fuck. What I was seeing was real.

I shook my head, trying to clear my vision. I pushed toward her, all while knowing that King Novakin was too cunning, too clever for us to beat him. Every time I thought perhaps I'd get a hand above him, he always had another trick up his sleeve, just waiting for me.

This battle was no exception. He'd planned for this. He'd probably orchestrated this winters ago just in case I ever tried to seize his throne. He'd always known this day would come, and he'd prepared for it just as I'd always feared he would.

A burst of pain from Ilara erupted toward me on our bond.

My heart stopped.

Ilara fell to the ground, and a guard raised a sword over her head.

"Kill her!" my father called from atop the wall.

"NO!" Rage clouded my vision.

Vengeance sang through my blood.

My dragon affinity tore through me, and in a shockwave of power that ripped through the realm, I shifted faster than the speed of sound.

Guards flew back.

Wind sailed through the yard.

My dragon unleashed.

Fire blazed out of my mouth, incinerating everything in my path.

I swung around. Ilara stood before me, begging and pleading me not to kill her.

I sucked in my fire. I towered over her, her figure so small beneath my giant dragon form.

Then thousands of figures of Ilara danced before my vision. All of the figures in the courtyard were suddenly my mate. The imaginary gods and goddesses were gone. The soldiers had disappeared too. Instead, it was only my mate as she knelt, sobbed, *begged* me to stop.

I morphed back into my fae form and cast illusionary clothes to hide my naked body. I locked my dragon affinity deep within me while the poisonous hallucinogen played deadly games on my mind.

My mate's scream again pierced my ears.

Screaming.

Screaming.

Dear gods, she was screaming, but from *where*? And was she really?

All of the Ilara's before me were screaming as distant battle cries continued to wage.

"Ilara!" I yelled for her, but the cries of slaughtering, bloodshed, and hallucinations rang around me.

And then the castle doors were opening. My mother was running out, my brother just behind her.

Another trick of my mind.

"Novakin!" Queen Lissandra shouted.

A hand grabbed my shoulder and pulled me back just as another whiz of a weapon careened past my face.

"Stay down, my prince!" Haxil yelled. "Ilara's still fighting, but your mind can't be trusted right now!"

My foggy vision showed my guards standing above me, their swords a blur of power as they fought and danced to protect me, but then a god appeared above them, and I struggled to comprehend reality from fiction. Goddess Armarus grinned while lightning forked through the air above her.

"Novakin!" the queen yelled again, and then my mother was right beside me. She gazed up at the king of the Solis continent. "This ends right now! You will never hurt my sons again!"

My mother pushed away from me and flew toward the wall. Black hair streamed down her back, and a dazzling blue gown swirled around her legs. Fire blazed to life around her—*her* fire.

The king's eyes widened, and his jaw dropped.

The entire wall of the castle went up in flames.

My father screamed.

Then my mother's cries joined his.

My mind spun. *What's happening?*

A guttural cry came from one of my guards, then the sound of a weapon tearing through flesh.

My father's cry of pain continued to career through the sky.

I tried to push up, tried to see what was happening, but a boot caught me on the stomach.

"Stay down, my prince!" Haxil yelled.

My heart exploded at the picture painted before me.

It showed my mother standing on the wall beside my father. Fire engulfed both of their bodies as their dual screams of pain pierced the air.

The courtyard abruptly grew quiet.

Swords fell to the snowy ground.

Shouts of disbelief came next.

And before my eyes, the king and queen of the Solis continent both burned in flames so hot that not even my mother could withstand her own power.

My parents' screams filled my ears until the fire melted their features. Before my eyes, their bodies turned into piles of ash.

And then I heard nothing at all.

CHAPTER 28 - ILARA

"Norivun?" I said quietly just as the bargain's mark, the king's crown, flared on my mate's inner wrist, then disappeared from existence.

I swallowed the knot in my throat. My mate's bargain with Lord Crimsonale was complete, which meant the king was truly dead.

I cradled Norivun's head. "My love, I'm going to heal you. I'm going to rid you of the poison inside you."

The crown prince lay on the ground, his face a mask of shock. Soot coated his cheeks. My brilliant white angel wings spread around him, holding him. Protecting him.

Fatigue barreled through me. I was so tired, so *very* tired after the battle in the yard, but I couldn't stop now.

Haxil, Sandus, Nish, and Ryder stood around us,

forming a cage of muscle and taut wings even though all of them were bloodied, injured, and barely standing. Ryder had a cut so deep in his abdomen that his face was entirely white.

I would heal him next, then the other three before I turned my affinities to the injured castle guard. I would heal as many as I could until my magic ran dry and unconsciousness claimed me.

The prince reached for me but then pulled back. Along the bond, disbelief and wariness consumed him.

"Is it you? Is this real?"

"Yes, it's me, my darling." I called upon my angel affinity until light blazed from my palms as the soothing dark followed. I dipped my magic into his body, seeking the powerful hallucinogen that coursed through his bloodstream.

Heat blazed from me, followed by the dousing cold. Concentrating, I focused on what Matron Olsander had helped me recognize during the queen's healing session. *The queen.* An intense burst of pain filled me. *No, I can't think of her now.*

I closed my eyes and unleashed my angel magic, letting it naturally seek out the ailment.

It spread like wildfire, blazing out of me. It incinerated every drop of the poison in Norivun's blood, seeking it out, burning through the potent drug until Norivun's blood ran clean, and the hallucinogen had been whisked away.

Gasping, I pulled my affinity back into my body.

Exhaustion hit me so hard, but I breathed deeply and allowed myself a moment of rest. But only a moment.

There was so much yet to do. So much.

Around us, bodies lay on the ground. Injured soldiers. Dead fae. Shocked guards.

Charred earth lay in a razed crater where Norivun's dragon fire had been unleashed. And a gaping hole in the castle's wall stood before us, containing the obliterated remains of the king and queen.

A lump formed in my throat just as the crown prince's gaze sharpened, his eyes no longer coated in a glassy fog.

His head whipped around, and then he bolted upright. When he beheld the destroyed castle wall, he paled.

"Norivun, I'm so sorry." My arms closed around him as the first hint of clearness billowed toward me on the bond, no longer warped in the ugly, cleaving edges of a poisoned mind.

The prince's attention swung toward the ash, to where his mother had killed his father in order to protect her children, using her own fire to kill them both.

"No . . ." He shook his head. "She didn't . . ." His body grew stiff, and he pushed to a stand. "It was a hallucination." He shook his head again. "That wasn't real. She didn't kill him and herself. Please tell me she didn't."

"Nori." I stood too, stepping closer to him. Tears made my throat thick. I cupped his cheeks, then pressed a kiss tenderly to his chin as he continued to gaze at where his parents' ashes remained. "I'm sorry, but she did. It was real. She's gone, my love. She killed the king and herself in the process. And I think she did it all to save us, to save you from having to kill the king. If she did it, you couldn't be accused of anything. But that meant she could also face the supernatural courts. I think she chose death instead of possible imprisonment."

Nuwin's cry rose in the distance, and then the younger prince moved as fast as the wind on a gust of his air until he was at our sides. His face turned ashen. "She locked me in a ring of fire, so I couldn't intervene, and none of the soldiers could get to me." Anguish twisted his features. "Oh fuck, Nori. Oh fuck!" He fell to the ground, hands twisting through his hair. His sobs followed.

Each of the prince's guards hung their heads, and one by one they brought a fist to their chest before bowing. "All hail the queen!"

Stark faces met me every which way I looked.

A sea of fae stared back at me.

Collectively, they all turned toward their fallen queen. Then every Solis Guard and castle guard soldier that still stood brought fists to their hearts before bowing toward Lissandra's ashy remains.

The looking glass's magic still showed the truth of the king. It continually blazed through the sky like a meteor.

I didn't need Norivun's sensory affinity to know

that all of them were beginning to understand the truth. Reality was sinking in to all of their expressions. Anger. Betrayal. Disgust. It was evident on their faces. Looking glass magic couldn't lie. The king had deceived them.

"All hail the queen!" each of them shouted, their last tribute to the monarch who had ruled their land with a kind hand and soothing embrace as their shouts of respect rang through the courtyard.

Nuwin's sobs continued. The youngest prince remained collapsed on the ground.

I ran a hand along his back, but I knew it was a trivial touch. Nothing I could do would comfort the brothers.

Fisting my hands, I wished so deeply that I could turn back time and stop what had just occurred. The pain and torment streaming from my mate barreled toward me on our bond, so great that I nearly barreled over.

"Nori," I whispered.

But his expression remained distant, his features devoid of the light that had grown in him over the past few months.

"She's really gone?" he finally said.

A tear leaked onto my cheek. "She is. I'm so sorry."

I felt it the moment acceptance hit him. A torrent of lashing agony streamed along our bond.

My mate's head tipped back. A slamming wave of his power cracked open the earth beneath our feet. An anguished scream tore from his throat. It blazed through the sky as fissures appeared in the courtyard. The castle walls began shaking, and the entire remaining outer wall trembled under the force of his unleashed magic.

The land vibrated around me, robbing me of breath and hope as the tormented cry of a destroyed son burned through the realm.

CHAPTER 29 - ILARA

I sat beside Norivun in the council chambers. Lord Crimsonale and Lady Wormiful had arrived only minutes after Norivun's magic had been unleashed upon the castle. Dozens of fae from the factions had been with them, more appearing with each minute as word spread of what had occurred.

But they'd all been too late.

While the king had been destroyed, the queen was also dead.

Even though we'd saved the continent, we'd failed Queen Lissandra.

I placed my hand on my mate's thigh. His muscles jumped beneath my palm, stiff and unyielding. It was the only reaction my touch elicited.

Norivun sat on his chair around the circular table. Nuwin stood by the window. All four of the crown prince's personal guards had positioned themselves around the room. I'd healed them before we'd entered the castle, but even though their flesh was smooth and their injuries gone, haunted looks remained in all of their eyes.

"Would you like me to get you anything?" I asked Norivun.

He didn't reply. Not even a flicker of recognition passed over his face.

My breath caught. He hadn't said a word since his magic had unleashed on the realm.

Outside, the constructo fae were hard at work, but the fissures Norivun had created in the soil had gone so deep it would be a miracle if the land was once again whole by spring.

I removed my hand and leaned back in my chair. My eyes drooped, but I fought the sheer exhaustion that barreled through me. We were all tired, dirty, and beyond fatigued, but we couldn't rest yet.

The door to the chamber banged open, and Lady Wormiful bustled into the room, a female I didn't recognize right behind her.

I straightened from beside Norivun. "How is the reconstruction going?" I asked Taberitha.

The Kroravee archon was pale, her movements stiff. The female just behind her entwined their fingers together. I knew in a heartbeat that she was the archon's eternal mate.

"The constructo fae are all working to fix the damage, but it's so extensive it'll take weeks if not months to fully repair. The castle's offensive magic was depleted entirely. Lady Busselbee is coordinating our strategy fae to reconstruct it. It'll likely take the rest of the winter to replenish it entirely." She sighed heavily. "If only we'd arrived sooner."

She waved to the window, to where over ten thousand fae had appeared in the past hour from all over the continent. The depths of the rebellion had gone deep, much deeper than I'd ever realized.

"Thank you." I dipped my head, feeling so out of my depths with the catastrophe that had unfolded around us.

The king and queen were dead.

The castle and grounds were in ruins.

And my mate was a shattered wreck.

Norivun, by birthright, should be the next king, but already whisperings had erupted through the halls, hushed talks of who should wear the crown.

As much as I didn't want to deal with it, I knew a certain fairy was stirring such talks. He was acting now while my mate was destroyed and our continent was in upheaval.

Just as we knew he would.

"Have you seen Lord Crimsonale lately?" I asked, a slip of annoyance creeping into my tone.

Lady Wormiful shook her head. "No. Last I saw him, he was speaking with Lord Woodsbury and Lord Pinebeer in the castle hall. They were whispering about something."

So, he's already strategizing to take the throne.

Nostrils flaring, I dipped my head. "Thank you for the update."

She nodded and turned, tucking an arm around her mate's waist. The female, Gysabelle, if I remembered her name correctly, glanced over her shoulder at me. She was a wisp of a female, thin and small. Delicate looking. The exact opposite of the Kroravee archon. An air of pureness clouded around her, and I couldn't help but recall the one time Taberitha had spoken of her.

"Gysabelle's my light."

The meaning of that smacked me so hard that I slumped back into my chair.

Taberitha and Gysabelle weren't that much different than Norivun and me. The prince had always said I was better than him. Kinder. More forgiving. The light to his dark. Gysabelle was the same to Taberitha.

And right now, our mates needed our light more than anything.

I ran my hand over Norivun's shoulder. His black wings hung listlessly behind him. Nuwin wasn't in a much better state. The youngest prince still stood by the window, a ghostly expression on his face.

Only a few hours had passed since they'd lost their parents, and nary a word had been uttered between them.

"Can everyone please clear the room?" I said to the faction fae and the others who stood in small groups discussing what had occurred.

Several males gazed at me curiously. With reluctant bows, they all did as I asked.

When it was only the crown prince and his brother left in the room, save me, I crept along the mate bond, caressing it, stroking it. A rumble of awareness came for the briefest second from the other end.

The crown prince lifted his head. Stark despair coated his features.

With a feathered touch, I pushed my love and devotion into him as I kissed him softly on the neck.

"I love you," I said quietly. "I'll always love you, and I'll always be at your side until our end comes and we venture to the afterlife. I'm so sorry this happened, my love. She was a great queen. A devoted mother. Her spirit lit up this realm, and always, we will remember her."

He stared at me, unmoving, and then his arm whipped out, and he pulled me onto his lap. He rested his head on my shoulder, his huge frame dwarfing me. I wrapped my arms around him, holding him tight, and then he finally opened himself completely to me on the bond.

Pure *agony* barreled into me.

My throat tightened, and tears clouded my vision. "I'm so sorry." I stroked his hair, his chest, his back, his wings. Everywhere I could touch.

His arms curled around me more, and he lifted his head. Dark eyes clouded in grief met mine. "I didn't save her," he rasped.

I stilled. They were the first words he'd uttered since his primal scream had torn through the realm and cracked open the ground.

I cupped his cheeks just as a stifled sob came from Nuwin. "You couldn't, my love. None of us could have.

She sacrificed herself to save you. To save all of us. She knew that if she killed the king, none of us could be held at fault. She did it to save you. She was your mother until the end."

He pulled me into his arms again, holding me tightly. Arms circling him, I held him just as fiercely, and for the first time since I'd ever met the crown prince, his walls completely fell.

I held him in my arms, soaking up his regret and aching sadness, wishing so desperately that I could take it as my own. But Prince Norivun Deema Melustral Achul, first son of the king, Bringer of Darkness, Death Master of the continent, son of Prinavee Territory, and crown prince and heir to the Winter Court's throne had to bear that burden.

A tear slipped out of his eye, and then another. He crumbled in my arms, and then he wept and wept for the mother he would never see again. For the mother who had loved him until the end.

For the queen who had ultimately saved our realm.

CHAPTER 30 - NORIVUN

THREE WEEKS LATER

I sat in the council chambers with every territory archon seated around the circular table. The scent of ash hung heavily in the air. The constant casting magic from our constructo fae releasing their telltale essence perpetually assaulted my senses.

Never in my hundred winters had I ever seen the castle in its current state. Repairs had still been underway following the gods' wrath when Ilara had been locked in the dungeon, and then the war my father decided to wage on his own soil had only added to its crumbling structure.

Regardless, the constructo fae continued to work. Soon, the Court of Winter would again be whole, and a new reign would ensue.

Now, it was only a matter of determining who would wear the crown.

I ground my teeth. I wouldn't let my mother's death be for naught. I would fight to rule as she'd wanted. I would be the king she'd dreamed I would one day become, if only I could convince the council.

Nuwin sat on the chair to my right, my mate on the chair to my left. A flicker of relief filled me that Ilara no longer had dark circles under her eyes.

After my mother's death, I'd fallen apart, had been barely able to function, let alone able to run a continent. But Ilara had been there, holding me up when I'd been too weak, guiding me along when I feared I would become lost. She'd been my pillar. My strength. She was not only my heart and my beating soul, but she'd been my resolve in the initial aftermath.

And that caring and determined nature of hers hadn't only been for me. She'd seen to Nuwin, had healed my guards, had nursed more soldiers than I could count. Those who Murl had declared would perish had survived because of Ilara and her divine angel affinity.

She'd worked tirelessly around the clock, never faltering, never fading. Even when she'd grown so weak from expelling all of her magic, she had only allowed herself enough time to sleep and eat before she'd awoken and done it all again.

The day after my mother's death, in which I'd been more ghost than prince, I'd finally found my way back to her. Guilt hit me hard that she'd dealt with everything that first day on her own, but I wouldn't fail her again like that, even though Ilara had empathized with me completely, telling me she'd been in the same state when she'd first learned the news of her parents and brother, before she'd known the truth and believed them dead.

Despite her understanding, I wouldn't put her through that again. *Never* again. She'd done enough already.

I took a deep breath and returned to concentrating on our current meeting. The territory archons were bickering once more.

My fingers drummed on the table, and irritation washed through me because my love, my mate, my queen had once again shone more courage and fortitude than anyone else in these chambers, and it burned in me so deeply that not everyone saw her for the magnificent female that she was.

Of all the fae here, Ilara deserved to be their queen. Her strength and unwavering resolve to save our fae and her deep-seated loyalty to our land would make her the finest queen our continent had ever seen—as fine as my mother had once been.

Nothing like the Kroravee witch who I'd sent packing the moment my head cleared enough to begin ruling once more.

I'd made sure that Georgyanna had been banished to the netherlands of Kroravee, stripped of title, wealth, and family name. Her parents had been aghast, but the look of vindication on Ilara's face had strengthened my resolve. If that witch so much as showed her face in Solisarium again, I would unleash my dragon on her, and I made sure she'd known that.

But despite making it clear that the Olirum Accords

had been banished for all of the females in the Rising Queen Trial. Despite knowing that Ilara was the only female who would ever stand at my side. Despite Ilara slaving herself to our nation. Despite me picking myself up and standing tall once more. Despite *all* of that, not everyone thought we deserved to wear the crowns of the Court of Winter.

Lord Crimsonale's eyes narrowed as he gazed at me from across the table. Gone was the conspirator who'd worked with us to spread word across the land of who my father really was. Gone was the noble who'd ensured that every city and villager had learned the truth of the deadly veil that had poisoned our soil.

Oh no. The greedy bastard who faced me now wore so much arrogance and righteous entitlement that I wanted to burn his face off.

"So let me get this straight, Lord Crimsonale." I leaned back in my chair, letting my wings slacken. "You believe that you should be the king of the Solis continent. Not me."

"Well, I didn't actually say—"

"You did actually," Nuwin interrupted. "Your exact words last night were, *The Achul family has spread enough terror across the land. The time has come to change the blood that sits on the throne.* That was what you said, correct?"

Lord Crimsonale clenched his jaw but didn't deny it. Michas, not present today, also shared that belief from what I'd heard from the whispering among the staff.

I eyed my brother. While still grieving in his own way, Nuwin had also shoved the pain of losing our mother to the side. He'd remained steadfast in the past three weeks, the first to defend me should anyone utter so much as a word of contempt in my direction. He'd also been the first to declare to anyone who would listen that Ilara and I had been working all along to save our land. And that I'd, in fact, been working for full seasons to save the innocent fae my father had sought to destroy in his twisted plan to gain control of our realm's continents.

Those on the Cliffs of Sarum had voiced their agreement with my brother. Some had even traveled to Solisarium to preach about my upstanding character.

Ilara's family was also shouting their declarations from the rooftop. Despite Ilara urging them to join us in Solisarium, they'd declined, understanding that our seats on the throne weren't guaranteed, not after what my father had done.

So after a brief visit with us last week, Ilara's entire family had returned to their mission, Birnee and Finley joining them as they traveled from village to city, from territory to sea, showing everyone what we'd done with looking glasses that Cailis had continued to forge every chance she got.

Ilara's newest friends and our servants had also become quite boisterous in their praise of us. Meegana, Beatrice, Balbus, Haisley, Patrice, and Daiseeum all declared us rightful and beloved rulers, and if any servant so much as muttered otherwise, they'd gotten an earful. Or so I'd heard.

All of those fae supporting and cheering for us was an incredibly humbling experience. For the first time in my entire life, fae on our continent weren't calling me a monster. They were calling me a fair ruler.

"So what will it be, Lord Crimsonale?" I arched an eyebrow. "Will you support my ascension to the throne while Ilara Seary is declared the rightful queen, or are you challenging us before this very council?"

Anger flared in Gregorian's scent, sharp like iron. "I simply bring concerns, my prince. King Novakin deceived all of us. The Achul family has ruled for so many centuries that it nearly destroyed us all."

"My *father* nearly destroyed us." I corrected, "But not my grandfather or me."

Lord Woodsbury wrinkled his nose.

I angled my sharp gaze toward him. "I suppose that you are in agreement with Gregorian, Lord Woodsbury?"

The Isalee archon squared his shoulders. His wings rippled. "I am, my prince. Lord Crimsonale makes a fair point. I've lost faith in the Achul family."

Nish muttered something from the corner of the room, probably something along the lines of the archon holding a grudge since Ilara hadn't married Arcane. Although, knowing Nish, it was said in much more colorful terms.

"This is growing tiresome, Lord Crimsonale." Lady Busselbee looked down her nose at him. "You're simply hoping to gain control while the land remains in unrest. But if you can make such a claim, who's to say the rest of us can't? We cannot allow such lawlessness. Solis tradition dictates the oldest child of the king ascends to the throne. Making a decision otherwise would entirely uproot everything we stand for."

"Exactly." Lord Pinebeer nodded flagrantly. "This is entirely preposterous. Our territories are still so newly united that creating this kind of upheaval could only lead to further arguments and battles. Who's to say each territory won't act to gain their independence again? Such an act would create chaos, and we'd lose the strength we've gained as a united continent."

Lord Crimsonale blew forcefully through his nose. "You're pulling at straws. I'm simply saying the Achul line shouldn't rule, not that we shouldn't stay united as we've been."

I drummed my fingers again. "So it's just *me* you don't want as king."

Lord Woodsbury sighed. "Perhaps Lord Crimsonale's idea to declare you the archon of Prinavee Territory and him the king of the Solis continent would be a beneficial compromise by all."

"Compromise?" Sandus called from the corner. "That's not a compromise. That's stealing the bloody crown."

I held up my hand as mutterings began around the table again. "There hasn't been a Prinavee Territory archon since my father was declared king of the Solis continent after he united the territories. That title was absolved once a king was declared."

"But that was only because your father had been archon of Prinavee Territory. Who's to say there shouldn't be a Prinavee Territory archon again, except this time, in addition to the king?" Lord Crimsonale countered. "Perhaps that is the role that suits you best."

"Lovely," Nuwin said, rolling his eyes. "In that case, *I'll* be the Prinavee Territory archon, and my brother will be the king. Perfect. Solved. Now, how about we all head to dinner? I hear the chef is serving a delicious plate of ustorill roast with herbed potatoes and all the usual sides and fixings." He made to stand from his chair, his black wings catching in the light. "Shall we?"

"Sit down, Prince Nuwin," Lord Crimsonale growled. "You shall not be declared the archon of Prinavee Territory."

"Ah, no? Perfect, then Norivun and Ilara will be declared the king and queen as they rightfully should be, and we'll be done with this nonsense."

Lord Crimsonale's nostrils flared.

The squabbles continued. Crimsonale and Woods-bury repeatedly protested my ascension to the throne while Busselbee and Pinebeer staunchly opposed their propositions.

Strangely, Lady Wormiful remained quiet throughout most of the discussion, perhaps because her steadfast alliance with Lord Crimsonale was unraveling before my eyes. From what I could gather, the Osaravee Territory archon had failed to mention his ultimate plan to steal the throne from their enemy while leaving his ally high and dry as he gained complete rule.

"Enough!" Ilara abruptly declared, standing from her seat. Her white wings spread out. She'd grown so proficient in her angel affinity that she regularly left them on display, her healing light only a second away if needed. "By birthright, *Norivun* is the next king of the Solis continent."

Lord Crimsonale snorted. "As you're probably unaware, Lady Seary, when succession is passed, the king's council must—"

"Agree as a whole to pass along the crown to the firstborn." She leveled him with a hard stare. "Yes, Lord Crimsonale, I'm aware. But that same law also states that in order for a firstborn to be removed from the throne, there must be due and forthright proof that he or she is of unfit mind. You cannot possibly tell me that you have proof that Prince Norivun's mind isn't fit to rule?"

"I would say being Death Master for more seasons than you've been alive would be cause to consider exactly that. His bloodlust is legendary, not to mention the way the fae of our land fear him, the way his very presence evokes disgust, not respect. Or how—"

"Not another word," Ryder growled from the corner. "If you believe such atrocities, then you don't know your crown prince at all, and you're a complete and utter fool."

"Exactly my thoughts," Ilara stated, her violet eyes flashing at the Osaravee archon.

I stayed still, inhaling all of the emotional scents floating through the room. Anger. Disgust. Arrogance. Impatience. Mistrust. Hope. And curiously, amusement as well. I figured that one was from Taberitha, although why she found any of this funny, I wasn't sure.

But before I could comment, the Kroravee Territory archon rose from her chair and faced Lord Crimsonale. "I think Prince Norivun has shown his true colors over the previous weeks, don't you think, Gregorian? Even though his father declared him the villain of our land, Prince Norivun's actions have spoken otherwise. I think such revelations, if anything, *disprove* everything you're suggesting."

Lord Crimsonale's eyes narrowed in her direction. He scoffed. "You're siding with *him*?"

Lady Wormiful sat again. "I'm siding with *reason*. Not with any particular member of this council, or—"

"Ock," Lord Woodsbury cut in. "If anything, the fact that Prince Norivun wed the female who was supposed to marry my—"

"Oh, give it a rest already." Nish let out a frustrated sigh. "She was never going to marry your delinquent child, Lord Woodsbury, not even if Norivun wasn't her mate."

A few of the archons gave my outspoken guards frustrated looks at their continual outbursts, but Taberitha snorted quietly, and the scent of amusement rose from her again.

At least one of us was enjoying this meeting.

Sighing, I ground my teeth. "I can see that we're not

going to get anywhere today, so I propose we retire for the night and carry on discussions tomorrow."

Magic rumbled along my limbs. As much as I wanted to silence Lord Crimsonale and Lord Woodsbury and squash their conspiring, I couldn't. Doing so would only prove the point that they were trying to make. That I was a monster and was unfit to rule.

But when I made to stand, my mate placed her hand on my arm.

Ilara's throat rolled in a swallow. "I propose a different idea." She lifted her wings, the feathers shining like snow. She eyed the Osaravee and Isalee archons. "If you're so convinced that Norivun isn't fit to rule and that the entire continent will be in agreement with you, then I propose we have a vote. Not among the fae in this room, but out there"—she waved to the window, to our vast continent—"with all of the fae of our land. If you're so certain that my mate doesn't bear the qualities needed to rule this land, that our fae truly do fear and hate him and are in agreement with you, then let *them* be the decision-makers. Let the Solis fae determine who their next king will be."

"A vote?" Lord Crimsonale sneered. "We don't allow citizens to *vote* on the king."

"And why shouldn't we?" she challenged.

A moment of fear stole over me, of knowing that the citizens of our continent would likely vote to burn me at the stake rather than see me wear the crown, but as I watched my mate, I didn't voice my concern.

Ilara stood like a queen, her resolve to stand by my

side unwavering. And her conviction, while possibly misplaced despite what her family, village, and our friends were trying to achieve—that our fae would vote for me as their ruler—made me prouder of her than I'd ever been.

She truly was a queen of the citizens. She wouldn't serve for herself or rule with only her intentions at heart. She would lead with every male, female, and child who lived on our land as her guiding light. I knew deep down in my soul that her rule would be just and kind—like my mother's had been.

My breath caught at the memory of my mother, but I locked that pain down as far as it would go.

Lord Crimsonale snorted, and Lord Woodsbury leaned over to the Osaravee archon and whispered something in his ear. With each word he said, Gregorian's expression grew more smug.

Finally, he nodded.

The Isalee archon leaned back in his seat, and Lord Crimsonale stood and clasped his hands beneath his wings. "All right, Lady Seary. If a vote is what you want, then that's what you'll get. Mind you, that would mean that if the vote is in favor of *me* and not the crown prince, then I shall wear the king's crown."

Ilara's throat again rolled, but her conviction held firm along our bond. "Do you agree, Prince Norivun?"

Despite knowing that my loss would come swiftly, I didn't dispute her. I couldn't. I wouldn't shatter my mate's belief in me even if it ended in my demise. She truly felt that our fae would find me worthy of their love.

I knew they likely wouldn't. For too many seasons they'd hated me, but seeing her resolve and unwavering faith in who I was . . . for me, *that* was enough.

Standing, I bowed before straightening, then declared. "I agree. We shall allow the citizens of the Solis continent to vote for who they deem worthy of the crown. Me or Lord Crimsonale. We shall let our fae decide."

CHAPTER 31 - ILARA

It took a month before the fae of our land could cast their votes. The entire continent needed to be alerted to this new, strange way of deciding who ascended to the crown.

And the council had to create a separate group of fae with affinities in documentation in order to ensure the votes were tallied accurately and efficiently. Thankfully, magistrates at the supernatural courts provided assistance, allowing us to create a system that worked smoothly and easily.

It was so different than anything that had ever been done before. For centuries, the king of the Solis continent had been determined by birth and birth alone, but when the day came that every adult male and female arrived at their council building to vote within their city or village, the prince and I stayed in the castle, sequestering ourselves to his chambers as the servants, his guards, and our friends and family waited impatiently in the great hall below.

But not Norivun and me. We opted to enjoy the day alone. We hadn't been able to spend nearly enough time together with no one but the two of us.

A fire roared in the hearth, crackling and snapping as snow flew outside. The castle was still being repaired. There was still so much left to do, but come sunrise, these chambers might no longer be our own, and the castle's state might no longer be our concern. But we would enjoy it while we could.

"You know, I still don't know what your sixth affinity is," I teased.

Norivun chuckled and ran a hand through my hair. "I wondered if you'd forgotten about that."

"I haven't. We've just been too busy for me to demand that you show me."

His lips tugged up, and he ran his hand down my back. "And what do you think it is?"

"Honestly? I have no idea. Will you please just tell me?" I batted my eyelashes.

A deep chuckle rumbled in his chest before he stood. "How about I show you?"

He held his hand out to me, and smiling with curiosity, I let my fingers entwine with his. He pulled me along to another room in his private chambers before he ignited a fairy light with his magic.

This room was small, with only a few chairs, a piano, another bookshelf, and several instruments.

The prince pointed to one of the chairs. "Have a seat."

I did as he said and glanced around as I waited for something magical to appear.

But the prince merely went to the piano and sat, then placed his fingers upon it. "I've been wanting to play this melody since that first night you came to me, the night you joined me in my chambers and declared that you saw me for who I really was."

His fingers met the keyboard, and then . . . he began to play.

Music strummed from the piano, a soft melody at first that grew stronger and sharper and more complicated with every press of his fingers.

My throat tightened as the symphony of sound barreled around me, igniting the room in crashing waves and haunting twists.

The prince played with his eyes closed, his body moving slightly while his hands drifted effortlessly over the keys. He played as though his heart connected with the sound, as though his very essence was poured into that music.

And it struck me with complete shock and bold pride that my mate held a creation affinity. His sixth affinity was the ability to create beauty through sound. His masterful touch created some of the most emotional music I'd ever heard. A song of rapture and love, loss and hope, redemption and acceptance.

Tears shone in my eyes when his hands finally quieted.

He turned to me with an apprehensive look. "Now you know, my love."

I rose and went to him, wrapping my arms around his neck as my tears began to fall. "You're amazing, utterly and completely amazing."

He chuckled softly, then pointed to the mantel, visible through the door in the other room. "Well, if that's the kind of reverence I get, then I'll also tell you it isn't just music. Do you see that painting?"

I turned and peered toward it, at the painting of a scene of Solisarium. It was a perfect rendition of the castle, of the splendor of our city.

"Yes, it's beautiful."

"Well . . . I painted it."

My attention whipped back to him. "You can paint too?"

He gave a single nod. "My sixth affinity is a diverse creation affinity, the ability to create art and music. It's nothing mighty or powerful, and according to my father, it was an embarrassment." He shrugged. "But there you have it. That's what my last affinity is."

I gazed at him in wonder, then looked at the painting again and the piano he'd just played as though the instrument had been created for him. "You truly painted that and composed that song?"

"I did. My mother used to love listening to me play."

My throat tightened when an aching wave of his sadness barreled toward me on the bond. His mother's death was still so fresh. I knew it would be many, many full seasons until his grief began to pass.

Hoping to distract him, I cocked my head. "What else have you painted?"

His lips curved in a cheeky smile, and he pulled me onto his lap, nestling me between his strong thighs. "Do you remember the tapestries lining the throne room hallway? The scenes from all of the territories?"

I nodded. I'd first seen those resplendent master-pieces on the night Norivun had taken me to the Betrothed Ball.

"I painted those too, and do you remember the music from the Betrothed Ball?"

I nodded. "It was beautiful. Hauntingly so."

"I composed that."

My jaw dropped, wonder filling me. "That's amazing."

He shrugged. "Not all think so, like I said. It's a friv-olous affinity, nothing that strengthens my rule."

I gripped his shoulders and leveled him with a heavy stare. "I think it's *magnificent*. You're like Daiseeum. You too can create beauty. Our continent needs that. We need music and art to remind us of the beauty of our land. Not everything needs to be about death and power."

"That's what my mother always said." He ran a hand along my cheek. "I've been wanting to paint you."

I shivered. "I want you to."

He leaned forward and kissed me before we both settled back, and another moment of silence passed.

"Do you truly think I stand a chance at becoming king?" Norivun asked quietly as I leaned against his chest, listening to the beat of his heart and depth of his breath as the warmth from the fire in the other room filled the air around us.

"I do." I ran a finger over his shoulder, right where his mating mark was. His muscles jumped beneath my light touch. My attention kept drifting to the painting above the mantel and then to the haunting music he'd just played for me. "It's been long enough since we first began to spread the news of the truth of your father. Everyone now knows what you did for the innocent fae that had been living on the Cliffs of Sarum. They know that your father wanted those fae murdered, not you. And they've seen how you've been working full seasons to save all of them and how all along your father was actually the villain. Not his crown prince."

"I was still the Death Master. I still *am* the Death Master. I've taken more lives than I can count."

"Someone has to be the executioner, my love." I placed my palm flat on his chest and raised my chin to meet his gaze. "But you've borne that burden long enough. We can find another if your soul grows weary."

His eyes narrowed, and he ran a finger along my cheek. "But then I wouldn't be able to torture Vorl and ultimately decide what I'm going to do with him."

My breath hitched before a nervous smile tugged at my lips. Vorl was still being kept in the dungeons. Still in the same cell that he'd been in for months on end.

Norivun had visited him frequently during the last

six weeks. I had no idea when my mate's rage would be sated or when his vengeance would abate. Perhaps it never would.

"Do you think he's suffered enough?" I asked, despite knowing that Vorl would always be a vile male who sought to hurt others. But now that his thumbs were permanently disfigured, he would have a harder time accomplishing that task.

"No." My mate's response was quick. Definitive. Leaning down, he flicked my chin, then kissed me softly before his tongue slid along my lower lip. "I plan to keep him for many months to come. I told you that I was going to take my time with him."

I shivered as a lick of his darkness gathered around me.

"Perhaps it's best if I'm not king." He continued his slow procession of lingering kisses. He kissed along my jaw, throat, and down my collarbone. Heat began to grow inside me. "My thirst for punishment may be too great for some."

"Not me." I gasped when he lifted me, and I straddled him. My dress bunched around my hips before he swept my underthings to the side. He inched his trousers down until his full length was revealed, and then he slid me onto him inch by inch.

"And that's why you're perfect for me, my love. You accept my darkness. You understand it." His lips curved when he kissed me again, and then he hissed when the remaining inch of him filled me completely.

"Gods, I will never get enough of you." His breaths came faster, and I began to move.

My belly tightened as warmth spread through me.

He lifted me, his hands gripping my hips as I rode him. The strain along his mouth grew, our bodies moving and writhing together. His fingers tangled in my hair, and the need to own him, claim him, nearly overtook me.

We came together, the prince's roar guttural as I cried out in ecstasy. I rode the waves, savoring every bit of the climax that he'd wrenched from me as the fire continued to crackle and warm my back while the fairy lights hummed.

And when we both came down from the high, he pulled me to him, our breaths mingling while his cock stayed buried deep inside me.

"I love you." He kissed me tenderly. "My light. My wife. My eternal mate. My love. My *queen.*"

"And I, you. My darkness. My husband. My eternal mate. My king. We shall always have each other. No matter what the future brings."

We sat like that for a while, enjoying the quiet and the feel of one another. The mate bond inside me hummed, burning brightly between our connected souls.

I eventually lifted myself and straightened my clothing and hair before wiping away the essence of our lovemaking with my cleansing magic.

"Hungry?" I asked my mate.

He nodded. "Famished."

But I didn't get a chance to ring the golden cord by his bed. In the other room, the door burst open, and then we heard Nuwin, Cailis, my parents, my friends, all of the prince's guards, and his personal servants fill the space.

We quickly walked into his living area to find them all grinning and bursting in happiness.

"Is there a reason you've all barged in here, into my private chambers, when I could have been in the middle of making love to my wife?" Norivun asked dryly, yet his tone held no malice, merely amusement.

My father cleared his throat, flushing at the prince's comment, but Nuwin merely beamed.

The younger prince fell into a bow before everyone behind him did the same.

My heart began to race, and I eyed the clock. The voting had closed. If the magical system in place had worked as flawlessly as the fae who created it claimed it would, then it was possible a decision had been reached.

I threaded my fingers through Norivun's. Hope pounded in my chest.

Norivun stood entirely immobile, not even his chest lifting with breaths.

Nuwin raised his head and gave us a cheeky smile. "All hail the new king and queen of the Solis continent. King Norivun and Queen Ilara. Let a new era of reign begin!"

CHAPTER 32 - NORIVUN

Ilara and I stood on the shores of northern Mervalee, the crashing waves from the Brashier Sea pounding against the shore. Behind us, the music and celebrations continued. We were finally celebrating our eternal marriage with all of our family and friends. We'd invited as many fae as had wanted to attend. Every single fairy on the Solis continent had been invited to celebrate their king and queen's union, and the turnout had surpassed everything my mate and I had dreamed of. Thousands and thousands of fae were in attendance.

"They truly want you to be their queen, my wife," I said teasingly as I stroked a finger along Ilara's cheek.

She shivered and ducked her head. The moonlight caught on the nightill flowers woven through her crown, the flowers holding a special meaning since it had been on the southern tip of her territory that we'd claimed one another and sealed our mating bond.

"And they want *you* to be their king." She kissed me slowly, suggestively, and I was about to start looking for a hidden cove along the shore in which I could properly and thoroughly fuck my wife when a brush of something pierced my Shield, and then filled my mind.

"Norivun."

I stilled.

Ilara pulled back, the same rigidness consuming her. Her magic subtly shifted around her when her Shield also lowered, and then she gasped. "Did you hear that?"

My heart began to pound. I whipped my head left and right. The party raged behind us. All of my guards, Ilara's family, Nuwin, Finnley, Birnee, Meegana, Beatrice, Balbus and Marcina, Patrice, Haisley, Daiseeum, Ilara's entire village, and every other friend Ilara had made during the Trial danced and drank, their smiles and boisterous conversations drifting through the air.

But nothing looked out of place.

I ran a hand along the back of my neck, shaking my head. I was imagining things. I had to be. "I don't know what that was."

"I'm so proud of you. Of both of you. My darling boy and the daughter I never had."

Ilara squeaked, and I spun around.

My eyes widened when a female appeared along the beach, walking toward us in the moonlight. She wore a cloak, and her long silver hair hung down her back. Hair as straight as an arrow.

But her face was different. Her height altered.

My heart began pounding so hard that I feared it would beat right out of my chest.

The female stopped before us.

My affinity punched through the illusion mask she was wearing.

I stumbled back, my hand going to my chest, but the female rushed forward, stopping me from making a scene. She gave the party in the distance her back before releasing her illusion mask entirely.

Ilara gasped. "Queen Lissandra!"

My mother brought her fingers to her lips, shushing her. "My secret cannot be revealed, but I couldn't miss tonight, not the night where the realm celebrates your union and your ascension to the throne."

I shook my head. "How? You died on the castle wall with Father."

Her lips curved. "I didn't. I killed the king with my fire but not myself. I created an illusion to make it appear as if I did, but I mistphased at the last moment and have been living on the shores of Osaravee ever since. Now, I'm just a nameless fae female, living in her home territory, returned finally after many winters away."

"What? How?" I stuttered and shook my head, my thoughts careening in my mind like a trapped bird. "But it's been *months*. Why didn't you tell Nuwin and I that you were alive?"

She laid a hand on my cheek. "I'm sorry. I would

have told you sooner, but I needed everyone to see your grief and feel your pain. I needed everyone to truly believe me dead if I'm to live in peace. It troubled me greatly to keep this from you for so long, but I knew when enough time had passed, and my death had started to turn into a memory, that then I could tell you."

Tears pricked my eyes, and through the bond, Ilara's disbelief and happiness barreled toward me.

"We all thought you dead," I whispered before pulling her into a tight hug.

I swallowed my mother's frame, but she only laughed and hugged me tightly in return. "And it's important that everyone continue thinking me gone. I wish to live in peace, Norivun. Away from the court. Away from Solisarium. I've suffered enough. Now, I just wish to live my life on the shores of Osaravee. A life I should have been granted long ago. A life that *I* chose. That's all I want, that and to see you and Nuwin happy."

"Does Nuwin know?" I asked, nearly choking as I gripped her and breathed in her scent.

"Not yet. I wanted to tell you both first. My king and"—she reached a hand out and tugged Ilara closer to us—"my queen. How proud I am of you both. I knew the stars would align, and my vision would come true. You just needed to stay together to beat the tyrant on the throne."

Disbelief continued to fill my soul. My mother was alive. She was well and truly *alive*.

We laughed and hugged, and the aching pain that had settled inside me since my mother's supposed death eased.

"How often can we see you?" I asked, finally releasing her.

"As often as you like. I plan to wear my illusion mask indefinitely to keep my identity concealed. When you come to visit me, if you both wear illusion masks too, no one will even know that the king and queen regularly visit an old fae female on the southern shores."

Ilara laughed and brought a hand to her mouth. She jumped in glee before flinging her arms around my mother.

We stayed like that for I didn't know how long. Lissandra told us about the life she was building for herself and how for the first time in hundreds of winters, she was no longer in pain. No longer suppressed. No longer caged by the king.

"And I have you to thank for that, my darling girl." She cupped Ilara's cheeks as the moonlight shimmered off of my mate's angel wings. "You clever, brave, magnificent girl. The perfect female to be mated to my son."

Ilara hugged her tightly again before letting her go. And when my mother's illusion mask fell back into place, she wandered toward the party, toward where Nuwin was currently flirting with half a dozen females.

We watched her walk across the sand, her head high, her aura potent, her Outlets open.

And as the moon shone down on us, and Ilara gazed up at me with tears in her eyes, I knew that no matter what might come for us, in the end we would always have each other and our family.

And that . . . *that* would always be enough.

AUTHOR'S NOTE

Hello, dear reader. You know it's funny that whenever I write the last sentence in any of my series, I always have a tear in my eye. I love Ilara and Norivun so much. They've become so real to me, and they're truly like friends. I'll miss writing their journey, miss spending my time on the Solis continent, and I'll miss all of the exciting things that their lives still have in store for them, but I can say this . . . this series ended exactly as I always saw it—Ilara and Norivun fighting for their throne, while the queen gave the ultimate sacrifice to save them all.

In my original plotting of this book, Lissandra was going to die and truly enter the afterlife, but in the end, I couldn't kill her. She suffered so much and had always been so kind. That must have been weighing heavily on my mind, because one night I woke up from a dream in which Lissandra cast an illusion around herself to hide her death. And in that moment, I knew the final plot twist in this story had fallen into place.

My characters often come to me in dreams, my mind busy at work crafting stories even when I'm sleeping, so in the end, I changed *Crowns of Ice*, and I hope I was able to bring a smile to your face when you read that last chapter.

Anyway, enough ramblings from my jumbled author mind. I'll end with saying that I hope you enjoyed this series, and I thank you so much for loving my work enough to read it until the very end. So *thank you*. From the bottom of my heart, *thank you*, for giving this series a chance and gifting me with the ability to chase my dream. Ever since I was a child, I dreamed of writing stories for a living, and because of you, I get to do exactly that!

ABOUT THE AUTHOR

Krista Street loves writing in multiple genres: fantasy, sci-fi, romance, and dystopian. Her books are cross-genre and often feature complex characters, plenty of supernatural twists, and romance in every story. She loves writing about coming-of-age characters who fight to find their place in this world while also finding their one true mate.

Krista Street is a Minnesota native but has lived throughout the U.S. and in another country or two. She loves to travel, read, and spend time in the great outdoors. When not writing, Krista is either chasing her children, spending time with her husband and friends, sipping a cup of tea, or enjoying the hidden gems of beauty that Minnesota has to offer.

THANK YOU

Thank you for reading *Crowns of Ice* the final book in the *Fae of Snow & Ice* series.

If you enjoy Krista Street's writing, and you live in the USA or Canada, sign up for her new release text alerts to receive a free, digital epilogue told from Ilara's point of view. To sign up, simply text the word **ILARA** to **888-403-4316** on your mobile phone.

Message and data rates may apply, and you can opt out at any time.

If you live outside of North America, and you would like to receive the bonus epilogue, visit:

www.kristastreet.com/ilarabonus

And if you enjoyed reading *Crowns of Ice*, please consider logging onto the retailer you purchased this book from to post a review. Authors rely heavily on readers reviewing their work. Even one sentence helps a lot. Thank you so much if you do!

To learn more about Krista's other books and series, visit her website. Links to all of her books, along with links to her social media platforms, are available on every page.